W9-BYU-521
Saint Peter's University Library
Withdrawn

THE INVISIBLE VOICES

THE INVISIBLE VOICES

By

MATTHEW PHIPPS SHIEL

Short Story Index Reprint Series

BOOKS FOR LIBRARIES PRESS
FREEPORT, NEW YORK

First Published 1936
Reprinted 1971

INTERNATIONAL STANDARD BOOK NUMBER:
0-8369-3929-8

LIBRARY OF CONGRESS CATALOG CARD NUMBER:
74-160950

PRINTED IN THE UNITED STATES OF AMERICA

TO

JOHN GAWSWORTH

IN FOND REMEMBRANCE OF DAYS
OF SUGGESTION, DEBATE AND
COLLABORATION

CONTENTS

CHAPTER I

THE PANEL DAY

WHEN Greta Chesson received a letter from her sweetheart, Harry, and by the next mail a letter from one "Whip," she said to Netta, her half-sister, "That Whipsnade Prince is coming : I won't see him" ; so, putting pyjamas and her *Comparative Anatomy* into an attaché case, she trotted in along Cap Ferrat to the tram, and was off to Monte Carlo.

For the letter from Harry (Ransom) had in it an idea that had hit him, and now hit Greta, too : *Why* should he and Greta wait to go through their examinations before getting married ?—since married people can still read betweenwhiles. *She* was reading for Intermediate in Science, *he* for Student Interpreterships : for though she, on marriage, would become very wealthy, it would still be well for him to have position and salary, seeing that she had the fixed purpose to endow research with the money—she being a strong-headed soul with her own views on things, and the larkiness of that twinkle-twinkle of her narrow eyes' sidling had a star behind it—a broad face, broad brow, square jaw, which meant what they said, as he was aware, for they had been sweethearts four years, since they had been fourteen ; and he himself approved of her intention, was proud of the self-will of her ideals, being himself rather " high-brow " in his own niche and choice of path, taking life pretty seriously—at present (on Sundays) he was the " acolyte of an angel " (" *angel* " being some church-officer of that Catholic Apostolic Church of Edward Irving).

As to the letter from " Whip " (Whipsnade Prince), this also was the offspring of an Idea, " Whip " radiating ideas as radium spits out beta bits—lived on ideas, his own or others. If it was not Lord Orpen—some company director—who dropped him, in passing at some club-door, a tip as to underwriting something, as to being a bull in something, then, an idea would spring within Whip Prince himself, as primroses in Spring ; then he might be suddenly in funds for some months, then to skip out of another little fix by some idea—which occurred to him of itself out of the earth's fertileness, without work ; for, as others work to come at money, so money worked to come at him, the stars in their courses operating to keep dancing a spark so naturally uplifted, speaking an accent so Oxford—though, in fact, he had never been near Oxford, his brag that he was an ignoramus being true enough ; and, indeed, he would doubtless have been less clever an adventurer, if he had ever crammed Greek grammar. But sometimes when faring prosperously " Prince Whip " (as Mayfair named him) did preposterous things—had lately bought a yacht, then couldn't pay her crew, and had had to sell, after finding himself borrowing a hundred pounds from a Savoy Hotel American. And now he was visited by the idea that that would be good business to marry his cousin Greta himself, and get hold of that lump of money ; he had twice come across her in Society, to find her quite a likeable minx. So he wrote to Cap Ferrat to say "expect me——"

But Greta guessed his game: and, to get out of the ordeal of saying No to what was really a reasonable proposition, fled away from Prince.

The proposition was "reasonable," because he was the next heir, if she died unmarried before coming of age; this by the will of her father, the late Sir Richard Chesson, City-king, Member of the Stock Exchange (he had left £575,000); Whip's father having been the baronet's brother.

Now, Whip had felt pretty certain that, with his customary luck of a Piccadilly prince, the girl would decide to die before marrying, and had found himself saying "Blessed are the dead: she might be inspired to expire now"; but when she got to be about nineteen, and no sign of dying, the odds began to look bad; he decided to act.

So, on reaching Nice, on taxi-ing over to Villefranche, he strolled on over Cap Ferrat to Greta's Villa dei Gigli—white home within a white garden, having white terraces of gradients going down to be ever gabbled on, betongued, by the harbour's wavelets wagging—to find, however, no Greta, to find Netta, to find himself saying to himself "By Jove, rather sweet: hair waving round forehead—soft stuff, like chromos of moonlight-scenes—eyes so grave—grey—soft stuff"; then to find himself submitting to "*tea*," like a captive in the clutches of her and her Lady Dale-Eldon (companion-housekeeper, elderly); then to be led by her to step in amid many lilies; and now she spoke out to him of Greta: the kind of human being that Greta liked best was boys, because, as Greta said, she could see into them, sympathize with them—cared less for men, women, girls ; and Greta was going to marry a boy whom she had long been attached to.

He said " Let me see—Ransom—I am said to know everybody—yes, rather, I know Ransom ! 'fresh young manhood,' as they say—rosy—hair parted with a passionate accuracy, brushed wet off his frank young brow—know him well, saw him at Lord's some weeks. . . . But—doesn't it rather seem to you that that would be—er—appropriate, if *I* was the boy——?"

" No," Netta said : " you see, Greta has her own notions—doesn't consider that such a mass of money should be spent on private rioting ; her design is to endow science—you'll hear her say 'whole-time research in bio-chemistry on the Unit System.' You, perhaps, don't even know what that means ; and would never see with her in this."

" No, by Jove," Whip muttered, and added : " I'll look into it. . . . Now I'll go and dress, come back for the evening."

But she said " Haven't I to go to the *Rodney* ball ? "—for dancing was going-on in a battleship and destroyer then loitering in the bay; so Whip was balked there also ; but after Netta had watched his thin legs stepping away inland, and had said to herself " Nice lips, firm—teeth too *long*—but vital eyes, Mediterranean-blue—movements quick, quick wits," she had to 'phone to Greta, at the Hôtel de l'Europe (Monte Carlo), " Our Whip isn't gone away—call him Whippersnapper—coming again to-morrow."

" What for ? " Greta demanded.

"Heaven knows!"

"Make him go to the devil, Netta: I am wasting time."

But again the next day, and the next, Netta had to telephone that Whip was at "The Welcome," straying with a Villefranche carnation about that Corniche du Littoral, enduring the dull drone of the trams' overhead-contact, amused at spinsters of England thin and stale, who went gazing through glasses held by a handle, carrying tennis-rackets under the sun; he took Netta out in a motor-boat; and now they were intimate, he and she, chaffing each other's accident of sex.

On the sixth forenoon, though, she could 'phone "That young gentleman departed last night, thank heaven."

But that was not so: again that afternoon he turned up at the Villa dei Gigli.

"But whatever for?" Netta asked him.

"Why, to see you," he answered.

"All nonsense."

"Don't think that I am come to propose to you."

"No, I won't think so."

"You're old. Twenty-seven, I reckon, and I only twenty-five. I'm not going to marry a lady older than myself."

"No, and you are not going to marry a lady who would laugh if you asked her."

"Would you laugh? I don't think so. Very well, I'll test it: please—let's marry."

"Oh, my! this is for my sins this day."

"Ah, you see: you don't laugh, you say yes."

"Look here, leave me in peace, will you?"—in the thick of bandying which badinage, they suddenly saw Greta's face, broadish under its pancake béret cocked, she stepping along with her attaché case.

Her astonishment at so butting into Whip, whom she supposed to be well away, may have amounted to shock, which shock may have been in some connection with what was now about to befall her ; anyway, she came paleish, weary-looking ; and when Prince presently went away without any reference to his motive in coming to the Riviera, she complained of headache, then dropped asleep in an easy-chair on the verandah—an odd thing for her.

Toward night she sat to write to her Harry Ransom, to invite him to come to discuss his bright-idea of marriage now ; but that letter was never finished ; in the midst she found her brow bowed down on the scrivania she wrote at, as though she had sleeping-sickness.

However, the revolution in her habits during the last days having made her lose time, she drove, compelled, herself to her usual studies that night ; in a 'foreday hour, lonesome in the soundless house, she had her bulky skull, a dark-brown shapeliness, bent down over the task of discovering, by differentials, for what number of N cells, coupled in series, C is a maximum ; but she did not discover : that head was under a dreadful strain, wrestling still, but really beaten ; and suddenly it seemed to her a sure thing that some footstep went treading round the table she was seated at ; upon which she was up and away, fled with her sob to Netta's bed. . . .

In panting it to Netta, she collapsed, her arms hanging abandoned, her eyes stared sightless.

The following day she presented all the appearance of death, and though two doctors said that she was not dead, during four days she kept them in a state of frowning and curiosity at her sort of coma of the Sleeping Beauty, until on the fifth noon her lids flickered. But she continued to be comatose : there she lay, awake, having some intelligence apparently, not technically paralysed, but no lust, interest, her neurons suspended, knee-jerk dead, hormones not functioning, salivary glands themselves gone moribund, pulse characterized by dicrotism, scleræ of hœmolytic icterus, indifference to rocks dropped near her ear, little response to the faradic current, indifference to radio Schubert, which her soul had loved. Her nerve-system, overworked, had snapped like elastic, they asserted ; profounder than salvage she had foundered ; and the prognosis was death within three weeks, unless some power or other could be found to penetrate, rouse, resurrect her.

As to Netta Fenton, in six days she was six years older : for those half-sisters were nearer and dearer than sisters ; and added to the loss of her darling was the problem on her back in what manner to bring about for Greta, Greta's heart's-desire as to financing science. Let Greta die a minor, unmarried, and Whipsnade Prince got the fortune, to finance Piccadilly. Netta, though, could marry Greta quick to someone—to a gardener : but to put so much power into a gardener's hand . . . little her gardeners knew about bio-chemistry, except the bio-chemistry of lilies. There was Harry Ransom—intelligent, steady—but, after all, a boy: to dab suddenly upon a boy's back several hundred thousand pounds ! But there was Sir Thomas Ormsby : *he* was ideal, man of science, unmarried—

might not mind marrying, and being a widower five days after. He could hardly be *asked* to—the thing was delicate—but Netta could hint. . . .

On such a rack she had been, so distracted, that she had not written anything of the event to friends, until the sixth evening when, after making a list of twelve, she sat to the task of letters. But she found it a mountain ; the more her haste for the night-post the less her speed; tears interfered, her lips shivering for the pity which is in things, her thoughts wandering. She managed the letter to Sir Thomas Ormsby. . . . " You know of Greta's intention to endow organic chemistry . . . she only inherits, before twenty-one, on condition of being married . . . it has seemed to me possible that you, being unmarried, may be interested." . . . But now a doctor was announced, and she, having to dash off to him, dodged the job of the letters, saying to her Lady Dale-Eldon " Do write them for me—here's the list—just copy the one I've written "—she was gone trotting ; but her fretted head forgot that the one she had written contained more than news, contained a suggestion, contained that statement, " you being unmarried . . . "

So that two married ladies in England and one married man got letters telling them that they were not married ; so did nine unmarried men.

To " Whip " Prince nothing had been written, nothing even yet to Harry Ransom ; but Ransom understood that something very rum must be happening at Cap Ferrat ; and from Ransom Whip had it : for, interested now in Ransom, Whip one evening had an impulse to step aside from the Strand into King's College, where he was guided down to an underground room, and there Ransom sat, undergoing coaching. Whip suggested dining at "The Savile," saying "Then we can discuss—I am not long back from Villefranche"; but Ransom, no diner-out, smiled, answering "Perhaps you don't know what long-tots are?—rectangles of figures to be added-up: one can't, if not in practice; they are in my preliminary exam. And I am in another stew just now—in doubt whether to abandon everything, and be away to Villefranche: for something sinister has happened to Miss Chesson—no reply to any letter——"

And Whip, who could decide like lightning, decided then to be back at Cap Ferrat, to see to his interests, to see Netta Fenton.

Near the time when he was arriving at Nice, Netta was receiving from Sir Thomas Ormsby a wire in reply: "I am coming to do as you desire"; and, comforted, she went out in haste to arrange at the Villefranche *mairie* for a civil marriage at the Villa dei Gigli: "Greta Chesson, aged eighteen; Sir Thomas Ormsby, aged forty-eight."

But when she came home another wire awaited her: "Am now leaving London in conformity with your wishes. Killik"—Mr. Ernest Killik, senior partner of the firm of Killik, Murgatroyd and Baggitas, solicitors, of Lincoln's Inn.

"Which *wishes?*" Netta asked herself; but, as she asked, began to gather.

And within an hour came upon her, to her dismay, another announcement of the same thing; then two tumbled in together; then during the afternoon four: from which it appeared that eight gentlemen, to whom her Lady Dale-Eldon had written "you being unmarried," were willing to have in their hands the disposal of five hundred thousand pounds, at the price of being married for some days ; and were travelling in trains and aeroplanes to that end.

" Now, look here . . . " with a sort of half-laugh at the inexpressible, Netta dropped upon a sofa, then, smitten anew by the social dysthesia of the thing, threw fingers to face, breathing " But, ah, how agonizing ! what in God's name *am* I to say to eight of them ? "

Some minutes after which " Whip " appeared before her stare. . . .

" *You ?* " says she.

And he : " Pleased, are you ? "

" What, Sir, is it you want now ? "

" You, I think."

" Hm."

" Tell me : I hear that Greta is ill."

Her lips shivered toward tears. . . . " Come, you can see her."

They passed out to an arbour of marble, a part of the garden bounded by harbour-cliff, where two rows of pillars rose in gross masses from a ground of slabs, supporting a grille of rafters overgrown by roses, by grossness of ivy, vine, violets ; and on the remote brink of the scene of sea more blueness, of mountains distant, a tower, a little crowd of villas, enveloped in blueness of the heaven of heavens ; out of the bowels of which blue universe came forth music of Utopia, a superheterodyne set—then rendering Liszt—being there beside the deck-chair in which the sick lay near the cliff's brink, a slit of her eyes visible, fixed, unlighted. . . .

When Lady Dale-Eldon went away on their

coming, Netta and Whip sat beside the *chaise longue*, and bent silent.

Then Whip : " I say, will she die ? "

" Yes. It is the eating ! "

" Poor chit ! "

But, then, he was born lucky. . . .

And presently she, with a face in pain : " And I am in another misery. . . . She has, of course, to be married quickly, if her wishes as to the money are to take effect : so I wrote to Sir Thomas Ormsby, suggesting that he might like to ; then I got Lady Dale-Eldon to write the news for me to different friends—told her she might just copy the Ormsby letter, never dreaming that she'd be putting that in, too ; and now nine different men are on the way, coming upon me. *How* am I to say to eight of them 'After making you take this journey, I have selected somebody better than you ?' The excruciation of it ! "

As she spoke, Whip had flushed ; and he said " Serves you right."

She stared. " Serves me. . . . You say that to me ? "

" Of course, I say so." He sprang up. " Where do *I* come in ? I thought that you cared something for me."

Her stare followed him stepping about ; and she said " But about that child's chief wish ? About the public good ? Must I not—— ? "

" Oh, leave the public good out of it ! Providence is the managing director of the public good, not you and I. But, then, what nonsense ! How can the girl marry, if she can't say a word ? Marriage is a consent——"

"Mons. Soriac, the mayor, has arranged to waive——"

"Can't! What Court, do you suppose, would uphold a sham marriage like that, faked to do an heir out of his rights?"

"But"—her eyebrows up—"if nine responsible men are coming to marry her?—one of them a solicitor?"

Whip spun round upon her. "The solicitor should be ashamed of his unconsciousness of law—if he knows the facts. Probably they don't know the facts—the girl's actual condition, or the existence of another heir's interests. If a marriage-rite took place, the other heir would simply apply to the Court to disallow it, and the case wouldn't last fifteen minutes."

"And *you*"—with an underlook—"would do that?"

"You may bet!"

"Oh, dear, I have been living in a dream—all's up!" Now she covered her face, weeping.

His head, as he paced, turned to murmur at her "Cry, if you like."

Then a silence filled with the wireless, the music now over, some voice now saying its say out of the void of heaven.

But nimbly in an impulse Whip was on a knee to her, pleading "No, don't cry! Look here, I die if you cry."

"I never thought"—on a sob—"living in a fool's paradise——"

"But don't cry. I'll do whatever you want—there. There's always a way out, some idea will be cropping up; but how can it, if you cry? Don't cry."

" No, I'm not "—on a sob—" I dare say I shall live through it—but perplexity on top of bereavement—all at once——"

" Yes, poor ! But don't cry : let's see, let's think "—he leapt up now to step away, to throw himself down on the cliff-brink, facing the sea ; and in every pause of the radio talker she could hear him siffling an air through his teeth-edges—this being his way of " thinking."

Then he beckoned her with " I say ! Sit with me a little ? . . . Uplifted, this. Here's where Jehovah will sit on Judgment Day, having beneath his feet a sea of billions of sinners, looking rather blue. But don't cry "—as she stood beside him—" it will be all right ; I see a way——"

" Way ? she said ; " there's no way."

" Oh, yes, there's always—Look here, we'll make it a lottery : that will give *me* a one-in-ten chance to inherit, and will rescue *you* from your mess with those nine : for you'll put the blame of it upon *me*, you'll say to each, as he comes, that after you wrote to him *I* turned up, and refused to admit the validity of the marriage, unless he won in a gamble between him and me ; then, you'll say, you got me to agree to a gamble between ten—or eleven, if Ransom comes—your reason being to increase to eleven the odds against my winning. That will——"

" Aye, smart," she put in, " but will that be quite true ? "

" Is anything ? "—he laughed—" we have to compromise : living is compromise. The sun pretends to be round, but isn't really. Look at my friend, the bishop of Shipley : the good fellow proclaims in church ' On the seventh day do no work,' knowing, as he proclaims it, that men are working to broadcast the church-service in which he proclaims it. One lies a little, doesn't one ?—the grease of life which keeps the machinery from shrieking."

She eyed him aside, smiling her tiny smile. " Aye, I see the kind of little sinner you are : one lies a little Piccadilly-way, even when one is not a bishop. . . . But do you suppose that those nine responsible gentlemen are going to draw matches, to see who draws the shortest match—— ? "

" No, not exactly matches," he put in—" something less *banal*. You hear that man spouting now on the wireless—famous novelist—telling his favourite tale he is, the B.B.C. giving a series, each writer telling the tale of his career which he himself likes best, one every day, except Sundays. So, if you associate some particular day and its tale with each of those nine—or each of us ten say—or eleven—— By the way, are you pleased with me for being willing to convert my certainty into an eleventh chance ? You haven't mentioned that you are pleased. The sum involved is considered a lot."

Her grave gaze meditated on him before she said " I don't mention everything ; some day I may, if ever I come to know that you don't ' lie a little '—to me."

This had the effect of making him blush, look rather shy ; and hurriedly he said " So, if we associate each—Who, by the way are these nine ? "

Netta answered : " There is Sir Thomas Ormsby, of the College of Science and Technology—big, his big brow half-way down his face ; then there's Killik, the solicitor, getting grey in his beard ; and you may know the painter, Paul Watts, whom girls' eyes turn aside to follow—tall—dash of darkish moustache—rather charming ; then there's Lord George Orchardson, the motor-racer, with his compelling expression, rigid lips which say 'You shall!' to his cars ; and Gerald Jewson, son of the Royal College president—at concerts *he* is the viola—longish hair, excess of neck-tie ; and Sir C. Alexander Caxton of the Foreign Office—bush of white eyebrow, white face of rock, raw-looking, raw sort of voice ; and the Rev. Strong Darrel—red like red-ink, red face, red rag of goatee-beard, to aggravate a bull—talks short in cablegrams, like Morse-tappers rapping out peremptory cablegrams in spasms, voice strong, authoritative ; then there's little Mr. Coward—thinner than you—olive-dark—elfin face, hair black, with some silver in—horsey—his home is the Hotel Métropole—or the Maelstrom, say—lives in a whirl, but unconcerned himself, bets on every race, I think, but doesn't care ; and there's Mons. Makla Pascal—little, too, with a great square head ; and there's—No, that's all."

Whip said : "Yes, I know most of them—Coward and I are intimates, Caxton, too, a little, and Paul Watts. . . . So, then, you'll write 'Thursday,' 'Friday,' 'Saturday,' on slips of paper, then let each of us take one haphazard out of a bowl, and whoever takes the day whose tale has some characteristic or other marries Greta, unless it is I—for *I* get the money without troubling to marry."

Netta meditated, hesitated ; scented something, doubted something ; felt somewhere in her that

Mr. Whip Prince was parting too easily with the certainty of half-a-million, merely to save his nerves from the irk of seeing a lady leak tears, and might be tricking her simplicity somewhere. But, then, he might not be ; if he was not, he was being wonderful, and it was horrid to suspect him ; doubtless he was accustomed to think lightly of sums of money, he was "Prince Whip," living in a light assurance, aloof from the world which works and worries. Suddenly she said "I—see. But what characteristic is the winning tale to have ? If I say 'the day whose tale is the best,' who is to be the judge of 'best' ?"

"*We* will be the judges," Whip said, "we'll vote : nobody to vote for his own day's tale. But not 'best' tale—we aren't a crowd of critics—let the winning tale have some more definite characteristic than 'best.' Suppose we say 'the winner is the tale that *cannot have happened*.' How would that do ? Something definite."

Netta meditated it. "Well—yes. The most improbable tale. But—why not the most probable ? That seems more natural."

"You think ? No, I thought of that, but 'most improbable' is more definite, easier to judge. 'The tale that cannot have happened'—put it like that. That's quite definite."

But Netta was not at rest. "And if none of the tales is a tale that cannot have happened ? These are professional tale-tellers : is any of them going to tell a tale that cannot have happened ?"

Now Whip, on his defence, suggested "One of them may tell a fairy-tale."

But Netta again objected. "Or two of them

may: then how will there be any judging, if both never can have happened?"

Now on a puff of laughter Whip said "Deah me, how suspicious of the future! Won't you ever marry for fear your husband may have a secret addictedness to steak-and-onions? If we think of possibilities, we will never open a letter, microbes may be on—don't you know. These aren't fairy-tales—not likely that there'll be one, there can hardly be two. 'Tale that cannot have happened' will mean the one farthest from any possibility—and that will be easily seen. If we trust the future, the future proves trustworthy. 'Take no thought for the morrow.' A young couple who venture to get married without money are well-off in a month—I know one boy who picked up a shilling the morning after his marriage. But don't trust the future *too* much: that makes it touchy. So I seldom bet: when I do, I win."

And Netta: "Is that why in this case you are willing to 'convert a certainty' into a tenth or eleventh chance? Feel that you will win, do you?"

"Well, I suppose—yes—that I shall win."

Her eyes dwelt on him. Then: "Been lucky in love, too?"

"By Jove, let me see—No, I have only loved One, who is not responsive to my keenness to please her."

"Named Patricia?"

"Begins with N."

"Ah. Little 'liar a little.' I foreknew the little lie before it lied a little. So in this case——" but she stopped at a sigh "Oh!" behind her—from Harry Ransom, who had travelled to Nice in the same train as Prince, each unaware of the other. He now, seeing only the sick, tripped straight to his knee beside her, and, noting her face bony, the still slit of her eyes musing unmoved on what none knew, he put his lips to moan pity on her pallid hand ; and more or less she, too, knew him : an expert observer may have determined that something not unlike a smile stirred her mouth. . . .

That being a Monday, on Tuesday " Whip " Prince executed in Villefranche a deed by which he agreed to regard Greta's marriage, if she married, as valid ; this he handed to Netta, who now, meditating on him with that mildness of her pensive eyes, with the tiny smile of that hint of humour hovering elusive round her mouth, abandoned to him her hand to be kissed.

By Wednesday morning a copy of the *Radio Times* had been acquired, from which Lady Dale-Eldon, who was to distribute the slips, saw that Friday's tale-teller, a writer of fantasies, was the one most likely to tell a tale that " cannot have happened " : so, knowing that Netta wanted Sir Thomas Ormsby to be the winner, she dog's-eared the slip that had on it " Friday I," and in handing out the slips haphazard from a bowl, managed to pick up that slip to hand to Sir Thomas. The Rev. Mr. Darrel got a Saturday—" Saturday II "—but Whip Prince, who had got " Wednesday I," said that he was bound to be off to Monte Carlo that afternoon, and got Mr. Darrel to exchange—to take " Wednesday I," and give " Saturday II " ; as to Harry Ransom he got a Monday—" Monday II "—last day of all.

Prince then went away, but everyone else, entering with gaiety into the spirit of the gamble, passed out to the arbour, where card-tables had been placed on the pallid carpet of leaves mixed with pallid tints of petals that strewed the slabs, like lucre of Elf-king's bankers profusely strewn—the tables bearing tulip-hues of liqueurs, wines, fruits, and there were chairs of various kinds, and music coming wonderfully out of wide Nowhere.

Then all at once Prince steps-in in his pressing way, to tell that he had managed after all to evade his trip to Monte Carlo ; and whereas the others had sat on chairs, he chose to sit on the cliff-brow, feet swinging over, while Ransom and Netta sat together in easy-chairs near the invalid, on the invalid's other side being Sir Thomas Ormsby, whose patient she at present was, " in consultation " with a pair of Villefranche physicians ; and he, every ten seconds, whatever talk he was having, shot at her a side-look from his sharp eyes, to catch her in the act of manifesting phenomena ; and a noise of gossip chattered, until now Elgar's " Pomp and Circumstance " smashed to its end ; and now out of the void a voice uttered " The next part of our programme will follow at once " : whereupon a stillness there, while the red Rev. Darrel, as if nervous—this (Wednesday) being his day—shook up and up his red right sock, which, crossed over the left thigh, showed above the shoe ; and now it sounded, the announcement : " This is the national programme from London " . . . " And now for that period *raconteur*, Mr. H. C. Morrissey, in his tale 'The Panel' ! " . . . " Mr. Morrissey" . . . the announcer proffering him in a voice of awe, as ushers profoundly bow : and the tale told was this :

The thing that Walter Gilbert could not do was to preach—and he was a preacher. It was at St. Jerome (Devonshire), paying £95—for which not much is to be expected of the lungs beyond breathing, but the little congregation persisted in expecting orations less grey ; in other respects the new man had crept into their hearts. Rumour told of his sick-bed tendernesses, tramps across country to see a paralytic. It was noted that, as he went with his swing along lanes, smiting his thick stick upon the ground, he was fond of glancing at the sky with a sort of glad half-laugh ; if he met anyone, the same half-laugh, as he flung out on his hand his " How-d'ye-do ? " He seemed attached to children, and would carry a small boy on his shoulder. Big he was, with a light-coloured moustache, and wore a short morning-coat, not the parson's frock. He was winning somehow. But he could not preach. And Baldchin, the farmer's daughter, who had been at boarding-school at Bath, uttered judgment that he was " not a gentleman."

One Saturday night he sat writing the morrow's discourse in the parsonage, an old house embowered behind a mass of boscage. The week had been so full, that he had found excuse to put off that task till now—those two cartloads of words, that work of Hercules. If he had only been content to utter simply the limpid thing that was in him to say !—but no, he must be ornate, must do better than his best. " Anything will not do," he said constantly, spurring himself. But either his wits were not bright, or preaching was the thing for which he was not made : his congregation regarded his outpourings with a half-smile of tolerance. Sometimes he was near to despair ; would thump his forehead, say " Dunce ! Thick-head ! "

This night he wrote till one, and then the Sunday-morning task was over. He read the thing over, and was not dissatisfied : rose, went to bed.

But at breakfast he once more read the sheets, and this time with loathing. How little of the heart with its yearnings and out-goings was here ! He did not know that even works of art seem to their creators, after repeated readings, flat and dull. Yet at ten he was at the fatal scrawl again, reading. . . . The thing would not do—this leaden thing. It seemed to him improper that the word spoken in " The Temple " should be other than inspired—and he fell to his knees, his forehead striking a wall, to pray . . . for some miracle to help . . . if not, then for some work in the world which he could better do. And now something moved, gave—at his forehead, where it rested upon the wainscot. He put up his hand, pressed. A panel flew back, and there was revealed to him an opening in the thickness of the wall : he had touched some spring ; in the opening lay a packet of papers.

He hurried to a table, untied a ribbon : a blank sheet of foolscap ; then a parchment, engrossed : " This is the last will and testament of me, James Anthony Pritchard . . . and as to the residue of my estate realty or personalty . . . upon trust to pay the annual produce, rents, dividends or interests thereof or thereon to the said Alice Jane Woodhouse . . . £175,000 . . . and from and after her death or decease upon trust to transfer, convey, or assign the said lands, hereditaments, premises, funds, trusts, stocks——"

A will thirty years old. . . . And, tied by itself, a packet, which he sat reading till at eleven the bell ceased its tolling for the service ; then rose, flurried, frightened, in his hand the sere sheets—in a woman's writing.

He stammered no leaden things that day. When he sat down, pallid, the discourse finished, St. Jerome was thrilled.

He remained there another month, continuing without fail the series of burning sermons, full of humour, brilliance, wit. But it was noticed that something of his simple-hearted jollity had passed from him. As to James Anthony Pritchard, as to Alice Jane Woodhouse, he made inquiries, but learned little.

At the end of this time he was suddenly called away to a living in Wales, where he remained two years ; and here again occurred the same poor beginning, bursting suddenly into the same fine surprise. He received then an invitation to a curacy in Derbyshire, which he felt a call to accept, and thither went.

The church was in a valley, somewhat remote from Lyston, the townlet, and near the church the parsonage, an old-time manse, half wooden, where Gilbert lived alone. By a lane at the back of this you ascended a hill, went down into a dell, and so to the manor-house, the dwelling of " the Doctor "—a shaded place, a stately home, where, strolling in its park one day, Gilbert came upon a Miss Rosey in a hammock, bowered all in brown shades. She lay asleep, wrenched hip-hilly, shins revealed, the gracious curves of her girlhood on exhibition ; but, as he gazed, her flush deepened, and she was up, laughing. He, too, laughed, saying " I am only a bungler, not a thief—was innocently strolling, waiting for the Doctor to come home."

His laugh was too loud, his hands too large : she noticed them with a mental pout before saying, " It is of no consequence—I fell asleep over the book you set me reading."

" *A Modern Utopia* ? You like it ? "

" Seems goodish. And *you* approve it. I rather pin my faith to your literary decisions, do you know ? "

Her head perked saucily. . . . Sometimes he had a dread in his heart that she was laughing at him.

They then walked among the trees; and he said, " What I wanted to know was whether the Doctor will be able to preach to-morrow."

For Dr. Grandford, a fine orator, who always " took " the morning sermon, Gilbert preaching at night, had lately been showing signs of break-up.

" I'm *afraid* he won't be able," she said. " Do you know, he took yesterday to a *stick* ?—making him look so quaint, my poor dad ! "

" That, then, is two sermons for someone between now and to-morrow. Can't you write one for me, Miss Rosey ? "

" I can at least give you all the sympathy I have to spare." Then after a silence : " But do you find it, in truth, a very great—bore ? "

" It is far from easy."

" And I wanted to ask you : do you, as one somehow suspects, imagine that you do not preach—nicely ? "

" My heart knows that, Miss Rosey."

Her manner became earnest. " But you *do !*

Will you believe me? And more and more you do. Your sermons are becoming 'freer'—my father's word, and approbation from him is something. If crude people think differently, why trouble? I, at least, like——"

She stopped, he looking down upon the path, sensitive to the gentle purpose of her words; and he murmured, "You are kind to me, kinder than anyone I ever knew"—as a footman came announcing the arrival of the Doctor.

An hour afterwards Gilbert was still alone with Dr. Grandford in the library, the Doctor standing, a forefinger smoothing down the strip of silver whisker on his pale face. He was large, white, conveying a suggestion of immaculate cleanness, dignity, uttering deliberate phrases; and Gilbert sat before him, hearing him say, "You surprise me. You mean that you have been so—incautious, as to let yourself, ah, fall in love with Rosey?"—Dr. Grandford being "a younger son"—aristocrat.

Gilbert looked upon the ground, fingering his shovel-hat. "I am afraid, Sir, that something like that has happened, and I thought it well to mention it to you in the first place. Of course, I know——"

The Doctor smoothed his strip of whisker. "But have you grounds for imagining that such a notion would be received by my daughter with, ah, acquiescence?"

"No, Sir; no grounds. That is, I have thought it not impossible. I may be presumptuous. . . . Miss Rosey is very good and gracious to me, Sir."

"There is no question of presumption," the Doctor said; "but you must see that there are—reasons. You are not, ah, firmly established; and my daughter has been richly nurtured. I may mention, too, that a calamity just befallen me would prevent any deficiency in you from being remedied on *her* side——"

"Calamity, Sir?"

"It has made me ill, you see"—with a smile. "I tell you in confidence; my child is aware of nothing. The extent of the disaster one does not yet know, but the concern in which most of my personalty has been involved has, ah, failed: the consequences—debt, mortgages on my realty here, impecuniosity. If the worst be true, I may have to depend upon the income of the little church—and you see me daily grow feebler. In fact, I now largely depend upon your efforts, Mr. Gilbert, and have been comforted by the knowledge that my trust is well placed. I have observed you, and, ah, like you. But as to this matter of my daughter——"

"Do not let that be an added trouble to you, Sir!" Gilbert cried: "I, for my part, will—at any rate, it can wait."

"Well, but that is not what I wanted to say. I do not feel the impulse to thwart your inclination to that extent. Having gone so far, I should, if I were you, ah, speak to her. You will find your mind freer in consequence. But I do not conceal from you my anticipation that you will find your suit—unsuccessful."

Gilbert grasped his hand. . . .

In the grey church, with its effigies of centuries and melancholy half-lights, a thin congregation the next morning saw Dr. Grandford in hood and surplice, at the choir-end behind the pulpit, listening to Gilbert with a sideward head, with a slight twitching of his brows, a kind of surprise in the expression of his face. The surprise was general! People leant forward, intent upon a new utterance. In her curtained pew Rosey contemplated her lap, slightly flushed, frowning. There were, then, unsuspected powers in him? Yet something troubled her, jarred on the nerves. One Dr. Deighton—winey old practitioner of Lyston—swore in his pew, muttering, "That's not his own sermon, by Heaven!" This thought occurred to others. Yet, if not his, whose? Would he dare to preach a published discourse, which any of his hearers might have read? Nor was he, they knew, the species of person to shirk his burdens by the cheapness of petty theft. As for Gilbert, the words which were filling his mind were these: "I now depend largely upon your efforts, Mr. Gilbert." This had been a goad at his will.

After the service a Lady Garbril, who, with her brood of girls, had accompanied Rosey home, asked in the drawing-room "Did anyone notice anything odd in our sermon?"

The Doctor was silent: still on his face that look of puzzlement—those twitching brows.

"Did *you*, Miss Grandford?"

Rosey was somewhat restless, peevish. "It was a little—unusual, I think," she said curtly, turning her neck.

And in the evening Dr. Grandford, contrary to his wont of late, again drove to the church—a fuller church—a sermon as brilliant as the morning's: in the midst of which a little "Oh!" broke from him—three choir-boys heard and reported it: Gilbert in a flight of eloquence, had said:

"You cannot bind a zephyr in an embrace: it will escape you; it will away to the mountain-top and flout you; it will wheel with wings to the mid-sea to mock you!"

And the same night the Doctor summoned Miss Rosey into his presence in the library, where his hand rested on her rumply head, she seated on a footstool by his easy-chair, rather pale: for his face was hard....

"Rosey, I have to tell you—something. I shall not detain you from your music; but it is as well that you hear this without delay. I know it to be possible that words may be spoken to you by Mr., ah, Gilbert, which may set up a new relation between you: and in order that there may be no kind of doubt as to your course in such an event, I have to tell you my impression that Mr. Gilbert is not a man of, ah, honour."

She turned sharply, her face all inflamed, upon him. "Oh, I say, Dad!"

"You are moved, Rosey."

"Because—this is so strangely *unlike* you! And I am so certain that you must be wrong——"

The Doctor frowned. "You make me conjecture Rosey, that I did well in ordering this interview. Am I to understand that you are—*attached*—to Mr. Gilbert?"

"I am pleased with his society, Dad," she answered, with innocent round eyes of surprise.

"I see. Then, you are no doubt a close listener to his discourses. You may, therefore, chance to remember a sentence of to-night's harangue beginning, 'You cannot bind a zephyr in an embrace.' Now, I say that I know that sentence—have read it, or heard it, before. So that, having heard it from Mr. Gilbert, I was able to know that to-day's sermons are certainly not his own. And you cannot, I think, hold a man honest who takes to himself credit, aye, and possible emolument, advancement in his career, on the strength of another's expressions. You see that, I think."

"Not his *own*, do you say?"

"No."

The roses had whitened in Rosey's cheeks. "And *you* know whose they are?"

"No. I should, however. I have certainly heard or seen them."

"He must be a very foolish man to act in that way," she muttered. "It seems so sudden and incredible—unless there be some mistake—some other point of view. But, of course, it can be nothing to me——"

She stopped, an aching in her throat; and the old man patted her hair, until she sprang up and ran from him. . . .

Well, the bankruptcy crashed ruinously upon Dr. Grandford: there was a month's confinement to his bed, then came a migration from the manor-house to the parsonage—the footmen gone—strange men walking with an air of ownership in the halls of an ancient race. . . .

Rosey now knew the truth, and her lips were pressed. When, a week after taking lodgings in Lyston Town, Gilbert found the chance of speaking, of which she had been clever to balk him, when he said "There is little in life for me, Miss Rosey, if you do not care for me," it was a patrician who answered him, poor-proud now: the Doctor, hearing her, would have pronounced her manner and voice-inflexions the perfection of tone. "You surprise me. May you not have allowed your fancies to overreach your instincts, Mr. Gilbert?"

"Miss Rosey——"

"I am sorry if you suffer. You will let the question drop now. You have business with my father?"

The Doctor had waited with peevish impatience to see if the series of sermons would cease; but they had revoltingly continued. At every fresh sight of the frequented church he had had an impulse to interfere. At last he summoned Gilbert.

With a multiplicity of "ah's," he lying a-bed, Gilbert sitting near, he said that circumstances over which he had no, ah, control had, to his annoyance, and, he might say, sorrow, compelled him to think about having another curate. He recognized the value of Gilbert's zeal, and had actually reported of him in that sense to the bishop, who, he had reason to think, might, on his approaching visit to Lyston, have something to say to Gilbert.

The double blow fell upon the simple, tough fibre of Gilbert like a sledge upon a block of oak. Stunned, he never winced; started forth upon a headlong walk, away from men, over the country, everything seeming to have slipped from him. "I now depend largely upon your efforts, Mr. Gilbert"—those words had puffed him with a boyish pride, pricking him to utmost energy! And it had ended in this: dismissal—from all he cared for in life—from the old man, from her. To live without tie, all unrelated to the world—brother to nothing, son to nothing—this was his bitterness. The night came down upon him far from home.

" Rosey ! " he cried to the four winds.

Had he done anything—neglected to do anything ? The sermons ! Those sermons of another mind ! They were a rather sore place in his consciousness. Ought he ever to have preached them ? God knew his motive, that it was pure. At their first discovery, he had promised himself never to utter them on any occasion when there was a chance that any benefit might accrue to himself from them ; hence, on going to a new place, while he could at all consider himself as being more or less on his trial, he had spoken his own words only. Then, the finding of the sermons had seemed to him so directly " an answer " to his cry for help ; and now it was Dr. Grandford's expression of dependence upon him that had led him to keep the church, by these means, a centre of interest. He could not manage to blame himself—looked deeply within, and found all clear and selfless. For an upright nature to commit a deception for the good of others may be a greater exhibition of self-sacrifice than to tell a truth at any cost ; so he tossed his head backward in cloudless appeal to God. But the sermons had nothing to do with it ! he thought : it was all the crookedness of his own fate ; no one knew of the sermons, or could know. When some spears of rain hurtled upon his face, he turned back, walking still in the same haste ; and again and again he was uttering " Rosey ! child ! "

Rosey was at his lodgings waiting for him ! The bishop's visit to Lyston to confirm a flock of young people was only a few days off, so, as Rosey was to return to the cathedral-town with him as governess to his girls, she had been paying farewell-visits, and had undertaken to tell Gilbert, in passing, that a Mrs. Grimes, the quarryman's mother, near to death, was eager to see him. He was out ; she would wait ; was shown into his sitting-room ; stood at a window, twirling her parasol. Then of two oak-sticks of his she took one, looked at it ; then, as if it were hot, put it quickly from her ; then walked listlessly upon her parasol, to and fro. On an escritoire lay a manuscript in faded ink, which, as she passed, caught her eye ; and fixed she stood, unable to shift her gaze from the sheets. That hand—she knew it—that running scrawl ! *Two* people could never have written so peculiarly, and so similarly. And the sentence she read told her that here was the last sermon preached by Gilbert. Not now did she wait a moment, but hurried forth, fluttered, into the rain of the already late night.

The way to the parsonage lay through lanes, then a darksome avenue of larches, which she had reached when she was aware of a breath bearing her name : could see nothing, but the " Rosey ! " reached her heart. The next moment she collided with Gilbert, was in his arms, her lips found out. . . . There was a scar on her upper-lip, mark of a cut, which, kissing her, he felt and tasted. . . . In an instant she was fleeing like a roe, pursued by the wild pain of his cry, " Rosey ! "

But she stopped, stood away from the path, fearing, hoping, that he might follow. He, however, had no notion where she was ; and she, panting, pressed against a tree-trunk, could hear him pass away from her. She stretched out an arm after him, saying " I did love you ! "

In the parsonage, wet, with a pale face, she walked straight to the Doctor's bedside.

She said calmly, " I have been to Mr. Gilbert's rooms, where I chanced to see his last sermon. It is unaccountable—and I do not know what bearing it may have upon your opinion of him—but, judging from the packet of letters I have of my mamma's, that sermon was certainly written by her."

The Doctor's hand went sharply up to his brow.

" My—my *good* child——"

" I thought I would tell you, Dad."

She walked away, longing for solitude. As for the Doctor, he sat up, smoothing his whisker down, deep in thought.

For two days he did not refer to Gilbert; but once, when Gilbert was announced, Rosey was surprised to notice a twinkle in the Doctor's eyes.

On the Saturday arrives my Lord Bishop—a little, brisk person with a bird-like perk of the head. He had heard of Gilbert's pastoral qualities from the Doctor, and had it in mind to place him well. At dinner he asked " Is he—tell me, now—a man of liberal utterance, this Mr. Gilbert ? "

" I can at least promise you a very, ah, tolerable discourse from him to-morrow evening," the Doctor said with a twinkle, ending in a frown.

" Mr. Gilbert cannot preach ! " Rosey blurted with a flush like anger.

" Rosey ! you are candid "—from the Doctor.

The Bishop's head perked from one to the other.

" There is—come, now—a difference of standpoint between the new age and the old," he said, puzzled. " Well—I shall keep an open mind, and judge for myself."

There was "confirmation" at both services, the bishop preaching in the morning, Dr. Grandford constraining himself to attend both times, and read "the lessons." As Gilbert's coming departure from Lyston had got abroad, and he was understood to be in some measure on his trial before the bishop, expectation of special effort from him was on tip-toe, when his snowy robes slowly mounted the pulpit, Rosey now bending a pallid face over the hymn-book still open in her lap.

His brow, massive, slanting, bald on the top, was beaded with moisture ; he had a way of shaking a bent forefinger, as he preached, but this night he buried both fists in the cushion, leaning forward on his arms, with a slow enunciation ; there was a mournfulness in him this night ; he spoke, did not read ; and the drop from the clever flow of utterance of the last months to this stolid talk was marked. But the sermon differed as much from his own laboured discourses of other days as from the borrowed sermons. For the first time he uttered himself. As perfect love "casteth out fear," so profound sorrow does not admit of embarrassment. He did not stammer, was clear and calm ; and the speech of this grieving spirit held the people in such a grip that evening as when a brother utters his plaint to brothers.

Something or other moved Dr. Grandford ; his face showed it ; his hands rather trembled : for in a flash the whole secret of motive and character had illumined him—the reason why those borrowed sermons had not been preached on Gilbert's first coming to Lyston—something of the reason why they had been preached afterwards—the reason why one of them was not preached *now* : he divined the whole. This man he had supposed capable of appearing before the bishop in borrowed plumes for his own preferment ; but he was a better man.

He said, as Gilbert was leaving the vestry, " Will you, ah, Mr. Gilbert, lend me an arm to the parsonage ? "

And so they went, the bishop walking in front with Rosey, to whom he said " You told me—come, now—that Mr. Gilbert could not preach ? "

" I was mistaken, my lord," she answered.

And the Doctor behind, leaning upon Gilbert : " I must speak to you—now. I have misjudged you. I must humble myself before you. The matter is this : for some months you have been preaching to me a series of my own sermons——"

" Sir, Sir," Gilbert muttered.

" I did not know *that* fact—till a few days since, or should have told you. It was a circumstance discovered by Rosey at your rooms which opened my eyes. They must have been written by my wife at my dictation at least thirty years ago, and I had forgotten them wholly, except a single sentence. I knew, however, that they were not yours, and thought—but let that pass. I say to you now that I divine your motives, and, ah, honour them."

" But, Sir, Sir "—Gilbert was all in a mess of shame.

" What you have to do in the first place is to appease my curiosity : by what miracle did you obtain these writings ? "

" I found them, Sir, behind a secret panel at St. Jerome's parsonage, at Hurley, in——"

"You have been there, then? I don't think you ever told me?"

"No, Sir? That may be because I was there only two months—a mere incident."

"Well, but this partially explains it: for before inheriting the manor here, I, too, was incumbent at that very St. Jerome's."

They had reached the parsonage, where the Doctor led Gilbert into the study, saying "The fact of the secret panel I can explain. In the parsonage lived with us my wife's sister and their grandfather, a Mr. Pritchard—the house was, indeed, his property—an eccentric person, of great age, wealthy, a man of essentially worldly mind, who yet conceived it a good investment for the future of his soul to hear a sermon once a week; and, as he was almost bed-ridden, unable to attend church, upon me was imposed the task of reading to him a weekly sermon, which he liked to buy, liked to be specially written for him; and I was glad to do them, for for each I got £5: to a young man with a command of florid language such as he loved the labour was not great. He took possession of the sermons after hearing them, and, I suppose, treasured them behind this panel."

"But, Sir—the will!" Gilbert now cried out, starting to his feet with sudden recollection.

"Will?"

"James Anthony Pritchard's will!—bequeathing £175,000 to Alice Jane Woodhouse—wrapping up the sermons——"

The doctor's face on the red chair-back went white.

"She was—my wife's, ah, sister," he said: "Rosey is her—heir."

" The will is in the hands of a lawyer in London, Sir," Gilbert said—" duly signed and witnessed."

The Doctor's eyes closed.

An hour later, when Gilbert rose, he, too, rose, scribbled some words, handed them in an envelope to Gilbert, saying " As you pass by the drawing-room, you might hand this to Rosey."

As the bishop, tired, had retired, Rosey, with dejected eyes, sat alone. When he came, handed her the note—a cry from her ! She read : " Have no longer any fear that Mr. Gilbert is not at all points worthy of us."

And instantly her sadness changed to frolic. He had sat awkwardly by her, and when he " sighed like furnace," says she " Anything wrong ? "

" Rosey——"

" Well, Mr. Gilbert ? "

" Rosey !—breath of my life—zephyr from——"

She was up, and gone from him, saying " You cannot bind a zephyr in an embrace "—with a curtsey : " it will escape you ; it will away to the mountain-top . . . " but now with a run, a trouble and murmur of love, she was crouched before him, her mouth upturned.

On the telling of this tale, Netta switched-off the utopian thing which was echoing near Italy what was being said in London, thus switching-on a chaos of tongues about her, Mr. Gerald Jewson, of the viola, saying to Mr. Paul Watts, the painter, " It had ' stuff,' some interest, but too *voulu*, manufactured—don't you think ? " to which Watts answered soft, not to offend any listener, " Clergymen in our age are essentially uninteresting persons, and should be kept out of art, for art is sincerity, and they aren't real people. This curate of the story, born an honest boy, became dishonest without knowing, because his education had made dishonesty his second nature. Those men can no more be straight than they can draw a straight line, or make a straight saw-cut."

" Oh, come, Watts ! " came from Lord George Orchardson, the racing ace, of the stressful expression of face : " it is dangerous to damn a whole class, man. Who invented the granular carbon transmitter ? parson !—the Rev. Hunnings. I bet *he* could make a straight saw-cut. Who invented the torsion balance ? parson !—the Rev. John Michell. *He* could make——"

" Well, yes," Watts said, " I knew of those : two out of hundreds of thousands—honour to them ; nominal clergymen ; *they* probably preached neither other people's sermons nor their own ; if they did, they were hotly honest sermons, scorning what all the others assert."

But now Sir C. Alexander Caxton—he of the white eyelashes, every inch " a permanent official " —observed, " Opinions differ, you know, Mr. Watts : how interesting the English clergy can be is shown in George Eliot's *Scenes from Clerical Life* ——"

" To which she was a foreigner," Watts put in : " her parsons aren't actual parsons. If they had been——" But now his attention was distracted to Netta asking " But can it have *happened*, Mr. Coward, do you think ? " near her now being the little Mr. Coward like a jockey in Elfland, who lived in the thick of things, making wagers on races, at one of the great hotels ; but he answered with a guffaw " Oh, Lor', don't ask *me*, blest if I know " ; upon which Whip Prince, chancing to catch Netta's question in the chatter, sang out to her " Surely ! why should it not have happened ? "

" No, Netta," now came from the red Rev. Mr. Darrel, who turned upon her from conversing with Mr. Killik, the solicitor—" cannot have happened. That tale-teller knows nothing of the clerical life he tries to describe. Here are a rector and his curate. They are associated for months, years. Yet they do not discover that both had once been incumbents at the same place. That could not be. Then you have the rector remembering a phrase that he once wrote, yet not remembering that it was he himself who wrote it. That could not be "—his voice strong, his phrases brusque, abrupt, like kettledrums rapping out spasms of patterings, so that several stopped talking to hearken, and a discussion arose as to his remarks ; in the midst of which Sir Thomas Ormsby, the doctor, said in a secret voice to Lady Dale-Eldon, seated near him, " Might have happened. My sister Harriet lately sent me a hymn praising the Sabbath, asking if I could tell her the writer's name, and, on my writing to say no, though three of the lines seemed familiar, she wrote ' Thou art the man '—stuff written when I was a youngster ! As to the two having been incumbents at the same place, one of them incidentally, I can quite see that, if it did not chance to come out at once, it might never chance to come out. Clerics are given to dogmatic statements made with a bias, to stating as truths what they have a motive to desire to be true. This being Mr. Darrel's day, he has a bias inclining him to state that the event cannot have happened, and perhaps by habit of mind he states it."

"Well, perhaps," Lady Dale-Eldon admitted: "but aren't we all like that a little, Sir Thomas?"

"Not quite all, I think," Sir Thomas replied: "the new type of mind called 'scientist' acquires so absorbing an interest——" But now Netta bent across the invalid to say to him "Sir Thomas, do you think she listened?"

And the scientist replied "Yes, I think that once her right eyebrow stirred. I shall be sitting up with her some time to-night"—for he was sleeping at the villa, but the others, except Harry Ransom, in the town; so now a move was being made, and soon eight were going in groups along the road, only Whip Prince staying with Netta a little.

CHAPTER II

THE ADORE DAY

THE next day the same breadth of brow of that universe of blueness, vast sun-bath of summer afternoon; but the meeting in the arbour was different in this—ten this day instead of eleven, Whipsnade Prince being away; and Netta said to the Rev. Mr. Darrel "Were there not eleven bidden, where is the one?"

The reverend gentleman answered "Gone to Paris probably. Mr. Gerald Jewson, out for a walk, saw him take the Nice tram which catches the morning train northward."

Netta said, "Dear me"; then, turning to Sir C. Alexander Caxton, said "Mr. Prince has fled from being present at his defeat, Charles, because this is your day, and the Foreign Office always wins."

On which Sir Charles, whose pale face readily flushed, went pinky, answering "Well, the old homeland does hold her own in the new age, does she not? as of old—as of old. But Prince must have some other reason for fleeing: a first throw is never likely to win—this is my first game of chance; moreover, my tale-teller, Brereton, is too reasonable a soul to tell a tale that 'cannot have happened.'"

"He may," Paul Watts remarked: "nothing so fickle as the artistic mood; soon wearies of one thing—realist yesterday, dreamer to-morrow—from fiction to philosophy: Brereton was romancist in

Edwardian days, when he wrote of pretty suffragettes, now he is a realist——"

"But this is Thursday," the little Mr. Coward put in, pacing: "nasty day, Thursday, for betting, Sir."

And now from Sir Thomas Ormsby: "She's awake!—just woke"—sent out in a hushed tone to Netta.

And from Coward, who chanced to catch it: "It's that crash of the music woke her." He added, "Sounds nice, that loolaloo: what would be the name of that bit?"

Gerald Jewson answered him, "Nicolai—Overture to 'Merry Wives.'"

"Well, there you are," Coward remarked—"'wives': Sir Charles is a winner. If you are thinking of betting on a horse named 'Jolly George,' and you happen to hear somebody say 'George Johnson,' bet away on him, sure to win."

Upon which Lord George Orchardson remarked, "Now the Foreign Office is at war with itself: Sir Charles feels that he will lose because it is Thursday, and will win because someone has said 'wife.'"

And Paul Watts, lolling at his length in a chair, touching his darling dash of moustache, remarked, with an eye aside on the Rev. Mr. Darrel, "With men this is impossible, but with God all things are possible."

"Right, Sir!" Mr. Darrel answered in his hammer manner: "the riddle can be interpreted: Sir Charles will nearly lose, but win, or will nearly win, but lose. All things can——"

But now the wireless went silent; and in some moments the Invisible Man was there, and spoke:

"This is the national programme . . ." "Now for Mr. D. B. Brereton in his story 'Adore'" . . . Mr. Brereton" . . . who now arose out of Utopia, and spoke, recounting this story :

"I am in love with him ! now, how funny !" Dora breathed it up her cigarette, blinking up in the sunrise from the rose-garden of Glanna toward her husband's window. Though twice married, she was still as virgin as early snowdrops are, and love fell upon her with an astonishing freshness, exciting in her a kind of curiosity and amusement at herself ! She had conceived it as a semi-voluntary sort of whim, and now stood astonished that it was a thing that overtook one roughly, like hooligans at old Ballybrophy, with shillalahs.

It had happened the night before. Sir Robert (her husband), had gone to get her out of Bow Street police-station, whither a troop of them had been taken for window-smashing in Whitehall ; and in the evening, alone with him in Glanna Small Drawing-room, she had said, smiling, her eyes on the floor, "I hope you don't mind."

He, standing before the hearth-place, had answered "About the windows ? not in the least, since that amuses you. Smash away—smash *my* windows—burn down all my residences—I think you will not find me perturbed."

Now, this was a new notion to Dora—the notion of smashing *her own* windows : and she had stood arrested by her husband's sense. She had a quick gift of thought, a conscientious intellect, which followed logic whithersoever it led her : and she saw at once that, since window-smashing was *only* done to attract attention to a wrong, there was no reason why she should smash other people's more than her own. She then and there determined never to smash another, until she had first smashed some of the Glanna or Grosvenor Square ones—so conscientious, resolute and radical was her young intellect (she was now twenty). It was, for instance, one of her creeds that "everyone should work for his or her living," and so, though a millionairess, and an artist by temperament, she spent three hours most days in silver-smithing for wages.

She had said to Rhodes in a low tone "That is rather a striking idea, smashing—our—own windows."

Noticing her hesitation at the word "*our*," he had smiled one of his mysterious little smiles.

"Supposing I do," she had said, "you won't mind?"

"Try me and see," he said.

"But if ever I have to do time"—she glanced up under her eyes with a sly shyness at him—"will you mind?"

This had caused his broad bare face, all clumps of muscle, to contract into a little grimace. "Well, frankly, yes," he had said; "I could hardly help minding that. Many medals for 'Valour' from 'the Union' cannot make it an honour for a lady to have worn the dress of Holloway-prison—in *my* opinion, I mean! I know that I am of the unenlightened! But remember that I am a little somebody in His Majesty's Government—that my name is not unknown—and that you are of my household. Besides, I am considered to be responsible for your well-being. I think, then, that I should recommend you to draw the line—if possible—at doing, er, 'time'."

How politely (it had struck her then) he chose his words! At what a courtly arm's-distance he kept her ever! There had flashed across her memory how he had kissed her—slowly—pensively—on the lips—that evening before the wedding, in the conservatory at Ballybrophy: his first kiss, and his last: for during their six months of cohabitation he had made never a motion to repeat it.

Twice or thrice she had almost feared him—and flinched a little—musing in her heart at smiles of his—little mysterious smiles, and deep peers of his deep eyes, that appeared to read into the very secret of her nature. He was a strong man, come of a strong stock, all massive, four-square, with "common sense." His father had known how to take advantage of the discovery of that hæmatite ore in the Cleator District which has proved so adapted to the manufacture of Bessemer steel—hence the millions which had bought her: for she supposed that he had merely bought her as an ornament, like the Velasquez in the Glanna gallery—in which case he would surely not like to know that another had touched her lips before him. That would be like buying a Velasquez with a smudge!

Not much had she cared—till now. She had "Valour," and a light mind—"flighty" her sister Phipps had called it; and "*Dora is wild*" had more than once been said at Ballybrophy. She had six sisters, all but one of whom had been bought as ornaments of Society, their father resigning them with a sigh not unmixed with thankfulness, for the old Hall was no longer all there, and wanted paint.

But now Dora cared ; and something smote her inwardly at the thought "*suppose he knew !*" Soon after the discussion about "doing time," she had been playing Fauré's *Berceuse* on the 'cello, Rhodes standing over her, turning her music ; but, looking down at the peachy flush of her right cheek, her robe of dark-blue voile, hydrangeas at the waist, he had turned a leaf too soon, her hand had shot up, their fingers had met, and in that instant an awfully odd and divine thing had taken place in her, she had been as one born again. There she had sat with her face bent, blushing like a rose throughout her soul, thrilled like a string struck, drunk with honeys, and had roamed all the night-long in dream-lands of spice.

In the morning she rose, as always, with the lark, and from the little enclosed rose-garden of Glanna threw half-a-kiss half-an-inch toward his windows—furtively, with one winked eye—standing in trousers, brush in hand, one foot on a footstool ; and a wee enough lad she looked like that—women, indeed, being wee-er things than they seem ! their skirts giving them bigness, as fur gives bigness to a rabbit, until it is skinned—a wee but gallant lad, slim, lissom, like some spirited prince, in her suit of duck, immaculate as new snow, with its elegant legs and catchy *chic* of jacket—nothing spoiling the illusion, save her pointed toy-shoes with their heels, the *chiffon* at her throat, and then her roll of dusky hair, her glittering fingers. She always declared that she could not paint in woman's dress, because "she felt left-handed then" : so in all her négligé and private hours, when only her maid admired her, she changed into a fairy prince—a habit not caught from the Divine Sara, probably, for Dora was Dora, and took her cue from no creature on this sphere.

She had decided to do a miniature on ivory of *Him*—she had " exhibited " miniatures—and spent an hour in composing the study from a photo within the rose-rockery ; then, hearing eight strike from the stable-clock, she suddenly dropped brush, lens and cigarette, ran down an alley, mischief in all her mien, into the house ; and down a corridor she went bending on tip-toe, stealthy, stealthy, with ogling big eyes of pantomime, and balancing palms, till she was at a certain door, where she crouched to put a peeper to the keyhole.

He was in there, naked to the waist, in pyjama-trousers, with trapeze, dumb-bells, gymnasium-trappings, round him, and his body was spinning like a wheel round the bar—though he was forty last August. Then he was plying the clubs, and her eyebrows lifted in surprise at the hilly country of his muscular system, the bossy strong-box of his ribs and breast. That was what a man was like—no fairy prince there ; and the tempter of Eve was whispering at her ear " *Go* in to him—invent an excuse—join in the gymnastics—make him *teach* you ! ", to which she kept answering in a wretchedness of shrinking, " Oh, but I *wouldn't*—I *couldn't*—be so *bold*—good heavens—I'd die "; and now he chanced to step toward the door, upon which, all in a scare, she was up and away like the fleeing thief with backward leers, until she stopped to pant beyond the corridor.

She did not see him again until much later in the day from the top of a coach at the Coaching Club Meet : and then for the first time in her life she had a pang of jealousy. He was seated near Stanhope Gate, talking to a Lady Birkbeck all in white, with pearls and purple irises ; and though Dora knew that he knew that she would be at the Meet, he seemed to find Lydia Birkbeck too interesting to look away from her ladyship's face. Dora's eyes had quickly ferreted out *his* face in the long-drawn parade of faces ; but she was almost past him before he suddenly seemed to see her, and lifted his hat.

And at once there flashed upon her consciousness the fact that she had seen him rather often in talk with Lydia Birkbeck of late : she was silent that day.

Two evenings afterwards she pouted and said " I am sick of the Season : please be my courier to somewhere."

He bowed. " To where ? "

" Somewhere madly unEnglish—Morocco ! "

" I fancy you might find Morocco hot just now."

" I don't mind. I like the blazing dog-star."

He bowed again. " It shall be as you wish."

And he was always prompt : within a week London missed them.

In the end, after zigzag travel, they found themselves at Cairo.

There, on the second night, at Shepheard's, while sitting in the round lounge, waiting for Rhodes to come down, she saw across the throng of Turkish tables and divans those tigress-green eyes, that golden head, of Lydia Birkbeck.

Dora's bow was stiff. . . .

Her heart started at the question that arose in her, " Does this woman follow my husband about ? "—for though some people were there, the Cairo season could hardly be said to have commenced, and it was strange to see her ladyship there, who usually rolled with the social mill.

Lydia Birkbeck was talking closely—heatedly, it seemed—with a man whom Dora did not know, whose eyes, nevertheless, were fixed on Dora's face—a rather small man, with activity and will in his strong eyes—handsome, sun-baked—his very lips looked hard, as if they, too, were hard-baked—"army-officer," she thought.

But she gave only a glance at him and at his indelicate gaze at her, her mind was so taken up with the apparition of Lydia Birkbeck sitting there; and she thought with a touch of feminine venom "She little dreams, that woman, that her wealth, her status, all that she has, is legally mine, and I could strip her of all to-morrow, if I saw fit."

This unfriendly jealousy, by the way, was not without excuse—though hasty: for Lydia Birkbeck was a woman of extraordinary beauty (her grandmother was said to have been an Andalusian); it was her habit to be called "the best-dressed woman" in Society; she was, moreover, one of the "clever" women, gave political breakfasts, aspired to be "a great lady." With all which her reputation was not exactly like her tablecloths; and someone had said "she breaks all the ten commandments, for, though her father and her mother are dead, she still dishonours them." So, if the Birkbeck widow really had dreams of Rhodes, Dora's spleen was hardly unreasonable. Moreover, Lydia Birkbeck had once before supplanted Dora in a man's heart, and Dora knew it, though Lydia did not.

And when Rhodes entered the lounge, his eyes

seemed immediately to find out Lydia—though with some apparent surprise. He went straight to her ; and keenly Dora's eyes ferreted at the meeting of their hands.

But there was no lingering ; it was over in some moments ; and Rhodes came over to Dora. Lydia had not presented to him the man who was her companion.

Then Rhodes and Dora moved toward the *salle à manger* ; but at the entrance Rhodes left his wife's side a minute to say something to the manager ; and when he went back to her, he saw her face as blanched as the dead.

In those moments, while she had stood alone, some one standing close behind her had moaned, only loud enough for her ear alone, the word "*Adore*" ; and, once more, "*Adore.*"

Throwing half-a-glance backward, she had seen the man with the hard-looking lips, Lydia Birkbeck's companion, who had gazed indelicately at her. . . .

But *Adore*—that word at Shepheard's Hotel, moaned behind her by a man who somehow *looked* a scamp ! No one had ever called Dora "Adore" but one—her first husband, Sir Darrel Birkbeck : and at this thing her lips lay parted, her great eyes, with their gloomy glory, violet-dark, gazed aghast before her, like eyes startled at seeing fire break out, and the pear-shaped pearl-drops that poured in rays from her necklace rose and fell on her bosom like a hand that waves farewell. She whispered to herself "I'm dished."

She could not keep her hand from shivering on Rhodes' arm; and presently at table he said to her "Not quite well to-night? The neuralgia?"

Sometimes, as now, he thrilled her through, his voice went so tender and low.

"No, not that," she answered. Now she pouted: "This is *bête* here: I want to see Bethlehem."

He bowed, saying "You shall see it"; on which she lifted her lids to fix him with a look, and say "You are good to me"; and that night, when Egypt lay asleep, breathed-on by her breezes from off the desert, watched by her stars, Dora crept along a corridor to his door, put a kiss on it, whispered to it "*God bless you!*"

Four days later they were before Joppa—which must certainly be the choppiest port on earth—where trunks, and passengers, too, had to be flung to the boats, that now towered above the steamer's beam, and now were twenty feet down in the deep; nor are there any but the Arab boatmen nimble enough to deal with such a sea. At any rate, at the moment when Dora was, as it were, tossed to their tottery catch, Rhodes let out an outcry which sounded like the outcry of one in very fretful distress and anxiety; and during the trip to the shore she let her shoulder press on his arm, smiling, delighted with the Promised Land.

Then by the Joppa-Jerusalem railway they fared, and from Jerusalem were shambling on camels amid scarlet anemones at blazing mid-day for Bethlehem, when she took a framed miniature from her dress to present to him, with smile and bow.

His face lit up. "Well!" he went, "what a dainty thing! But—can it be that I am as handsome as this?"

"Oh, quite, I think!" she answered with a challenging little giggle.

"One for *me*, then! But—may I have this for myself?"

"I present it to you."

"Thanks—awfully! Wonderful taste—this background—the whole colour-scheme, I think. When did you do it?"

"I have been doing it for months."

"Really? And could you not do one of yourself, and give me that, too?—or sell it me. Then I shall have a pair for my bedside table."

She cut an eye at him, crying "I'll see!"—and laughed!

That evening, in that old market-place of Bethlehem, he bent down and kissed her hand; and one evening, a week later, they standing alone on the shore of the Lake of Gennesareth, as the sun vanished, when for four minutes all things stood forth startlingly distinct, lit to a trance of rose and scarlet and daffodil, then sudden dark, like the puffing out of a lamp, she heard him murmur "My peace I leave with you"—and she put her hand on his shoulder. They were chums.

At first, after hearing that "*Adore*" at Shepheard's, she had cried aloud in a crisis of "Valour" "I'll tell him everything! I don't care"—a good resolution: but she had put it off, lingering on the brink; and now it was impossible for her: this Palestine travel had engendered a fresh friendship, and her terror lest anything should nip it like a tender lettuce sealed her lips. That Rhodes must have some *reason* for his courtly coldness seemed fairly certain to her, in spite of her lack of learning in the manners and customs of marriage; and she was a world too delicately virgin ever to hint to him that she was conscious of any coldness ; but, whatever his reason, she now felt herself growing strong enough to overthrow it. Sometimes now, burying her face, she'd breathe " Soon now! " and be red as a cherry. Hence it was no longer possible to her to tell, to shock him, to shake the castle of cards she was building up. " Some day, when all's safe," she thought.

Moreover, as the days rolled by, that ominous raven who had croaked " *Adore* " commenced to seem to her nothing but a beastly dream. How *could* he know ? she asked herself ; and began to disbelieve her ears. Yet ever, in her happiest instant, he was with her, a skeleton's grin in the back of her head ; he gave her nightmares and neuralgia ; and she had learned to hate one person on earth.

Every day she sullenly assured herself that she had not done any wrong—had only been secretive, and that was her nature. When she had been the wildest filly of fifteen named Dora Bray, she had met Sir Darrel Birkbeck at a school-dance in Harley Street, he being then a subaltern of twenty-two ; and what Sir Darrel Birkbeck was doing at a girls' dance, like the devil in Eden, one does not know, for he was the most irresponsible and callous profligate who ever spent a night in quod. He was handsome (though his nose was put on crooked), and was of great estate : and three months after the meeting Dora mysteriously disappeared from Harley Street one afternoon—not for long—long enough to get hurriedly married, for Sir Darrel had bribed the Registrar to wink : and that night she sprang and pranced on her spring-bed in her nightdress, twisting at the amazed school-friend who shared her room—a wedding-ring.

She realized now that this had been her sole motive for the marriage—to exhibit a ring to that one girl and see her stare, to pose as a matron, and be a heroine for a week; and "Ah, the silly kid," she often sorrowed now, staring into vacancy with a lost despondency.

From the moment when she had parted from Birkbeck at the Marylebone Registry, with a promise to meet, she had never seen him: quick and sudden the Inspector General of the Home Forces had had him snatched from Piccadilly to Poona; and his letters to Dora had only lasted seven months—she used to get them from a paper-shop address in Great Portland Street—at the end of which time he "married" a Miss Lydia Dalrymple at Simla.

This was what Dora had meant in thinking to herself that she could "strip" Lydia Birkbeck: for, since Sir Darrel had bigamised, the Birkbeck estate ought to have become Dora's, by law, when cholera brought the baronet's reeling career to a finish some months after his second "marriage."

Soon afterwards Dora had slipped her wedding-ring into the hand of a beggar in Dublin; and had considered herself done with that little spree.

As to the one creature, her school-friend, to whom she had told her secret, Dora trusted her (she was at present married, and in Hong-Kong): so Dora could not think how "*Adore*" had come to be moaned at her . . . unless Sir Darrel had kept her letters . . . ? She had sometimes wondered, and shivered, as to those letters. . . .

And this, in truth, proved her mortally weak spot—her letters. She and Rhodes were back at Paris, and she had just returned in the afternoon from the hats and costumes of the rue de la Paix to her flat in the Grand Hotel—had on still toque and gloves—when a card was handed her—"Captain Harold Barclay."

A name new to her: and at once a dart of omen struck cold to her heart, a foreboding of calamity and bad weather without end. That forenoon Rhodes had picked a mote out of her eye in such a mood, that she had afresh blushed at the sense of "*soon*"; and now there was nothing but him for her; her life hung upon his smile; he was her colossus, and chock-filled her universe with his hugeness.

"Show Captain Barclay in," she said over her shoulder, standing by a piano; and there she stood averted, till he was behind her, and she span and saw him—the hard lips—the neat moustache—his little knit activity—neatly groomed—a square forehead over grey eyes.

"*Adore!*" he said the moment the door closed—and nothing could be more consummate than the coolness and dominance of that smile.

She, as he spoke, got back her colour with a rush. "What is it you want?"

"Your love," he said.

"Nothing else?"

"Why, no. That is much." He bowed.

"Ever been worried by a bull-dog?" says she: "my husband is out, but we have one in yonder."

He dropped upon a sofa with half a yawn, saying

"I always carry a weapon; and there's no need to be very cross, dear, since I foresee that we are going to be friends. To tell the truth—I'm in love: the instant I saw your face in *The Graphic* four months ago—I suppose I am headlong in that way. I look upon you as the cream and queen of girls; and—put yourself in my place—could I resist the temptation, knowing that you are in my power? for I have ascertained definitely that you have not breathed one word to your husband, or to anyone, about your being a widow—as you imagined yourself—when you remarried. That was *very* naughty, Adore. You *ought* to have told, don't you know. Your second-marriage certificate has 'Spinster' on it—which is against the law, by the way—Ah, naughty! But you like acting on your little own, don't you? and following your own little nose, and keeping your own little counsel—you are what the French call *détraquée—I* know the secrets of the wayward, wild little heart. So what terms are you prepared to make? Here's your first-marriage certificate, see; and here's a bundle of your letters to Birkbeck, who, by the way, was one of my second lieutenants in India—look, 'My darling Darrel'—naughty!—at fifteen—and look, 'Your adoring Dora'."

Dora had gone colourless again, and suddenly let herself down on the piano-stool, feeling her knees weak, feeling her all, her dear dream, her beauteous bubble, slipping from her: for there was a terrible cold strength in the face before her, an expression, too, of cleverness and rascally adroitness; and with her gloomy underlook she mourned with reproach to him "Is a thing like you in His Majesty's service?"

"No, Adore, I've been kicked out—I'm a disgraced and desperate devil—frank, you see. But you needn't be insolent; let's be business-like—I think you have a clear head. Tell me at once whether or not you admit that I'm your master?"

She threw up her chin. "No!"

"You don't." His eyes flitted quick an instant in thought. "But have you any suspicion that you are not Rhodes' wife?—that Darrel Birkbeck is alive and in hiding for a crime?"

At those words the skeleton of her strong-boned face stood ghastly suggested—strong-boned, for it was her square jaw, contrasting with the pathos of her eyes' softness, which gave her face its strange charm. She sprang a little up from her seat, bloodless; but after ten seconds said, coldly enough, "That is a foolish falsehood. His body was brought embalmed from Bombay, and was seen by his relatives."

"A body very like his, yes, which purported to be his——"

"No, *his*. No one in the world could be mistaken for him: his nose—Oh, that is a *feeble* fiction"—with bitter and pitying disdain.

"Well, have it as you like for the present," he said. "I'll prove it later. But, whether or not, don't think you're going to slip me. I never fail in love. I bet you I get you."

"Better be quick about it, then," she said confidentially, with an admonishing nod, "for I'm expecting my husband every minute, and then you'll be rather up a tree, I think."

"Adore, I am *never* up a tree—I'm an imperturbable devil. But I hope he won't come, for your sake. The instant he enters I hand him these letters."

Now her face rushed into an expression of red-hot rancour an instant, and her fist lifted a little to fell: for this man, with his fascinating manner, his quick and easy speech, his handsome face, and hard lips, had a great power of rousing hatred—in her, at any rate. She already loathed him with an evil intensity which was soon to fester into a disease in her.

But he was strong—there was no good in ignoring facts—his whim was her law; and when he said "But why lose time? You know you're in a fix, admit it frankly," she sprang up to a window, and there, suddenly weakening, implored helplessly with a cry-cry face, "God, tell me what to do, my God!"

"Don't think I'm hard, Adore," he called to her back, "I know how to wait . . ."

She span round upon him with a haughty chin. "How much money do you want for those papers?"

"Now you are near to crying"—he shook his finger at her. "Don't cry, Adore—there's no need. As to money, it isn't so much a question of money—I happen to be hard up—give me a cheque for two thousand pounds—or one thousand, that'll do—and then, of course—a kiss."

Under gloomy eyes she looked at him, mourning "Coward."

"No, I don't think I'm a coward, Adore," he said with raised eyebrows—"on the contrary, I seem to be rather audacious. Say that once again, and I jump up and kiss you."

"*Hateful!*" she went, cutting a nose of disdain and hate at him.

"That's right, hate me—feel strongly—it will all evolve naturally into love when you once buckle under to my rule. I am accustomed to conquer Kates."

She stood contemplating with one eye small that hard unmanageable head; then suddenly turned to run to an escritoire, where she wrote a cheque with furious haste, then ran, threw it at him. "Now the papers," she ordered haughtily.

He looked at the cheque, saying "Two thousand, Adore? I said one. Well, if you choose to give me two . . . And now the kiss." With startling alacrity, mastery, he sprang up to her.

"*Better take care!*" she cried high.

"Oh, there's no escape—absolutely," he said: "you may as well be——"

It was at that instant that she heard a key in the flat-door—and at this thing her pecker collapsed to craven flurry and demoralization. "*My husband*," she whispered quickly with a mean and secret beseechingness—"*please*—go . . ."

"The kiss first!" he whispered.

"Oh, as to that," her bosom panted, "you jest"—with a mean smile—conciliatory—a rictus rather than a smile, for now steps were heard coming from the hall; and he hissed at her "Don't think I jest! *Be quick!* I never feel fear or flurry—I'll kiss you to death in the very presence of ten Rhodeses——"

"But for pity," she panted, her palms together.

"Pity be damned," grimly his grim lips riveted themselves; and now when the steps were quite at the door, quickly he threw his arm round her waist, drew her, and had just time to brush the left corner of her lips with his, then slip papers and cheque into his pocket, when Rhodes was in the room, looking from his wife's white face to the stranger, and back to his wife's face.

A little giggle—light, hysterical—came from her. "Captain—Captain Barclay," she panted, "my husband—a friend of Lady Birkbeck—who called—Excuse me"—she was gone.

The pressing necessity upon her was to wash her lips quickly; and headlong her steps pressed toward her bedroom, where she dragged off her gloves, and set to rubbing away the skin of the kissed spot, rushed to use her tooth-brush, spluttering, as she brushed, with strong disgust, then again set to scraping away, with a face of pain, the pestilent spot of her leprosy, panting, with now a sob, and now an "*Ugh*" of detestation.

On going back to the drawing-room, she lingered outside a little, shrinking from entering: no sound—Barclay gone—Rhodes seated on the piano-stool, examining the working of one of those witty little toy-things that one buys for a *gross sou* in the streets of Paris; nor was anything said for some seconds after she was in, until Rhodes enquired, without looking up, "You been in long?"

"Not long."

Now he threw a momentary eye at her. "You look pale. Paris is hardly at its best just now as regards climate. I hope you don't attempt much tramping."

"No, I've been driving."

He pried into the mechanism of the *pantin*;

and presently : " Struck yourself ? What's that mark ? "

" Where ? "

" There by your mouth . . . Do you know what a *suçon* is ? "

" No, what is a *suçon ?* "

" French lovers have a habit of sucking the fore-arm, neck, of each other, leaving a red mark, which they call a *suçon* : then the two *suçons* act as mementoes. Well, you have a mark there very like a *suçon*. May I express the hope——? " he stopped, smiling a little down at the toy.

There was a new coldness in his tone which she felt through the jest, nor was she in any mood for jest—turned from him, her lips pulling, water springing to her eyes, saying dejectedly in tones that broke, " No, I haven't been having a *suçon* "—moving to a window, to look upon the courtyard and the Rue Scribe.

And presently he : " Who, by the way, is this Captain Barclay with whom you left me ? I don't remember hearing——"

She said over her shoulder " I know him as an acquaintance of Lydia Birkbeck."

" Yes, you said that—I think I saw him with her at Cairo. What regiment ? "

" His regiment ? I—have no idea."

" Ah, you haven't known him long."

" No."

" Agreeable man," he murmured, while she, having a sort of consciousness of one of his penetrating looks fixed like a blister on her back, let her forehead drop upon the window-glass, and stared, undergoing that gaze, till tears stung her eyes ; and presently she paced slowly out, her face bent, without saying anything.

She was subject to neuralgia of the fifth nerve—from girlhood—and for two days did not see him again, keeping to her room. On the third morning she received a note from Barclay :

> "Adore, I am eager to see you. Meet me, will you, in the lounge of the Hotel Victoria on Tuesday evening, the 7th, at nine. Please don't fail. I'll give you the letters. HAROLD BARCLAY."

So he assumed already the authority to summon her from Paris to London, to "meet" him ? Yet that was not odd, for he knew now that she was his, and she knew, too: she had said "for pity," admitting to him his dominion over her. . . .

But she came of a haughty race, descended from sovereigns, and a hot arrogance flushed her forehead, as she laughed aloud at that note—a dangerous laugh, which might have chilled even so cool a nerve as Barclay, if he had heard.

However, there could be no resistance : looking into herself, she found that she lacked the courage ; and, as he had given her only four days to obey in, she wrote in the forenoon a note to Rhodes, begging to be taken back to her doctor.

She drove to the hotel rendezvous that fourth night accompanied by a girl-friend, whom she left on the landing-couch, whence the meeting in the lounge above was visible. Barclay was there amid the palms, deserted at that hour. But the interview lasted only a minute, for at once he stood up to her, saying in an offended tone " No, Adore, it's no good,

I'll have nothing to do with you. Who is that girl? This is not business."

Her voice shook passionately like her body, as she said "Be good enough to hand me the papers which I have bought of you."

"Nonsense!" he said in a huff: "you know very well that this is not business. Come alone to-morrow night. I am not going to eat you."

Fury flew to her eyes, but she controlled—half-controlled—the rush of her blood, panting to him with passion "Look here—listen—I am absolutely in your power—see, I confess—God knows—absolutely—because the regard of my husband is precious to me. But don't oppress me—better not—*because I can't stand it*"—she was gone from him, leaving in his nerves a certain respect and whisper of apprehension, to which he would have done well to listen.

The next evening she drove alone from Grosvenor Square to meet him, and he gave her the papers, demanded no familiarity; but said at their parting "I expect you to write me within a week when and where it will be convenient to you to meet me next."

"But what for?" She reddened with sudden rage.

"You know," he said.

"How offensive a being you are!"—with a look of reproach.

"Oh, nonsense: that's only a mental pose; all girls love me in their hearts. I bet I won't be able to breathe for you in another month. Besides, when a girl has once kissed a man, as you have me—that was another naughty bit, Adore!—suppose Rhodes knew——"

"Ah, but you are persecuting me!" she cried menacingly: "I have never done you any wrong! One being has no right to do this to another!"

Those unblinking eyes stared admiringly at her. "Fascinating little mortal you are—I could eat you. And don't say that I am persecuting you, for I wouldn't. If ever I tighten the screw on you, it will be only to get you: I want you, I like you. And think what I am doing for you: I have given you the letters—I am hiding the fact that Darrel Birkbeck is alive——"

Again those words had the power to strike her white to the lips, though they were untrue, and she was sure that they were untrue. Her parasol bored a hole in the carpet's plush, she bending over the hole. "Repeat that fiction, if it pleases you—it cannot affect me—I only wish that that was all. But I have purchased of you, at your own price, some papers of mine which you held: does not the relation between us end now? Fair's fair——"

"But, Adore, do you suppose that those are all the letters? I have more."

As this villainy left his lips, he staggered a little, struck with venom on his neck by her parasol, which snapped from its handle; and before it reached the ground—before she realized that she had struck—he had her seized and kissed. She knew then that the sinews of that little man were irresistible.

"Adore, you are not permitted to strike me," he said quietly, as she sank upon a divan, and from under her hands that pressed her face a sob broke out, another, and another, slowly tolling, she not troubling to scrub her lips clean this time, feeling them so defiled now, that all waters could not wash them spotless for the kiss of him for whom she had them.

She was so dejected, that she let Barclay hold her arm, supporting her down to her carriage.

After this every week that passed saw his kingship more established and habitual. At their fourth meeting he bid her send him a cheque for another thousand pounds, and she commenced then to suspect that the main motive of the tyrant's desire for her " love " was so to bind her to him, as to make her contributions to his bank-book an inevitable and natural habit, he intending to draw a considerable income out of Rhodes' pocket.

Meantime, he so persistently repeated the fiction about Birkbeck being alive, that she, without really believing it, acquired that kind of belief which people acquire in things that they hear continually repeated. She believed it in her sleep ; it was a disease in her dreams.

At their fifth meeting he said to her " Adore, you don't look well "—for she had been days in bed, so tormented with pain, that her physician had committed the folly of injecting her forearm with a quarter-grain of morphia sulphate—it was then that drugs began to be a habit with her. Before that week was over she was secretly taking cocaine, that dreadful drug which makes the blood to flare up suddenly. . . . She had none to guide, none to advise her, but alone went her way of pain, opening not her mouth. Her first impulses to throw herself upon Rhodes—upon her father—her sisters—make a clean breast of everything, were long since stilled within her, her feet too far gone on the steep path she had erred into, like the erring sheep that has ceased from bleating in the murk ; her habit of secrecy, the will to hide still in her mole-hole, had become too much an *idée fixe* in her bewildered mind ; nor was she given time to sit and think, but rushed thoughtlessly along her road like one pursued by a bull.

Meanwhile, the distance between her and Rhodes had weekly widened. He could very well see that she was not normal, that she had a secret, and his politeness acquired a chill of ice. She got to shun his gazes that steadily mused on her, to shun his presence. It is doubtful if she could still have been said to love—there was only room in her for hatred and pain : for when one is on the rack, one forgets what one is on the rack for, thinks only of the rack ; and that little captain with the hard lips who treated her now as a plaything, and now as a slave, who wanted her " love " and her money, who had her letters, became the mania of all her thoughts.

At their sixth meeting, as he and she were stepping out of Albert Gate to her brougham, Rhodes was there, and with him Lady Birkbeck and another man, walking. The evening was thick with mist and drizzle, but the abundant lamplight just there showed them all fully to one another. Rhodes lifted his hat with a nod and a smile, whose meaning Dora knew ; Lydia Birkbeck glanced backward with a little expression of surprise in one eyebrow ; and Barclay bit his lip a little, like one annoyed.

As for Dora, when she was alone in the brougham, her lids lay closed, and the expression of her face was one of excruciation, more anguished than any expression which neuralgia could stamp on it. From that night she entirely shunned Rhodes ; and everything in her nature changed to hatred. Sometimes her maid considered her a little delirious.

Some mornings afterwards, lying in a boudoir lounge-chair in her duck suit, an idle brush between her fingers, her eyes closed, her face bony and bloodless, she was thinking how Rhodes had never once reminded her of the miniature of herself for which he had begged her that happy day at Bethlehem—the humiliation ! to wait, and pine, and be slighted ! and suddenly she sprang in a passion to her feet, shivering. " I won't stand it ! I'll end it ! "

That was at Glanna : and, in the afternoon, motoring through Croydon for air, she saw a tool-shop, where she stopped and bought for sixpence a scriber—sort of awl, six inches long, with a handle : a quicker way, that, than the drug way, though the drug way was less drastic, hard. . . .

For two days she kept it in her dress ; sometimes took it out to look at. . . .

On the third morning she received a summons from the captain to his flat that night at eight. He had never before gone so far as this ; but he said " Please come, I won't eat you "—and when he said " please," she understood that a threat underlay it.

She drove with her maid, Martha, to Grosvenor Square in the afternoon. Rhodes was not about : there was an Autumn Session ; he was probably at Westminster. She went to bed, and lay under the influence of cocaine till twenty past seven.

When she rose, as her foot touched the carpet, she pitched headlong, butted into a wardrobe, and sat some time on the floor, stunned and sighing ; then pulled her darkened brain together, got up, got dressed. She had ordered a carriage for 7.45 ;

and, making of her palm a bed for her racked forehead, she crept darkly down the stairs into a book-room used by Rhodes, and put a note to him into an old book, which he might not chance to open for years, if ever :

"My dear,

"Perhaps you will not see me again. I am in very deep trouble. Forgive me that I could not make you give back to me a drop of this river of love that flows from me to you. But you will throw a rose on my grave, I think, for pity of my fate.

Yours, DORA."

She then started out for Gower Street, the scriber in her gown.

The notion of ending the captain's, instead of her own, life does not seem, so far, to have occurred to her, or not consciously occurred : she anticipated violence that night from those sinews of iron, and was firmly determined, at his first attempt, to lay herself dead at his feet.

A lift took her up, close-veiled, to his flat-door ; and her hand had risen to touch a button, when it halted midway : she saw that the door was a little open.

She wondered whether, for some reason, he meant her to enter without ringing. . . . ?

Uncertain, she decided to ring ; but now only touched the button momentarily, timorously. . . .

There was no answer : and she stood a little, letting her aching forehead rest on the door-frame, wondering. Then she put her ear to the door-opening—no sound in there; then, hearing the lift coming, to avoid observation, she slipped within.

In there all was dark, and she shuddered at the dumbness of the flat, at that sense of death and darkness of the grave which over-shadowed her life, for her shattered mind was now all haunted by ghosts and glooms and cobwebs of despondency. He must have gone out, she surmised, to get something ; and, since he had left the door open, would hardly be long. And now a thought struck her—her letters! If she could quickly happen upon, and seize, all of them in his absence, half the strength of the rack on which he kept her stretched would be shattered. She went wildly white, almost fainted ; but—she stepped forward.

The first door on her right was slightly open, and here there was a hint of rosy light from a fire which was dying within. Opening the door more, she moved into what was evidently a dining-room : for, dark as it was, the fact of a spread table, and the fire-glow glancing on glass and silver, could hardly fail to strike the eye. She, however, saw only *him*. There he was, looking out of a window straight before her—she understood that this was why he had not heard her touch of the bell : he had apparently dropped something into the courtyard, and was trying to see it, for he was bent over the sill—had not gone out !—there he was ! and she felt that he had the flat in darkness with no fair object.

Twenty seconds she stood watching him ; and, without knowing how or when, she had the scriber now in her hand ; and now her mouth was wide in a soundless howl, her eyes wildly wide, like the eyes of one dropping down a precipice in the night, as, step by step, tiptoeing, she crept . . . now run three steps . . . now *do* it . . . stick the steel deep into his back.

At the blow, a little oblique, he tumbled against the window-frame, then down before her he dropped. She got a little glimpse of his pallor, ghastly in the glow of the coals. . . .

Howling—soundlessly howling—her hands held up, shivering aloft as from a scorch, she turned to flee—a new Dora—good-bye now to the blue of the sky, freshness of morning-winds in March. But she did not flee two steps : for before her she saw two eyes, looking at her.

Not a cat's eyes, if cat-like ; they seemed to be staring out from the side of a sideboard on her right ; she could see nothing but the eyes ; and steadily they stared.

Probably she would have fainted without this, being so ill ; but at this sight she at once tottered—forward toward the table, caught at it, missed it, fell on her face.

It seemed to her years before she next opened her eyes. She was then not lying, but sitting, on the floor, against a couch, with a cushion between its head and her head, in her right hand the scriber—though she had the impression that she had left it in the body. The fire was not quite out ; and all at once she was aware of a shape lying quiet under the window with her in the dark ; at which consciousness, she was up and gone with skedaddling skirts, her palms out to strike open the doors in advance ; and a little gurgle and giggle of escape she gave on finding herself out in the light, then down the stair she fled cringing, and entered her carriage with a sense of wonder that the coachman did not apparently know what her hand had done.

She lay several days after it in a very hectic state, afflicted with a hiccup that continually clicked, with pins-and-needles in the left leg, and during those days was hardly quite a sane girl. Then there were long, deep sleeps ; and now her clouds and darkness began to roll from her ; until, one bright morning, she awoke rapturously to the fact that she was free to live and to love, and the enemy of her life was dead. To her astonishment, she now felt no genuine remorse, though she spurred and urged herself to feel it. All that first awesomeness, when all was emotion, was gone now : for now all her intelligence assured her that, if there is anything in "Unwritten Laws"—laws older, and deeper, and higher than those made with haphazard "amendments" and "schedules"—then, this must be among them, that she had had a natural right to sacrifice that half-human tiger, and merited a medal, as those who had sacrificed Marat and Caligula had had monuments raised to them. As to arrest and punishment, she was simple-minded enough, unversed in the world enough, to have no apprehension at all of such a thing for a daughter of her father. She had read of "the inquest," etc. ; it had been called "*a mystery*" ; and she supposed that the episode was ended, recovered health, threw off the power of drugs, and set herself again to court and flirt with Rhodes.

But one night, in leaving the Opera-house with a man, she caught sight of someone talking with her coachman in a tone which struck her as quite furtive, hurried, earnest. Her eyes rested on his face—he had bright-brown eyes, was slim, young, though the back of his head was grey ; and two evenings afterwards she started, on glancing from a Grosvenor Square window, to see the same man looking up. . . .

All at once now a Polar cold of panic struck at her heart ; and soon came crowding upon her the realization that there must be proofs *in plenty* connecting her with the death. *Her letters !* Though not a mention of them had been published, those must have been found in Barclay's flat ? supplying a motive for the act ? The coachman who had driven her to the flat . . . the lift-man . . . the coachman who had seen her enter the tool-shop to buy the scriber, which she had wildly left in the flat . . . many, many proofs accumulated upon her memory. And then those eyes, not a cat's eyes, that had *seen* her do the deed. . . . She was suddenly amazed now at her levity in imagining that she could possibly escape—when she had been *seen* in the act. Someone had certainly been there ! For even if the eyes which she had seen gleaming out of the gloom had been only a dream of her crazed fancy, *some*one must have put her to sit against the sofa after she had fainted ! Who ? and why . . . ?

At any rate, she could not long doubt that she was being shadowed and spied at. She had driven to an assault-at-arms at Bertrand's, and was about to leave her carriage, when the carriage-door was opened by the young man with the bright eyes, who intruded his face, smiling. She started so, that Rhodes, who was with her, glanced, and seeing her all short-breathed and pallid, asked if something was wrong?

"It is a pain," she answered, with shut eyes.

"Shall we return?"

"No."

"Better," he said gently.

"No"—she stood up.

That young man seemed to *intend* to terrify her—to wish to study the effect upon her of his apparitions; and her intense nerves, with their neurotic tendency, got a morbid enough horror of him, his image now filling her being, as Barclay's had once filled it. Once again she withdrew herself from her husband and from Society, slinking into the burrow of her secret misery, knowing never an instant's peace, ever apprehending that her arrest impended.

In the deep of night she would steal and kneel at Rhodes' door, with wringing palms and contorted form, breathing with tears "Have no fear—I will not bring disgrace upon your name—I'll die——"

This was her terror—her most frenzied terror—that through her wayward and aberrant breast pain should ever touch him, shame bend his head. Compared with that, all else seemed small. His honour was so touchy, his morality so conventional. She remembered often his little grimace, as when one tastes an acid, at the idea of her "doing time" for her suffragettism. But how if she were arrested for—murder? He would go to Samoa, to mourn.

"Not quite well yet?" he kept suggesting gently to her, at luncheon, at dinner, or meeting her in Glanna Old Garden one evening.

And she would look at him with her gloomy

eyes before replying "Not yet : it is the pains."

One night he was preparing a speech in the Grosvenor Square book-room, when, on opening an old blue-book for some statistics, he saw the note she had left before going to Barclay's flat. She had forgotten that it was there . . . !

He frowned deeply over it. "You may never see me again . . . in deep trouble . . . river of love that flows from me to you . . . throw a rose over my grave. . . . "

This made him moan. Thumb and finger pressed his eyes inward under his frown, and so he sat a long time ; then, gazing at a study of her in pastels by Sargent over his desk, a groan broke from him.

He rose suddenly to go seek her—had reason to think that she was at home. But she was not in any of the reception-rooms ; and, after peeping about, he finally knocked at her apartments. "Lady Rhodes in ? " he asked her maid.

"Her ladyship went out an hour ago, on foot, Sir—with a bag," she answered, with downcast eyes.

"Bag ? "

"I think there is something strange, Sir . . . Yesterday a trunk was sent away . . . I was to give you this when you enquired after her "—she handed him an envelope scribbled in pencil with "Sir Robert."

> ". . . am leaving you . . . I wish I had the courage to tell, but, then, I haven't . . . a being is made so strong, and no stronger, and all his piety or wit cannot make a mouse into a mastodon . . . I will only say that I have done something considered

wrong, and been found out . . . There is one thing that shall not happen: you shall not suffer intolerable shame for having married me . . . I am going into hiding, and they will be sharp if they catch me, for I shall brace myself to pit my wits against theirs . . . Have no fear for me: I take with me some hundreds of pounds, and I shall work for my living, as one should. . . . Only one thing pains me deeply, that I shall no longer see you, and be near you . . . I tell you this at the last, and God know that it is the truth. . . ."

In that great room with its row of blinded windows, its gilt, and moulded ceiling, Rhodes remained the night through, a lonesome and stricken figure, hour after hour, with a brooding underlook loaded with gloom. Early the next day he summoned a detective to him.

" Find her for me, Pole," he said, pinning the detective with his eye—" devote yourself to this alone, throw money about. She is cunning, she is sharp : but Europe is a small place, after all ; and I know men—you look to me a tricky and unconquerable fellow. Find her, and you will find *me*—grateful."

This Pole was a little man from Stubbs's, with a moustache which did not cover his barefaced smile, a little goatee-beard which his fingers milked, and a complexion pinky-white, suggesting consumption. But there was something quite quick and vivid in his way of leaning forward on his chair's edge, and in the quick-flitting sheet-lightning of his light eyes.

" What's she done ' considered wrong,' Sir ? " he asked—his speech betraying the Cumberland man.

Rhodes shrugged.

"Ey, you know, Sir Robert Rhodes."

"How do you know that I know?"

"You think that she killed Barclay."

Violently Rhodes started.

"I—you assume——" he stammered.

"Ey, we have to be frank with each other, Sir Robert," Pole murmured, with his eternal smile: "you think—you know—that she killed Barclay; and I think you know why, Sir?"

"No! I do not know; I may have guessed——"

"Stay: I think you know that she married Sir Darrel Birkbeck before she married you?"

Rhodes' lids fell. "Yes, I know that."

"Well, Barclay had letters of hers written to Birkbeck in India before Birkbeck committed bigamy over there; and Barclay persecuted her with them—that's why."

Rhodes sat forward with a stare. "But how in God's name do *you* know all this?"

"Oh, Sir Robert, I am more or less in everybody's secret. All this is now well known to the Yard, and I am never a thousand miles out of touch with the Yard. Her letters to Birkbeck were found in Barclay's flat; a weapon which she is known to have bought was found, etc., etc.; Scotland Yard were only waiting to have their case formally complete before arresting. And since this is so, what is your hope, Sir, in setting me to unearth her?"

"My hope," Rhodes said, his brow in his hand, "is to get out of Europe with her. To tell the truth, if the dogs get her, they get me, and it is both of us or neither."

Pole sprang up like Jack-in-the-box. "I see how it is. Good day, Sir Robert"; and he muttered, as he went away with quick steps, " Ey, I have better hopes for you than you have for yourself."

Not far from the house he touched on the arm the brown-eyed fellow who had become Dora's terror ; and he said, " Ey, McLaren, bird's flown."

" Slipped me nicely—for the minute," the other said : " you in the chase, too ? "

" Aye. Give me half a chance to catch her first, and I leave you whistling."

" Blowing my whistle, you mean. Ten millionaires don't get her now out of England."

Pole's eyes twinkled. " Suppose she's innocent, after all ? "

" Suppose the sky was red ? " from McLaren.

" It is sometimes."

" Never so red as that lady's hands, though."

" Nor so blue as the Yard when it jumps to conclusions, and gets left."

" Oh, you do like to set yourself up, Pole ! See through a stone-wall !—nobody else in it ! From the first you put it all upon the other one, and nothing can move you."

Pole tapped him over the heart. " Which of the two had the strongest motive to get rid of Barclay—Birkbeck's first wife, or his second ? "

" Pooh ! it isn't a question of motive," McLaren answered : " both women had the strongest motives; but *who* did it ? What about the awl ? "

" Ey, yes—the awl which wasn't an awl. Well, you go your way, and I'll go mine. Good luck."

This sort of talk was constantly taking place between these two during the next six weeks—in which Rhodes would have been very offended to know that Pole was not hunting for Dora at all. Pole, convinced that sooner or later the Yard would discover her, had put the quest upon McLaren, goading McLaren to eagerness in seeking by constantly telling him, " let me once find her, and I leave you whistling "—trusting in himself to know when McLaren was well on the road to her discovery. Meantime, Pole, obsessed with the idea of Lydia Birkbeck's guilt, was giving his whole time and mind to the attempt to fix it on her.

During all which Dora was living in a cottage near Hampton ; and even the little maid who attended on her believed her to be an elderly gentleman, she being as skilful at disguise as at several other forms of art requiring *finesse* of eye and finger. She had fitted up an *atelier* in which she did " art jewelry," and the little maid, looking on akimbo, would exclaim " My ! it's a licker to me how you make 'em, Sir ! "

" I learned when I was your age," Dora answered one day : " I shall teach you, so that you may have a trade "—and had commenced to teach her hard-soldering.

Twice or thrice a week, meantime, she was in London, and often saw Rhodes : would sit, a little old man, in St. Stephen's Hall, till he passed through to the Commons—once with Lydia Birkbeck at his side ; or she would even linger in the dusk at a corner of Grosvenor Square, to see him.

That much of this was risky she knew. But a great emotion of weariness and woe was upon her, and she became ever more careless. Some of her diary-writing at this time shows her in moods so potently moved to pathos rather than pain, that her expression of them becomes fantastic ; sometimes her pen springs to poetic expression, as where she says, " Oh, whereabouts is my little bed ? I will set a grave-digger digging eagerly to seek it, as one digs to seek hid treasure " ; or again : " I have eaten of the ashes of the fire of love " ; or again : " Shed one tear for me, dear ; let it fall into my handkerchief, and I will set it as a jewel in the ouch of a ring " . . . " Love loves for ever, and the heart slowly withers, but tells its pain to none " . . . Anon there is something of the old jealousy : " I will cover his doorsteps with sand, to detect the footsteps of those who visit him. . . ."

One day, on seeing a copy of *East Lynne* in a window, suddenly there flew to her head the notion of going back to him in disguise as a servant, like a lady in that tale : if she revealed herself to the lady-housekeeper at Glanna, her secret would be kept . . . and, being subject to these sudden inspirations to escapade and adventure, instantly she was filled full of this thing. That very night found her at Glanna.

But in going up an avenue to the house, she saw him in the light of a full moon coming down the steps, and with him was Lydia Birkbeck. Dora slipped behind an oak, as they came toward her—Rhodes bareheaded, his face very pale and grave, Lydia Birkbeck with a handkerchief in her hand ; and it was clear that she had been weeping.

Dora's heart stood still. . . .

As they passed her, she heard Rhodes say " God only knows what is the way out, if there is any way " : and Lydia Birkbeck sobbed once.

Ten yards beyond, Dora saw Rhodes bend and kiss Lydia Birkbeck's hand.

Upon which she moved away very dejected and slow down a shrubbery-path, her mouth pulled down like a child's to cry: and she took the train to Hampton, her *East Lynne* dream riven to pieces.

The next day she wrote to Rhodes a last letter. . . .

He was in his Grosvenor Square book-room when it came to his hand soon after four o'clock:

> " . . . I am still alive . . . but *you* will say, as *I* see, that that is hardly fair play to you, since you cannot remarry while I live, and you and another may suffer . . . I have decided that you shall be free to-day as my clock strikes six . . . It is hard to die in the Spring . . . but sleep, too, is sweet and slothful, like lukewarm baths of attar . . . Good-bye, Beloved . . . do not grieve much, but grieve a little . . . DORA."

Rhodes was already rather shocked and shaken when it came, having just got the news of the death of Lydia Birkbeck; and at Dora's letter he dropped, his arms cast over his table, his manhood collapsing now into sobs that gobbled forth broken gasps of "my tender darling! my mangled lamb!" It was a hard thing that he did not know where to find her, and that she should be dying. . . .

He flew—from his sobbing at the table to sobbing into the telephone. Was Mr. Pole there? No, Pole was not at the office. Rhodes' eyes appealed to heaven, and then his head fell.

Immediately afterwards, however, he heard running feet without, his door burst open, and Pole was there with words that leapt from his lips: "You must come instantly with me——"

"What's the matter? I was wanting you—look here——" he handed Dora's letter.

But Pole had hardly flung half-an-eye over it, when he threw it down, panting "I know. That's why I'm here. Let's be off."

In some moments they were in the cab that had brought Pole, and were away westward.

"Are we going to her?" Rhodes asked.

"Yes, Sir: and it was necessary to bring you, for a sound in the house—certainly the sudden sight of mine, or any other, strange face—would just cause her to do instantly what she intends doing at six. What I dread now is that Detective Inspector McLaren is at this moment on the road to arrest her, and, if he gets at her before us, all's up, for the moment he breaks into her presence, if he's hot-headed enough to do it, she lifts a vial to her lips——"

"How do you—know? What has happened?" Rhodes asked, all shaken, hatless, in a silk jacket, as they dashed past Hyde Park Corner.

"Ey, I went to Whitehall with the proofs of her innocence to McLaren"—Pole wiped his white forehead of dots of sweat—"McLaren was away, but Telford—pal of mine—says to me 'Lady Rhodes found at last'—full of it, had just put down the 'phone—of course, her photo is at every little constabulary. She's near Hampton Wick; been in disguise; but to-day—no longer caring—went out as herself, bought morphia tabloids, gave money away right and left, £180 to her maid. This, for *me*, meant suicide—didn't know *when*—and from Whitehall I made one dart for you, Sir, just throwing behind me for McLaren, who was expected every minute, 'Tell McLaren Lady Rhodes quite innocent—have proofs.' Whether that will have due effect I can't say. Ey, the man's mad to arrest—has spent so many weeks on it——"

"You know, then, that she is innocent ?" Rhodes asked : "how can you——?"

"Known it from the first," answered Pole with a down-look of disdain. "Stay—do you know, Sir, that Lady Birkbeck is dead ?"

"I have just heard it."

"Prussic acid—quick stuff—better than ten years of prison, for she wouldn't have been hanged for stabbing a cobra like Barclay. For years he has squeezed her of seven thousand a year—half her income—beside degrading her as a woman, turning to the fullest account his knowledge that she was not Birkbeck's wife, had no legal status. Who Birkbeck's first wife was he never let her know : only showed her Lady Rhodes' first-marriage certificate, and letters of 'Adore' written to Birkbeck after the date of Birkbeck's bigamous marriage, but Lady Birkbeck supposed 'Adore' dead, since 'Adore' never claimed Birkbeck's name and estate. Anyway, he had her well enslaved ; it isn't strange if she hated him : stabbed him in the back—dagger—then went hunting for papers connecting her with him—daring thing, hardened, in the presence of the body : not many men could have done it. Then, despairing of finding all papers, she conceived the idea—to suggest suicide—of throwing the body out of window, hoping that it might get so broken up, as to make the dagger-wound unnoticeable—had actually got body to window, had opened all doors behind her to fly instantly before body touched bottom, when she hears a ring, puts out lights, hides, and in comes Lady Rhodes with her 'awl,' as they call it——"

Rhodes' hand covered his eyes. "She took it to stab *herself*, apprehending violence: left a letter in a book for——"

"Ey, yes"—looking ahead out of the cab—"but, seeing Barclay hanging on the window, she stabs him instead, he having then been dead an hour; and as soon as I saw body, I decided that the two wounds were due to different weapons, used at different times. Then Lady Rhodes faints, leaving 'awl' in body; Lady Birkbeck lifts her to a sofa, puts 'awl' in her hand to incriminate her—that was a damnable thing."

"But natural, perhaps," Rhodes said: "she was not—infamous; and has suffered in her conscience. She recognized my wife, suspected then who 'Adore' was; and, remembering that my wife could have taken from her her position, but did not, she has since been stricken with contrition. It is this which has driven her to suicide."

"How do you know this, Sir?"

Rhodes heaved up his palms a little, saying "She confessed it all to me last night at Glanna!"

"Still, it wasn't contrition, Sir Robert, that did it, or not much. Fact is, I've haunted Lady Birkbeck of late: and it was only when I let her see and know that she hadn't a leg to stand on, that I got her confession for the sake of the other——"

"A confession in writing?"

"Here it all is"—he drew out some sheets covered with scribbling—"posted to me an hour before death: ey, she was not so bad"—he looked out of window anew, milking his lean beard, looking, not at the Hammersmith trees now mantling with a blush of Spring, but ahead and backward along the road ; and presently he started, leaning far out, and suddenly screamed to the driver, " You've got to catch that taxi !—there, by the tram ! A tenner, if you do "—he had caught a glimpse of McLaren's head glancing out, and McLaren had seen his.

The pace, already spinning, quickened—little traffic here to hamper them—Kew bridge nearly in sight. A policeman put down their numbers in his note-book. Rhodes leaned forward, as if to ease and help the speed.

" How intolerable ! " he said: " is he far ahead ? "

" Not four hundred yards." Pole glanced at his watch, muttering " five past five."

Opposite the Waterworks he shouted to his chauffeur, " Think you're winning on her ? "

" Both the same H.P.," the man flung behind him—" no go."

" Oh, but is there no way of stopping him ? " Rhodes groaned.

Pole drew a revolver .

Opposite Zion House he put out his head, set to howling " McLaren ! Proofs ! Stop ! ! "—waving Lydia Birkbeck's confession in circles ; but McLaren looked behind with his mouth wide open in a laugh ; and now Rhodes dropped back from looking, his lids closed.

At the same time Pole put one foot out, so stood three minutes, until they were well in the country, when he steadied himself, taking aim, and sent three shots at McLaren's off hind tyre. . . .

Within six ticks now they were darting past McLaren's howling mouth, Rhodes grasping Pole's hand. In ten minutes the cab stopped, to ask a countryman which was "Rose Cottage."

It lay down a lane, in a field, beside a rivulet. . . . Leaving Pole in the cab, Rhodes stole to its back by boring through a hedge, and scrambling over a wall by a pump : crawling cautiously like a war-scout he moved, dabbled to the ankles in marl, passed through a scullery, took off his slippers, passed through a kitchen with a floor of red tiles—no sound in the house—out to a small hall and stair. Here in the hall was the open door of a sitting-room ; he peeped in : she was not there ; and up soundlessly he mounted.

Above, there was a space round the stair-head containing one door at right-angles to two others, all closed. But which of the three . . . ? Terror took him lest, in opening the wrong one, he should make some sound : her hearing, he knew, was so acute . . . He stepped to the nearest, turned the handle as furtively as a clock's hand crawls, opened, peered—a work-table, a brazing-lamp, tools —no one there.

Then to the next in that wall : and, as he was at it, he heard a distinct something—like a sigh. Sharp he wrung the handle, and dashed in.

From what he caught sight of, he could just divine that she had been lying on a couch by the window, in her wedding-dress, to die in, looking up into a poplar before the cottage, a tall home of birds, whose top the Spring winds rocked with their song of eternity ; but at the first sound of the wrung handle, she must have sprung up and emptied a vial of poison-tabloids into her hand.

And now in the farthest corner she stood, stretched to her height, ecstatic, her long train which pages had carried wrapped round her legs ; and her face was as white as the dress's ivory satin, and yellow as its ancient laces.

Rhodes, too, stood white, with a brow that had broken out into sweat ; but within some moments he was warm and himself, his mood now rushing, by a reaction, into a sort of levity or frivolity.

They looked at each other.

" Got you ! "—from Rhodes.

She pushed out her face toward him, shaking it, saying " Dear, it is useless."

" Is it, by Jove ? Got you safe ! Nabbed ! "

" Dear—listen—I am too faulty——"

" That's how I like you ! "

She looked at him under her gloomy eyes, moaning " Dear, do you like me ? "

" That is very much so—just as you are—never mind about other people—*I* like you ! "

Her eyes fell before his stare of passion. " But, dear—listen—you don't know me—I have committed a crime——"

" Not a bit !—by God's pity. I know everything. The dog whom you stabbed had been dead an hour before—killed by someone else."

She started, staring. " Dear, is that the truth ? "

" I give you my word."

She covered her face quick with her hands.

" Don't trouble," he said ; " everything is all right; you haven't done any legal wrong; don't care about anything."

Now she looked up suddenly, as if to speak—

hesitated—then blurted out hurriedly, " Dear, I was married before——"

" I knew ! " cried Rhodes.

" *You knew* . . . "

" Yes—ten minutes after our marriage I knew. A telegram came to me at Ballybrophy from London, asking if I was aware that I was 'about to marry a widow.' Came from a man who turned out to be the husband of a girl-friend of yours—civil-servant, home on holiday from Hong-Kong—busy-body—'felt it his duty'. . . I knew."

" *You knew* . . . Dear, it was only a nominal marriage ! " she said quickly, bending to him.

" I knew. I was told ; and, if I hadn't been told, I should have known perfectly. But I felt that you ought to *tell* your own of it before we could truly be friends ; and I waited, and waited, and you wouldn't . . . . "

" *Oh !* "—she caught her face in her hands, and a sound came out.

" Never mind now," he said, going to her, " you've told me now "—wrapping her thrilling through her cataract of laces in the ark of his arms ; her head fell to rest upon him ; the pills of death drizzled from her fingers ; and he was wishing to pick up her chin to kiss her, when the corner of his eye caught sight of Pole and McLaren looking up foolishly from under the poplar, and he broke into a chuckle that had a sob of love in it.

When this story had been told, Lady Dale-Eldon, turning her face from being observed, wiped a tear from her eye, murmuring " Beautiful," upon which Netta, who saw, paused with her arm extended to switch-off, watching her companion-housekeeper with that wistfulness of sympathy which resided in her eyes, with that humour about the tender mood of her mouth that ever tended toward trembling; then, as the tongues broke loose, she bent to ask Sir Thomas Ormsby, "Can it have happened?"

"Well, really"—from Sir Thomas—"I don't like to dogmatize, but—yes, as far as I see."

She turned to Watts. "You are an artist, Paul—can it have happened?"

"No," Watts answered, "or rather yes—can have, but did not. You mayn't be able to put your finger on any spot of a plot of incidents, and say 'impossible,' yet the whole may be foreign to what occurs in the world."

"And is therefore impossible," Sir C. Alexander Caxton put in.

And the little Mr. Coward: "Well, there you are: didn't I say Sir Charles was a winner, when someone said 'wife'?"

"Not quite 'impossible' perhaps"—from Paul Watts to Sir Charles—"but stretched. There *are* dwarfs, so the tale of Tom Thumb takes that *fact*, and stretches it for the author's own motives—is possible, but is never met in the modesty of Nature. There are callous men, so the tale of the Good Samaritan takes that *fact*, and stretches it for the author's own motive, making two different people handrunning ruthlessly pass a wounded man—can happen, but does not: the details possible, the whole foreign to what occurs in the world."

Now Sir Thomas Ormsby remarked, "Yes, but it may not have been a stretch *then*: the ancients were less kindly disposed than we who have been living two hundred years under the reign of science."

Then Gerald Jewson of the viola: "And, after all, doesn't 'tale' or 'tell,' mean 'stretch,' Watts, if it is fiction? *Fi*ction is *fin*gering, making-up, inventing, building-up a bouquet, pottering a pot: so actual events, not fingered, don't run on the same rails as events fingered, invented. Now, to *tell* is to tell an event: painters, sculptors, depict what is still; *you* would never dream of painting a race; but the *teller* tells of races, motions, events; anything else, like 'character-drawing' is not telling, is drawing—another art: so the more the characters in fiction are like actual people the better; but the events, being telling, must conform to the law of fiction, and be fingered. So the great world-tales are first of all melo-dramatic—the *Iliad*, *Macbeth*, *Genesis*: they may have additional merits, but this is the essential—thrill, blood-and-thunder—the one thing needful, and the one thing difficult, if it is *real* blood-and-thunder. The character of Hamlet, of Abraham, occurs in the world, but the tale of Hamlet, of Abraham—the ghost conversing—the sacrificing of a son—does not occur: those are 'stretches.' If someone says 'I'll *tell* you a tale,' he may have the tongue of angels, but you expect beforehand that he has something outstanding to *tell*, and will steer a course between what cannot happen, and what is for ever happening: if it is impossible, you laugh, if it is ordinary, you yawn—if it is fiction: for to tell is to give information of an event, of something outstanding from the general mass of the world, and, if it is fiction, the *e*vent must be an *in*vention, and worthy of an inventor. If a maid says to a mistress, " A letter's come,' that's telling a tale, if it is fact ; but, if it is fiction, that's not telling, that's not a tale, she is using her tongue wrongly, nothing outstanding invented in it, nc 'stretch,' as there would be, if she said 'A letter's come—seems to be an eyeball in it'!"

"I myself," Lady Dale-Eldon now said, "can see nothing untrue either in the details or the whole of that poor Dora's story."

And Mr. Killik, the solicitor : "What, not in a young lady of twenty stabbing a man in the back, Madam, and feeling no remorse after ? Really !"

"She'd be too relieved to feel anything but relief," Paul Watts remarked.

"Thou shalt do no murder, Sir !" came sharp from the Rev. Mr. Darrel.

And Watts : "Oh, quite so, Sir ; I have no intention of murdering anyone."

"The girl was not English," Sir C. Alexander Caxton observed : "the Irish character cannot be fathomed."

And Netta : "Oh, well, we are all at sixes-and-sevens : when you come to vote——" but now approached a parlour-maid bearing a salver which was encumbered with ices of different kinds and with tints of summer drinks that foamed : and this was now to become the interest.

CHAPTER III

THE ROCK DAY

AND anew the afternoon after, the Friday, the sun sat enthroned, transacting that Summer-time, and if some clouds were sometimes clustering round his throne of government, like gowns of moguls flowing loose, they were of such stuffs rolled in glory as cannot be peered at without weeping, so that " dark with excessive bright his skirts appeared " ; and the men came in the groups of two, three, which they were getting into the way of taking ; but again not eleven gathered, but one less, " Whip " Prince not presenting himself.

However, some information about him was now obtained: for when Netta out in the arbour asked " But where is the one ? " Harry Ransom answered " Prince is in London."

" London . ." her eyebrows up: " how do you —know ? "

He answered, " A King's College fellow, Willings —you know Willings—'phoned me from Paris this 'forenoon. Yesterday, as he was getting ready to fly to Paris to meet his mother, Prince arrived at Croydon by air from Le Bourget, and Willings, in running to talk to Prince, who is his father's trustee, deposited his bag that has his book of tots in, lost it, so 'phoned to borrow my tots."

" London . . ." Netta muttered again : " oh, well, one can't calculate a flea."

And Ransom : " No, specially when its ' hops ' are from Paris to London."

But here interest in Prince failed, invaded by talk of Sir Thomas Ormsby : for Paul Watts had asked Sir Thomas, whose day it was, if he was acquainted with the tales of his tale-teller Miss Maidstone Fox, to which Sir Thomas answered " I am afraid not: in general I only read one tale, the tale of the earth."

" Ah, a mystery-story," Paul Watts remarked.

And Gerald Jewson : " Roundabout tale : no end, no beginning."

And the Rev. Mr. Darrel : " A tragedy, Sir: began in a garden, and will end in a conflagration."

But Sir Thomas : " On the contrary, I think it is always ending, always beginning, and always its endings are happy."

This caused Paul Watts to flush, and ardently he said " Yes ! That's why every good tale has a happy ending, for good tale is true tale. One of the beginnings was a pin-head of plasm—not so long ago —three hundred million years—and already that has ended in birds and men—eagles and aeroplanes, larks and Beethovens——"

The gale of Beethoven's " Gallop " piece was even then being given ; but now this stopped, and now a voice announcing, " This is the national . . ." " And now for Miss Maidstone Fox's story ' The Vulture's Rock ' " . . . " Miss Fox " . . . whereupon a suaver voice noising out of the hollow of heaven, relating this tale :

Arli may be the littlest community of human beings extant with a *trattoria* in it—littler, I think, than Moli, that looks down from its peak upon Etna and Taormina. Its people are antique—and amphibious, like seals. Perched up there on a spur of the Apennines, they are mountaineers, but are equally fishermen—from their peak can nearly see the sand on which they keep their shallops. And all round the valley, which reaches down to the sea, hang giddy villages on the crags—like nests. Till you are near them, the imagination refuses to see why they do not topple over—or till a telescope helps, picking out everywhere a little square church-tower.

In Arli there lived a great man, a rich man, a wise. What if he could not read? He had seen the world and its wonders, and the house he lived in had real shingles, come from Genoa. This was the old Francesco Testi, bent down now, his locks all white, but his eyes still bright. He, like others, had started life as a goatherd and fisher, and see what he had grown to now—a king in Arli: the reason lay only in the fact that he had had the pluck to go off to Genoa, and to cross the sea in a ship.

It was whispered that Francesco had seventy thousand lire, kept for him in a bank in some far town, this all to fall to Simonetta, his grand-daughter, when he died, and to the husband she should choose. Simonetta was seventeen, and often, as she wandered solitary in the pepper-wood, felt hardly grateful for her thousand pounds. She was the queen of the village, but wanted to be its plaything. The lads worshipped her at a distance.

Now, it happened that one day Francesco went away. It must have been to that same city where his wealth lay stored, for when he returned he had it all about him in notes. Day by day the hunger to see them had grown upon him : so he had gone ; and on the night of his return showed them in his glee to Simonetta before locking them up in a cabinet ; and Simonetta, in a flutter, went and told her friend Marina, who fluttered : and so the flutter spread.

But on the morning of the third day after Francesco's return the notes were gone—and those brown faces turned whitish ; a hush fell on that mountain-side.

From far and near they came to assemble in front of the shingled house, speaking in whispers, waiting as the hours rolled round, hoping for a sight of the old man's scared face, relieving one another like sentinels.

At last, at dusk, Simonetta came to the door, a woeful sight, her eyes red.

"My grandfather thanks you for your kind feeling," she said, and broke down, sobbing. "He—would come—and thank you—himself, but——"

"Who stole the money, Simonetta ? Tell us that ! What does Francesco think ?" a voice cried out.

"He—doesn't know—it must be one of you."

A murmur, half of anger, arose : a theft like this had never been among them.

"What about that Pippo ?" shrieked a woman's voice.

Simonetta started, looked up. This idea seemed to appeal to her. But she shook her head to say "It is impossible : Grandfather saw Pippo at Milan, where he got the notes. Pippo is far from here."

Now a sharp exclamation from a man in the crowd—from Nicolo, the boatman, the fruit-carrier to the Vulture's Rock : and every eye turned to him. Here would be light and insight, if anywhere. But Nicolo, not prone to speech, shy like a chamois kid, hung his head, said nothing.

"It boots nothing to stand there making guesses," Simonetta now said : "it would be better if you went home, and tried to forget us. But oh ! I beg you, whoever has stolen the money, return it ! Nothing will be said. You would not kill an old man ? And, besides, he bids me say that whoever—mark that—whoever brings back those pieces of paper shall—shall—have me for his——You know what I would say, perhaps. And I would consent, too—indeed I would—to save him——"

She ceased her simple speech, closed the door ; whereupon the crowd formed itself into a series of committees to discuss the situation. Only one of their number took no part in the parliaments of tongues—Nicolo, the still.

He descended the mountain-side, turned into a piece of ground shut in by crags, the grass covered in places by patches of crisp snow which had fallen the evening before, he keeping his eyes fixed on the ground, seeking something—seen there the previous night. Fresh snow had come since, but little, for he soon gave out a sound of satisfaction, stooping down to examine his discovery—a great footprint in the snow.

Nicolo knew that only two feet thereabouts could make such a track—the feet of Pippo, the hunchback. Yet Pippo was supposed to be in Milan !

Pippo was a stranger in those parts. No mountain-climber he, but a Roman from the flats of the Campagna. Some three years before he had appeared in the midst of these solitudes, had settled down amongst them, no one knowing who or what he was, save this : that he was a learned man, a chemist, a reader of books. It was clear, too, that he must be rich ; people whispered that he must be one of those *far niente* ones of the outside world, and, for some crime, had come to this quiet place to hide : for he did not labour like other men, but spent his time in bouts of drunken madness, or in wandering over the mountains, dreaming in his monstrous head dreams of Simonetta.

At first she had only laughed at him, witching him only the more with her laughter, until one day, meeting her in a wood, he seized upon her like a falcon, and in wild words swore she should be his. Then did Simonetta all at once become a tragic cat, using her little nails. Her tongue could be shrill and shrewish, and she used it. All this was known in the villages.

But what no one knew was a little romance—his only one—which Nicolo had been for some time hugging in his bosom. He was thirty years old, a black-bearded man, but there was burning in his nerves in these days of the theft all the insurgent joy of a boy's first love.

It had come about in this way : one day, the sun overhead, Nicolo, having sat under a pine-tree far up the mountain, had in the lassitude of the hour carved " Nicolo " with his knife on the trunk. A week after, coming to that tree anew, he stood confronted with a marvel : somebody had scraped in the bark under his name " te voglio bene " (I love you).

Who had done this thing? Without daring to whisper it to himself, Nicolo believed in his deeps, with that belief of which a wish is the seed, that it was Simonetta.

Well, after discovering the foot-prints in the snow, he continued his way down the mountain, no longer in doubt as to who had stolen Francesco's notes—the only question was, where were they now? The world is full of holes for hiding.

He sat on a ledge of rock from which the sea was visible, letting his eye dwell on a speck out on the water: for though it was already dusk, he had the vision of a sparrow-hawk, and presently this speck began to interest him . . . a small boat, one occupant; and that one, he soon decided, no fisherman. When he had run down and hidden behind a clump of bush near the shore, he could have laughed when he saw the large body of the hunchback, as the hunchback jumped from the boat, and put his great strength to draw it up. Nicolo had discovered, without an effort, the great secret: the notes were at the Vulture's Rock.

This rock, standing seven miles from the mainland, was called by the old fishermen of Liguria in Roman days "*Rupes Aquilina*," because the summit resembles a vulture's skull. And the old name clings to it, " Scoglio dell' Avoltoio."

It rises in awful solitude out of the sea to a height of near two thousand feet, shaped like one half of a cone that has been slit down the middle—one side flat, the other convex. On the convex side, the south, life is possible, a few poor men and women actually exist there, this south side having a regular incline upward to the summit, and a bold climber may reach the top ; but there the brain dizzies to look down, on the *north* side, upon a wall of rock falling away from the feet, not perpendicular, but having an inward batter. Those who have reached and looked down, by stretching out over the vulture's beak, tell that it is a spectacle of terror, the world turns turtle, making the nervous system sea-sick. In all this wall of rock there is one break only—a ledge, three feet broad, which runs across it at a height of three-quarters of the rock's height from the bottom. Quite near the end of the beak on that side a few shrubs grow.

Well, before the sun rose on the morning following his discovery Nicolo was out to sea—had laboured all night providing his boat with a supply of "tasso" (dried strips of meat), with water, fruit, goat's-milk cheese, fishing-tackle, a pot-bellied fiasca of gentian brandy.

He had an idea that Pippo was too cunning to hide his treasure on the rock itself : what was simpler than to put the notes in a box and sink them in the deep ? The sea is an excellent confidant ; but, then, you must mark the spot by some float.

So for this float Nicolo proceeded to seek, his movements regulated by scrupulous method, he never moving over the same spot twice ; at night, the sea being smooth, he hung two lanterns out ; and in this way spent two weeks, ferreting on the sea round the Vulture's Rock. Then he saw that he was on the wrong track.

The next week he spent on the rock itself, examining its accessible side—the south. One of the men who lived there remembered *to have seen Pippo* coming down the hill on a certain night ; and, on calculating, Nicolo discovered that that was the night after the notes were stolen. That evidence was conclusive, for with what other object could the hunchback have ascended the rock but to hide his treasure ? The notes must be there, near the summit : hardly any soil in which they could be buried, so that made his task easier ; and with scientific precision, with the patience of Sisyphus, he scrutinized—to the wonder of the few natives—every spot from base to top : weeks rolled round ; and he found nothing.

At the end of this great investigation Nicolo was seated one evening near the extremity of the vulture's beak, as the rim of the sun was dipping, away in a red west, into the sea ; and he had begun to ply himself with the question " what next ? " when a pebble fell away from his feet ; following this, his eyes rested on the ledge of the receding north side, and he started. . . . If the notes were there ?

But he dismissed the idea as improbable ; if there, they must have been flung there, and would be past recovery by Pippo himself : no motive for such a waste of money.

Still, ever as this question " what next ? " recurred to him, so did the idea of the ledge. He was desperately unwilling, after all his quest, to entertain it, but it would not be shut out. As days passed, the conviction grew upon him that Pippo had wantonly thrown away the notes ; and he began, too, to discover something like a motive for such an act : despairing of Simonetta rich, Pippo may have resolved to make her poor, and that

—not love of money—must have been his reason for stealing the notes : so he had practically destroyed them. But, for some reason or other, he had not thrown them into the sea, torn them up, burned them—for *why had he climbed the rock ?* And he had not hidden them on the south side ; of that Nicolo's perfect search made him certain : so only one alternative was left ; he had flung them on to the ledge—in his malignity, or with some other motive, where it would be impossible to regain them, unless —the rock were scaled ?

To descend was impossible ; for anyone attempting this with the aid of a rope would swing out into air from the projecting beak. But to scale it ? One must be as agile as patient, as daring as muscular, an animal made up of the gorilla, the goat, the eagle, the ant, and possessing the inventiveness of a man.

The ledge being visible from the summit, but parts of it hidden by patches of foliage, Nicolo passed hours in examining the parts he could see, leaning his body over ; but though he could perceive nothing except pebbles, he abated no whit of the resolve he had formed to attempt the feat. After spending several days in brooding over plans, separating in his thoughts what was possible from what was not, late one night, when prying eyes were closed, he returned to the mainland, pulled up his boat, and started off over the mountain-passes to Ricci, the nearest town. He came back as secretly as he went, staggering under a load of tools and provisions.

When he next got to the Vulture's Rock he anchored his boat under the north wall, mooring it in addition to a spike which he drove into a crevice :

for there was no beach, the water deep. He then rigged a tarpaulin into a tent in his boat—his sleeping-place. After that night, for four months, he never saw a face or sign of human life, except a boat or two, out fishing from the other side of the island.

He began by driving spikes, alternating these by holes which he chipped for his feet. To the spikes he attached ropes. He was provided with means to sharpen his tools when they were down, but the basaltic mass he worked on was almost as hard as the metal he worked with. Splinters, sparks, flew into his face, blinded, cut him. Sometimes when he had driven a spike after half a day's cark, he found it loose in the hole it had made. His labour *lo fece magro molti giorni*, made him lean many days.

He came to depend in great measure for his food on what fish he could catch, and this often did not come up to expectation. Once he hungered three days. All the time, too, it was necessary to drink little water, for his stock of this also was small, and to return for these things among men would be to delay his work, and betray himself. So long as he remained where he was he felt secure from observation, for the fishermen on the south never came round to that appalling north side. To the ships passing afar he was invisible, as to the folk on the mainland, who had little intercourse with those on the rock ; and, buried from the sight of man, he said one day " Thou, God, seest me."

Then he found that he had miscalculated the length of rope, which began to fall short, so now he cut his tarred-canvas tent into strips, which he plaited, and thenceforward slept under starlight and dews of Nebuchadnezzar. But he prospered, if slowly : every day found him higher.

It was when he had nearly reached the middle point of his pilgrimage that, as he was striking his last blows before descending for the night, his sledge-hammer slipped from wearied fingers into the sea—into eight fathoms. All that night, all the next day, he was dragging the bottom with his weighted net, which seemed to gather to itself all the *débris* of ocean to taunt him, all but his hammer. At last, with an angry exclamation, he stripped himself, began to dive ; and whiter, whiter, showed the resolute face of the man in the moonshine every time he emerged to the surface. When at last he appeared grasping the hammer crimson was trickling from his ears.

Here was something like hurling a challenge at the Invincible. Frosts in winter riveted his limbs, like the limbs of some crucified Prometheus, to the cruel rock. There was a morning when he awoke, quivering, from his nightmare sleep to see his ropes, gunwales, the rock, crowded with icicles. To climb now was defiant ; but he made more than one attempt, only to slip back bloody. During several days of frost Nicolo became a fury fettered ; but when it was gone he began sullenly again, not troubling to be grateful.

His garments, always wet, hung in rags from him. The elements, wandering through the world in search of a plaything, saw him—hail, sun, sirocco, snow, took turns at him. Gradually his eye lost lustre, his ribs stood out, a feverish shivering seized on him. He became the ruin of a man. And with all this, the spirit, too, that had borne him up began to droop. The worst element of his malady was the temptation that seized him in the last days to hurl himself into the deeps beneath.

At last, one day when only a week's labour remained to be done, Nicolo, absorbed in his toils, feeling a thrill run through him, threw an eye upward : the sky was black ; the sea beneath was white, breakers battering against the rock. When he looked for his boat, he saw it miles away, a dot on the waters. To swim after it in such a sea was a task too great for man, and he was already very weak. Now he was a real Prometheus—chained to the rock which he had set out to conquer.

He worked now night and day, foodless, parched, sleepless, bowed under a gale which, tugging at him, swung him to and fro, crashing him against the crag. Had he been humble, he must have failed ; but a demon urged him to insurgence—and on the morning of the third day he reached out his now bony arm, drew himself on to the ledge, and, with a gasp, dropped upon the object of all his effort, to perish.

He lay there without sign of life all that day, the storm bawling over him ; but when it cleared Nicolo moved in sleep, awoke to new hope and motion. Now at last he had triumphed, had only to stretch out his hand to take the notes, never doubting the correctness of his theory that they had been thrown there weighted, nor could they have rolled off, the inside edge of the ledge being lower than the outer.

But when he rose, walked backward and forward over the narrow platform, no notes were there ; and now, his head fallen forward on his chest, he sank down afresh upon the rock, and moaned.

Presently it struck him that he was dying of thirst, and he decided to descend, intending to swim round to the other side, if his strength sufficed —he hoped it would not. But as he was about to step over the edge, a piece of metal at the very end of the ledge's length caught his eye : so, wondering what it was doing there, he went and picked it up—a big nail.

He was surprised to find two threads tied round it. One of them, he saw, went up from the nail along the face of the rock above him ; he could not follow it far with his eye, but concluded that it must be fastened to some shrub at the summit ; when he tugged at it, it snapped mid-way. Then he looked at the other thread, and was mystified to see it rise straight up skyward, not along the rock, but up into space, away from the edge of the peak, which edge narrows-in to make the point at the summit—straight up and up—till he lost sight of it in the azure, this seeming the slight link that binds Heaven to earth. When he pulled at it, it yielded easily ; and he commenced to draw it in, hand-over-hand. The length seemed endless, but presently a round object came into sight above his head. At this object the thread ended.

When the whole length had been thus taken in, Nicolo held in his hand a balloon, a couple of feet in length, made of gold-beater's skin, filled with a gas. When he tore it open, he found the notes in it. With these in his hand, his arms spread to Heaven, he dropped upon his knees.

But in that moment his eyes, uplifted, met a face peering at him over the summit, and, far off as it was, he recognized Pippo, guessing instantly that Pippo, having missed him, had come to see how the notes were doing. Within some moments more a pistol-shot pierced Nicolo's back, and, wheeling as he transacted the drama of a tremendous somersault, in the end he reached, he plunged.

So long it lasted, that waltzing dive, that the eye of a bewildered fisherman was caught from afar by the flash of a white something tumbling down the dark of the Vulture's Rock ; and this fellow came to save him. He was taken to the other side and coaxed back to life by the fisherwives, who are their own physicians, Medæas trained to an old-wife's sageness of their own in therapy. Hence after some weeks he could one day steal out of his hut when his old nurse's back was turned ; and when she, on missing him, hurried after in alarm, it was to discover him at the water's edge, looking toward the coast. Nicolo was humming a barcarola.

All the birds were crying aloud that bright morning when he returned to the mainland, and set to climbing the mountains ; as for him, his heart was a nest of larks : but then a woman trotting down with a basket of *lime* (sweet lemons) remarked as she passed him, " What became of you, Nicolo ? Walk fast—see the wedding."

Farther up a goatherd called to him " Ola, Nicolo ! Back, then, for the wedding ? They're all there by now."

" Whose wedding ? " Nicolo asked.

" Whose ? Why, is it not Signor Pippo's ? Was it not he who found the notes ? and the old man had sworn——"

Nicolo moved on, no faster than before. He threw an eye upward at the sky.

At Arli the holy father, looking glum, as though conscious that he was helping forward the action of a tragedy, had already begun the marriage, when a figure in rags, with long hair, walked up the nave. So long had he disappeared, that many believed him dead : so his coming back was like a ghost's. With bent head he moved toward the altar, stood by the side of the sad-eyed bride.

Ignoring this ghost in rags, the padre asked, " Do you take this woman for your wife ? "

" I do," replied Pippo.

And Nicolo replied " I do."

In another moment he had the notes held up before the crowd, who soon understood that the notes Pippo pretended to have found must have been his own, not *the* notes ; so that faces reddened with anger at the deed that had been done in their midst, and a grumbling began to grow wrathful. In one hand Francesco now had a bowie-knife, with the other he pressed Nicolo's hand, while the bride, trembling, glanced thankfully at her deliverer. Meantime, the grumble had grown to a row. Some had huddled up toward the altar, and when a voice called " pin the imbroglione ! " it was followed by a rush, which would have borne down Pippo, if he had not retreated quick, drawing a revolver ; and, his face having now in it a something that warned the boldest to beware, at the sight of that cold barrel there was a hesitation, taking advantage of which, Pippo, spinning on his heels, made a dash for a chancel door ; but someone ran cat-footed upon him while he wrung the door-handle, and by sharp practice snatched the revolver, as Pippo disappeared.

The Maria Dora, who ran the *fa da mangiere*, related every day afterwards how, panting, he had then rushed into her shop, shouting " Brandy ! " and had half drunk a bottle. " They have my pistol," he had said, " but let them look out when Pippo comes back."

Then with the bottle he had rushed from the shop along the Genoa road. That night, a night of tempest, resolute men, with weapons ready, waited for his appearing : but Pippo did not appear. A week afterwards a boy found his body at the bottom of a precipice far up the mountains, the bottle gone, but its top part still gripped in his fingers. It was never known whether he had died a suicide's or a drunkard's death.

And now, with some sense of fitness, the Francesco was for having Nicolo married to Simonetta at the Vulture's Rock—which would be costlier, but now he owned two thousand instead of one—his own and Pippo's—and could afford whims. But Simonetta felt that she would see the face of Pippo frowning down at them from the summit. So the event took place in Arli : for Nicolo, too, was unwilling. For years he would never venture near that tremendous strength from which, by much wrestling, he had wrung sweetness ; when he cast a glance at the rock's grandeur, he'd be heaving a " God help us," crossing his breast.

This tale ended, Lady Dale-Eldon's and Netta Fenton's faces took-on a lost look, disappointed by the author, for they saw nothing that " cannot have happened " in it, and deeply Netta wished Sir Thomas Ormsby to be the winner ; but she took heart when in the todo of tongues that broke loose she heard Paul Watts assert to Gerald Jewson, " *That*, anyway, cannot have happened."

Upon which Sir Thomas, who had also heard : " Why, Watts, can it not ? "

" Superhuman, Sir, I think, the hero," Paul Watts answered : " there is no such animal as ' a gorilla, a goat, an eagle, an ant, and a man ' in one. And, then, some of the details. . . . When the fellow was shot, and fell holding the notes, he'd be suffocated before reaching the sea, his fingers would relax, the notes would scatter."

But Sir Thomas answered " No, I think that psycho-analysts differ from you there ; you don't give enough weight to the Subconscious, which, they say, is nine-tenths in us—functions even in death, so that dead fingers will still subconsciously grip an object which the living individual had been eager to cling to. As to this hero being more than Man, do we know how much Man is ? If the ancients had had some knowledge of embryology, the riddle of their Sphinx would have been ' What animal is that which is an eel, a lizard, a linnet, a pig, a gorilla and a man in one ? ' and the Œdipus who solved the riddle would have answered ' A baby,' since a baby is all these in his pre-natal career. And the adult man is a super-baby when he is drowsing, as usual, but when roused is a super-man. Little do men in general dream what heights they can achieve, until some heat of motive deep within them drives them to stretch themselves high, and try."

At this the eyes of that " tough guy " of Brooklands and the Monte Carlo Rally, Lord George

Orchardson, brightened, as he said " That's a fact, Sir; stretch her, and you get three minutes more out of her. You may vow, ' This is the limit, here's the last word in cars of this h.p.', but wait, in a month she's outrun : no end to it—stretch and stretch—what's impossible in January is old-fashioned in March."

And now Sir Charles Alexander Caxton : " It is a pity, though, that this Nicolo was not an Englishman, since his grit was English. Is the foreigner endowed. . .? In digging the Simplon tunnel, they could make little progress, the rock was so tough, until some genius engineer suggested, ' Try English labour ' : then the tunnel was soon dug."

But this caused Paul Watts to eye aside at Sir Charles with a sardonic iciness, as he remarked, " That was brute bravura ; but Nicolo had to invent as well, and so properly belonged to the race which made modern civilization, which, after inventing cosmology, proceeded to invent electricity, which, after producing ' the father of knowledge,' went on to produce Volta, Galvani."

" Well, yes, that's so," Sir Thomas Ormsby said : " the history of England is the history of our adoption of the ideas of the Continent. We didn't ' invent steam,' you know, in the nineteenth century ; there was a steamboat on the Seine—Papin's—in the life-time of Milton ; and, as chemistry is called ' a French science,' so electricity, from Volta to Marconi, can be called an Italian. Europe would be Asia without its Latins. But, then, we Nordics, if we don't originate, dig deeper, finish the tunnel, carry on, add, and——" he stopped to say to Netta, who was on the point of kissing the invalid's fingers, " No, I think she's sleepy, don't touch."

Netta whispered " Perhaps she listened, and the tale tired her."

And Sir Thomas : " Possibly. I think it quite on the cards that some one of these tales may move her, and then—What kind of fiction did she like ? "

" Boys' stories specially—fond of boys—real boys, I mean, small boys. She'd read *The Boy's Journal*—poor Greta, poor dear. Once made me try to read one of the stories, but I failed. . . . Sir Thomas, mightn't we try her with a spoonful of tea ? "—for now an English " tea" was seen coming ; but Sir Thomas was against tea for his sick, whereas all the others, seeing in it a piquancy of foreignness there, enjoyed it with jest before making any move to break up the arbour party.

CHAPTER IV

THE DIARY DAY

THE next day, Lord George Orchardson's Saturday, once more came together the old eleven, Mr. Whipsnade Prince now again presenting himself; and says Netta to him "Your return is thrilling, Mr. Prince. You do us too much honour."

"Ah, you did notice my absence," he said.

"Left a void, you know."

"You mean me to disbelieve that, but I believe it: I saw your face light up when you saw me."

"So? There's nothing like cheek. *De l'audace, et toujours de l'audace.*"

"Oh, no *audace.* That would be unfair if you don't like me, since I like you so much."

"If you like me, kiss at my ear through a telephone-mouthpiece, get me through the post, throw at me a telegram; I live in an Age of invention: I claim my Age."

"Your old age, say. You're oldish."

"Respect me, then: I claim both my ages."

"I had to fly off, Netta."

"Well, if you *had*—Where to?"

"To Paris."

"Paris . . . Not to—London?"

"*London*? no . . . or rather yes, I did fetch London just for an hour; Paris was my objective."

" But somehow you seem to be hiding something. What can it be ? Do you ever 'lie a little'?"

" Yes ; but not to you."

" How can I be sure that *that* is not lying a little, since you lie a little ? "

Prince looked at the ground : no answer, and Netta : " Good thing it is only a little ; much isn't pretty ; and your occupation, you know, is to be prettier than common Tom. Better take care."

" Very well . . . I say, look at Jewson—a musician's rapture : that's how I shall feel when you forgive my sins—for I'm a miserable sinner—when you say 'your sins, which were many, are all forgiven you' "—nodding toward Gerald Jewson, who sat lost to all else than a musical emotion, his eyes closed, his forefinger moving a little in time to that lovely " Dance of the Angels " now coming from the radio, or say coming from that heaven in which the angels, their souls in their toes, were moving stately to music of the Muses. But this piece, being pitifully brief, speedily ceased, to be followed by a horrid drop down from heaven's ineffable dancing to voice of man, to " This is the national programme . . ." And now for Mr. Algernon Shanks, invetei ate teller of Bush and Veldt, in his tale " A Diary " . . . " Mr. Shanks " . . . whose manner and habit of utterance now arose out of the womb of Nowhere to recount this story :

Sept. 14*th.*—He of the silk-beard and the shirt is not the only stranger here : there are three others—putting up at " The Anchor." In coming home, I saw these sitting on Mrs. Higgs' well, drinking her shop ginger-beer ; and one of them, a rather villiainous-looking person, was exhibiting the old well-bucket to the others as an object of ridicule. . . .

Sept. 15*th.*—No sight at all of silk-beard and shirt to-day. But there are other things interesting under the sun, Henny. Such a flame now in the heart of Nature ! Norfolk is all a daub of poppies, mixed with scabious purple, wild-tulip yellow ; and everything calling out " holiday " ! Little Miss Pinker, the postmistress, seemed to wave it me from her shop-door ; the washing hung in the cottage-gardens flap it ; the sails of the fishing-fleet. " Only man is vile " : for in the evening Passmore, the coastguardsman, told papa that the three strangers at " The Anchor " are people suspected by the police.

I said to papa " Perhaps I had better lock up the gems and Purchester Instrument in the study-safe."

" Henny, darling," papa answered, " how is anyone to know that I have gems ? "

" Oh, Papa, that is hardly a secret," I said : " at least six villages know by heart that you spend your wealth in collecting."

This chance word " wealth " set papa pacing ! " I am glad you see fit to call it *wealth*, my darling ! " he said : " I *should* by now have possessed a collection worth mentioning, if I had not been robbed by Robert Strong."

I read the other day that " the " is the commonest of English words, and thought then that in Manor House the name " Robert Strong " must be ! It is a little like mania, papa mine : for who could believe that Sir Robert Strong ceased from troubling forty years before you were born ? So much spleen against mere dust. With how vile a villainy has that name been connected in my mind from childhood ! Blue-Beard was an innocent in comparison. And yet, was Robert Strong really any more infamous than other people who have done things ? He is *believed* to have destroyed the " instrument " which could have made papa's grandfather Earl of Purchester—otherwise mere Henny would have been " the Honourable " ! But I forgive, oh, Robert Il Diavolo. Thistle is still purple, Bobs, and hedge-daisy yellow. Your descendant, the Earl, graciously grants my dad fifteen hundred sovereigns a year, of which I enjoy what gems do not absorb. And, if we have not " the instrument " itself which you suavely destroyed, have we not, to console us, the supposed copy, cherished, though valueless ? May you rest in pieces. . . .

Sept. 17th.—The man has had the daring to address me ! Up went the dreadnaught cap with ear-flaps, and says he " Forgive me—a stranger here—what use do they put this old tower to ? "

" Drowned sailors are laid in there until the inquest," I told him, *tout en passant.* Perhaps there was no need to have been so *short.*

But what a handsome man ! I did not know that there are such men. The fellow kidnaps one's eyes, and beckons meditation astray from its everyday lanes. The beard is really silk-like, ink-black, his skin baked dark, the eyes dark-blue—very strange ; and his teeth so sheeny and even. It was under the churchyard Spanish-chestnuts, where he was sauntering—walks with a long-legged swagger, laggardly, stealingly, as if his feet lingered a little backward. But his sudden nimbleness ! Just before I overtook him a rabbit's rush through the bush attracted him, and in a flash he dashed into action like a cat—though he is forty, or more, and though he had in his hand a horse, with Mrs. Ball's eight-year-old Gordie sitting lost on its long back, with the gravest face. Mary said in the kitchen yesterday that he has bought from the Barnidge Stud a hunter, on whose stretched neck he pelts over England like Tam o'Shanter. As for the shirt, to-day it was a dark-blue serge, double-breasted, with red anchors on the collar-flaps. He had on box-cloth gaiters, moleskin trousers, a flash sash-belt, a hide-whip in his hand—the formidable, gaudy being.

Sept. 20th.—I was reading *Idylls of the King*, seated on the column in the priory-ruins, when he came in—about three. Lovely day—sleepy, bee-burdened. I could hear the beat of a steam-engine from Chinnery's rick-yard, rakes whirring somewhere, and dream-shouts from some boys playing cricket on the Morplepiece. And all at once he was there with me. His feet do not make much noise!

He snatches off a "full-share" hat. "This being our sixth encounter within five days," says he, "I hope you won't be thinking that I am for ever tracking you down."

I let my lips just mutter "No," and he made a step to withdraw, but hesitated, stopped, asked the date of the priory. I told him.

"This is the nicest little land!" he breaks out: "I first drank pap about here, too—my father twelve years vicar of Knapton over yonder—left when I was five. You a native?"

"Yes."

" You live in that old gabled home in Soame's Hollow that they name ' The Manor ' ; father, Sir Reginald Lestrange."

" Yes."

" Collects gems, your father."

I was rather astonished. " Ye-e-s," I said, " he has some gems."

" Now, I am going to be all out frank with you " —he stood propped upon the clerestory column, his legs crossed, big, big, but limber, belted with zebra-skin to-day—every day differently decked out to the eye, with crass and antic dandyism, like the pheasant-cock in April, to entrap the tail of the ninny hen's (not Henny's !) eye—" frank with you. Have been knocking about the world—seen the whole fakement—and don't care now if I strike root. But I'm the newest of new chums in my own country—not one decent friend in it—you follow me. Hence should much like to make your father's acquaintance : so, on hearing that he collects gems, I remembered some pretty little Gong-Gong river-stones, yellow-water, that I have on board that schooner-yacht you can see beyond The Steel : and it struck me that an introduction might come about that road. Your father could have those diamonds of me for—a song ; or for—nothing ; makes no matter to me ; or might merely care to inspect them. Now, then, I throw myself upon you. Tell me if, and how, I can get in with your father."

The man's eyes do eat one in a rather embarrassing manner ; and he seemed so *ingenu*, boylike, I felt that I ought to show a frankness not less open-hearted than his ; so I said " I cannot quite say at the moment. I am afraid you will hardly find my father very ready to strike up acquaintances, in spite of many diamonds. But I will think of what you have said, and see if I can do anything."

Off he snatches the flash hat with a hand all pinks and blues with tattooing. "That's out and out good of you!" (Greater British, but Lesser English, my Henny!) "For the rest, I can wait. Have learned that out in all the pow-wow. This my little haven. After bush and karoo, am a Little Englander. As the local rhyme says, 'Gimmingham, Trimmingham, Knapton and Trunch, Northrepps and Southrepps lie all of a bunch'—very true. England's 'little'; one feels like riding over it in a night; but good. Little thatched churches of flint here; fishermen calling 'lobsters!'; cottages hiding behind ivy, with Gothic window-slits, latticed—suits me all to pieces! Everything dainty and genteel: the wind, the rain, genteel—what *you* call rain; *we*'d call it moisture. I have a tent on the Piece, but sleep out in the heather on that rock they call Devil's Rock on the Chase. Yes, this is my land. And the daintiest lady that lives I've seen in it."

I accused him a little with an underlook, took my Tennyson, and stood up. In answer to his question, I said again that I should think of his suggestion, and if I came across him later, should tell the result.

I came home fully intending to say something for him to papa, since his proposition seemed quite fair and square; but at tea-time papa rather had Robert Strong on the brain, so I thought I would bide my time; then, for two hours, came in the two St. John-Heygates, Douglas and Aimée; after which I played papa the Largo, which always pacifies him·

and, as I left the piano, said to myself "Now."

Papa was reclining on the sofa with his eyes closed, fingering his beard; and I began to say "By the way, Papa——"

But *he* suddenly spoke: "I say, Henny, where are the gems and the Purchester Instrument?"

I told him that since we had heard of the three suspected persons at "The Anchor," I had locked up the casket in the study safe.

"Quite right," he said: "I am bothered about something I saw to-day—a man spying about the place."

"One of those three?" I asked.

"No," he said, "not one of the three, but an associate of theirs, a fourth lounger—outlandish popinjay—who is now about."

"*He* is not an associate of the three," I said.

Papa glanced at me, and sat up to say emphatically, "Pardon me, darling, he *is*, for I saw him head-to-head with them on Monday evening by Barnidge pheasantry, and when they saw someone coming they separated. This same man was here to-day peeping and peering—I saw him from my bedroom standing on tip-toe on the tump behind the lime-trees, craning his neck, taking stock."

This did not please me. Papa must have seen me flinch, for he took my hand, saying "It mayn't mean much, don't be nervous—let the house be locked up at night. Why should they rob from me? They probably divine that the eyes of the police are on them, and the gems aren't worth £5,000. I am not worth the robber's while! I, a scion of an opulent house——"

I asked him at what hour he had seen this person

peeping, and he said about two—an hour before the man had been with me in the ruins.

Anyway, that ended my intention to mention to papa the alleged gems in this gentleman's yacht.

But afterwards, when I sat and thought of it, I saw things differently. The gem which " the popinjay " was spying after was quite possibly not of the mineral kingdom ! Yet, if one does " track down " someone, and then begs that someone not to imagine herself " tracked down," that is hardly as frank as possible, perhaps ?

As to his hobnobbing with the three, how about that ? One does not know what to think now ! Perhaps he craves for any kind of society, being friendless ?—heaven knows. " Makes no matter " to *me*.

Sept. 22*nd*.—It was hot indoors, papa had fallen into a doze over his Gibbon, and I strolled down to the churchyard with my Spanish hand-lace head-wrap in my hand, a W. L. Richardson rose in my hair. The harvest-moon was at its full, so that one could read the names on the grave-stones ; and there, in a moonlight-trail, lay the " schooner-yacht," also the Yarmouth steamer moving, and one boat out at the lobster-pots ; the sea asleep ; hardly a sound. I was seated on a tomb by the cliff-edge near the Lestrange brick-grave, when I heard ghost-dog Shuck rush through the grasses—I had a thought that it was Shuck ! But it was he—his tread, as ever, singularly stealthy !

I was pretty stiff and regal : for one should not spy. " No." " Yes." Charming night ? " Yes." Something about nights in Algeria—I was rather startled, my attention not quite calmly concentrated, perhaps. Had I by chance spoken to my father about the diamonds? No, I had come to the conclusion that there was little chance that my father would be interested.

This, I could see, chilled; some compunction touched me; but I did not show it: and after some moments of huff he began to talk of coffin-ends sticking out of the cliff-side at our feet. "All out sad: one of the oddest, saddest things I've dropped on."

His eyes can be most mournful: mild as moonlight. I melted and said that it *was* so; at least one land-slip every year; whole seaports swallowed—Ravenspur, Hythe; one Cromer gone, the other going; and "soon where late we stood shall no man stand" . . . "Do you like Swinburne?"

He had "never heard of such a person." Ah, me. How about *that*, Henny? Frank, *naïf*, yes, but—into what strange territories are we straying, Hen-bird?

I dropped Swinburne like a hot iron, and said, "So, you see, some day no more of Norfolk will be left for the sea to eat: let it be enjoyed while it lasts."

"The whole bobbery is the same," says he very gravely: "magic-lantern—mirage—dissolving, like that ship on the horizon. . . . Can your eyes spot that ship, I wonder?"

I peered where he pointed, and said "No."

"Full-rigged brig, southward bound: bigness of a tooth-brush hair. Now track her close along my finger."

He put one hand on my shoulder, stooping, with the other arm extended. "*See her?*" But I was not thinking of any brig, but of this man's hand on me, and of the miracle of my sitting and permitting it, like a hypnotised hen. I think he did it with complete simplicity and spontaneity ; and his being smells heavenly of heather, and Havanna, and far harbours. But just suppose, I thought, that someone were to pass and see this man's hand where it was, and his ear so monstrously near to mine. And even as the fear pierced me, the thing that I feared was upon me.

Yes, papa was there behind us. How I knew it I cannot say, but I found myself in the act of springing up sharply. I ought not to have sprung up sharply. . . .

Ah, the thing was awkward ! I could not present a man whose name I did not know ; and to explain how a man whose name I did not know chanced to have his hand on my shoulder was not exactly like kissing hands. To a third person the miracle of the innate relationship between two personalities is Dutch ; and there was no possibility of explaining the excruciating thing which had come upon me all in the twinkling of an eye, so to say. However, *he* did the best, perhaps, that could be done—raised his hat, and became interested in the Lestrange brick-grave. *I* said " Papa " jubilantly, and went to him.

But the walk home was a pain. Papa never said one word, except " good night " to a group of fishermen before the Roman Kiln, and to me, in Hewelsfield Lane, " I think, Henny, that three days more will see the end of the harvesting."

Sept. 29*th.*—Such a revel now ! every brake crowded with berries ; the groves of mountain-ash glories of red rosaries; grouse and partridge driven from their last refuges in the barley for the sportsman's gun; the only gleaners left are geese and fowls; the flower-festival's over. Farrel—*that* is his name, Mary says, and there *was* a Rev. Harold Farrel who was vicar of Knapton thirty or forty years ago—Farrel was at the harvest-home Dedication-service; sat in the fourth pew, gravely agaze through it all: corn-sheaves over the Communion-table and aisles, loads of poppies, cornflowers, mangolds, loaves. He still sat musing when it was over, while all moved out. I saw papa's eyes light one instant upon him, and instantly turn away. Ah, papa has been silent, *polite* to me...!

Oct. 1st.—Yesterday a great gale, which is not yet over, and young Rogers, poor Mrs. Rogers' son, drowned. It began about eleven in the forenoon, and at two the day was darker than some nights. That silver pine at the foot of the tump has been uprooted, and at four woodard Truscot came running to tell papa that there was a great landslip, Mrs. Rogers' cottage gone, her son with it.

The gems, too, are gone: and oh, confess, Henny, a woman in you is wounded.

Before eight o'clock we had the house well locked up. Papa and I kept in the Panel Room, he pacing about, gazing upward when he apprehended that the roof might be rent away into the gloom, every ten minutes guessing how many miles an hour the wind was going. It was fine, though occasionally one quailed. Anon Mary peeped in at the door for company, and cast up eyes of pantomime.

All at once there was a violent banging at the

front—it was nearly eleven—and my instant thought was that something else had fallen from the cliffs. But in a minute when Eliza opened the Panel Room door, oh, my astonished heart, I saw Mr. Farrel. If that is his true name. . . .

There he was, all wet and muddied, in Wellington boots, a sou'wester, and Raglan mackintosh, all of a sudden before one's eyes like an apparition, like the very spirit of the tempest made visible. Deliberately he bows to me ; then deliberately to papa ; then, a little breathless : " Pardon me—am here to give you the office, Sir, that you are about to be stuck-up." (" Stuck-up " means robbed!) " Was under shelter in that two-arched kiln by the old-British hut-dwellings, when three men lodging at 'The Anchor' ran into the other arch ; overheard them putting up to grab your gems—they had waited for a night like this. I thought I'd not attack—night rather too dark—but would scrag them in the act : so when they went off, I ran full-split to you—should have been here before, but pitched headlong into a saw-pit. Your study, Sir : get me there instantly, and they're shopped."

My wide eyes shifted to papa's face ; and, if ever I saw him *pleased*, papa was now—pleased at something or other, and at the same time envenomed against this man. He was smiling bitterly up into Farrel's face, and his answer, to my absolute amazement, was : " But your warning comes late, Sir. The gems you refer to are already stolen ! "

Farrel seemed to start. " Already ? " says he ; " then, they've come it at a better run than I gave them credit for, and done some smartish work here, too. Have they drilled the safe, Sir ? "

The storm laughed awfully, and papa laughed with it, pale, bitter, but—inwardly pleased at something.

"I have not seen the safe!" he cried out, "nor did I know of the theft to the moment of your entrance. But I know now, having proof of it before my eyes!"

The man looked very puzzled; and papa laughed again, gaily-angrily, a little hysterically, perhaps.

I could not conceive then, but do now, why he was pleased. He had been chewing the cud of wormwood ever since catching the man with me in the churchyard, though he had not referred to it by one word: and now he had visible proof that the man was a robber, and I there to see the proof, when it was once pointed out to me. This was why he was pleased.

"Proof before your eyes," says Farrel, his eyes on the ground: "I'm afraid I don't quite drop to your meaning." All this time he did not once look at me.

Papa now stepped dominantly up to him, asking "Now, what, Sir, is the object of this *outré* warning?"

Now Farrel frowns. "'Object'? '*Outré*'? Am I not thanked?"

"No, Sir, not thanked," says papa, who can be killingly cynical: "you come late to receive gratitude."

"Came as soon as I could! Came like one o'clock! Surely, Miss Lestrange, that deserves whatever thanks it is worth?"—at last he appeals to me, smiling.

And at that appeal papa stepped back quickly to where I stood, to murmur hurriedly near my ear

"Observe the Purchester Instrument in his jacket-pocket."

I could believe neither my ears nor my eyes. There it *was*, sticking out, two of the lines of engrossment showing. If I was awake, there was no mistake ; but I did not know if I was awake.

And, if he had the Purchester Instrument, he had the gems, they being together. But why did he have the stolen thing sticking out visibly like that ? And why this visit, when he should have been in flight ?

I did not answer his appeal to me ; and "Very well," says he, "makes no matter to me ; I will intrude no longer."

"No, make the best of your time, Sir !" cries papa bitterly.

Again Farrel frowned, seemed to reflect, and suddenly asked "What's that about, Sir ?"

"The best of your time !" cries papa : "you have not long !"

"For what ?"

"For escape, Sir !"

"*Me ?* Escape ?—from what ?"

"The police, Sir !"

At this a dark flush of offence dashed across Farrel's forehead. But it was not offence at being charged with a theft, as one might have imagined, no, it was offence at the idea that the police could seize him ! His next words proved this : for his disdainful answer was : "European traps ? Escape from *them* ? The escaping would be theirs, I take it, if less than ten of them ran foul of me. But I can't reckon it up that your gems have yet been robbed ! How down-to-the-ground foolish that'd be, Sir, if, while we are chopping logic here, the valuables are being actually carried off ! "

The man is certainly an admirable actor—if he is an actor : so perfect an actor, that papa now put up his hand hurriedly to say to him " Stay, you shall see for yourself, you shall enjoy the sight—just come with me " : and, catching up the three-candle candelabrum, he waved the man out, and went, I following them, out and down into the study.

Instantly, as we entered, the wind puffed out the three lights—proving the window now open ; but by the passage-light I could still see Farrel dash to the window, and, apparently, examine the sash and shutters two seconds, then back he dashed to kneel two seconds more before the safe, whose door now stood obviously open. Seeing which, papa said " You see, you see " ; and he began to add " As to that document which you have, since it can be of no value to you, I will agree—" but, even as he spoke, Farrel had afresh twisted away toward the window with his squirrel activity, and had leapt the twenty feet down into the courtyard.

Papa and I stood there in the half-dark, hearkening to his running feet rapidly ceasing to be audible in the uproar of the storm.

Papa had not referred to the Instrument in the Panel Room, thinking that the man's carelessness in having it visible in his pocket might result in its recovery ; but in the study he changed his mind, and was going, he says, to offer Farrel something for it, valuing the Instrument far above the gems ; but at the mention of the Instrument, Farrel was gone.

And, with all this, I don't think that in every bit

of my contradictory being I believed him to be a thief! Or, if I did, then in some bit of me I did not believe him to be a mean thief. Something in me held that there must be some excuse somehow, and I was his ally and advocate against himself, and against myself, and all things.

The next thing was to telephone the Northrepps station; and then to await what the morning might bring. I didn't really sleep all night.

And the morning's first event was hardly less wild and incomprehensible than the night's—a note brought by Rawlings from Farrel to papa. This was it:

> "Sir,
>
> Refering to what has happened to-night, I will do myself the honour to call upon you at two to-morrow.
>
> Your servant,
>
> RALPH FARREL."

"Referring" with one r . . .

Then, after the note, followed a visit of Grimes, the constable, with an officer from Cromer, to examine the safe, etc. They said that "The Anchor" three had fled, but that Farrel was certainly still lurking somewhere about. "He'll prove a fly fish to catch, too, I'm thinking," Grimes said; and he said, when papa showed them Farrel's promise to come at two o'clock, that that was "only a blind"; but papa inclined to think, and so did I, that possibly it was not "a blind," "for," papa said, "his visit to me last night, after the theft, proves him a sufficiently audacious miscreant"; and in the end it was arranged between them that the police should lie in wait at The Manor on the chance of catching him at two, if he should really come.

"There should be a good many of you, I think," papa said ; and the detective, an efficient-looking fellow, answered "*We*'ll look after that, Sir." The thing was terrible to me. . . .

Oct. 1st.—I wrote "terrible to me" at ten a.m., and am now writing at eleven p.m. So much has happened ! I can hardly write.

No, I did not wish him to be caught like a rat in a trap ; I understood that it was wayward of me, but I did not wish it. I spent two hours in my bedroom with deep searchings of heart, and, as my clock struck twelve, I was up, determined at all costs to warn him, if I could find the means, as he would have warned me.

In a few minutes I was out by the back and across the brook. I had scribbled across an envelope : "Miss Lestrange will be in the priory at 1.30," and had decided to leave it on Devil's Rock, where I knew that he sleeps, on the chance of his seeing it in time. I knew of nothing else to do.

I ran a good part of the way, the wind, still high, pressing against me. Passing within two hundred yards of his tent on the Piece, I could see a man lurking within it—one of the police, I believe, watching for his coming. But he is hardly ever at his tent, I knew ; probably at that moment was roaming the country somewhere in his vagabond way, if he was not in some hiding-place hereabouts.

In half-an-hour I was on the Chase—not a living thing, save two woolly little nags with hairy fetlocks in the bracken. He wasn't on the rock, I could see ; but when I had stumbled to it along the rocky little sort of footpath, I called out "Anyone there?" knowing that the rock is hollow on the further side. Oh, my heart beat foolishly, it is such a lonely place, and I thought that the man's phantom would start up, and be madly at me. "Anyone?" I called once more, but only the mouths of the winds yowling weird things answered me. I then went up the sloping side; and the instant my eyes were level with the top, I got such a shock!

In the heather and gorse that covers the top I saw two camp-stools, a camel-hair sleeping-bag, a lion's skin, a calabash-basin all carved, a cigar-box, a campaign-cap, and a hotch-potch of other objects, some of them weighted with rocks. At one spot, lying together, were a coffee-mill at the end of a post, a coffee-pot, a spirit-lamp, a palm-needle, and one of the fancy shirts: and on the shirt I saw papa's steel casket; yes, there it was.

It was hard for me to believe my eyes. But there it lay—open to the sky. It is true that not once in ten years, probably, does anyone go on or near Devil's Rock, but how did he know that the police might not hear that he sleeps there, and go to it, and see the casket, I asked myself? did he, or did he not, know that the police were seeking him?

I took up the casket, fully expecting to find it broken open, and the gems gone—but it was still locked. I shook it—the gems seemed to be there. How, then, had he got out of the casket the Purchester Instrument which I had certainly seen in his pocket, I wondered? There was no question of his having a key, since the casket opens by turning the notches in the three knobs to certain numbers known only to papa and me.

My head was all in a whirl, I did not know what in the world to make of this network of mysteries, so I simply left my envelope, weighted with a stone, on his sleeping-bag, and ran with the casket.

I was too flurried to stop to open it. When I got home, I went straight with it to papa in the Panel Room, and I said " Papa, I have found this on Wensome Chase."

Papa's eyebrows slowly rise, he eyes the casket, he eyes me ; and his first interest is not in the casket, but in me.

" You have been on the Chase ? "

" Yes."

" Ah, I didn't know you had gone out. And you—have found—the casket—on the Chase. That is remarkable. Empty ? "

" No ! The gems seem to be in it. Let us see."

I quickly had it open, and there the gems were, arranged in their different squares, and, over them, folded, as usual, the Purchester Instrument.

" Here they certainly are," says papa, ridiculously lost, a castaway on a sea of perplexity : " and you—found them on the Chase. On—which part of the Chase ? "

I fancy I hesitated one tick; but said " On Devil's Rock."

" I see. You have been on Devil's Rock. Extraordinary. What—led you thither ? "

" It is where the man generally sleeps."

" The man—er—Farrel ? "

" Yes."

" I see. You knew where he generally sleeps. And you found the casket there. In concealment ? "

" No—quite openly laid on the rock."

Silence. Then papa : " Is it restitution—or what ? Restitution does not alter the fact of theft, nor the necessity for the punishment of theft."

I thought this bitter of him. He said it too bitterly.

Just then Mary came in to mention the coming of some constables, and I went up to my room to rack my brains over the ten different mysteries of the man. How had he managed to open the casket to get out the Instrument last night ? Why had he come to warn papa after the theft ? Was it merely to see me ? Why had he not fled with the three, if they were his accomplices ? Why had he left the casket exposed there on the rock, and had the Instrument sticking visibly out of his pocket ? Why had he run away so abruptly when kneeling before the safe ? What was the motive of his appointment with papa at two ? What, what. There was no answer to any of them ; and suddenly I saw that I must hurry, if I was to be in the priory at 1.30, as appointed, and I ran down by the book-room stair, out through the kitchen, and over the brook.

While running down the footpath to the ruins, I saw his head look out of the chapter-arch, and all at once my heart started to find myself in with him. Oh, I was foolishly breathless, and gallopingly I panted at him " One word with you, Sir. If it is really your intention to present yourself at The Manor at two o'clock, that will be at your peril, for the police will be——"

This word " *police* " appears to irritate some nerve of him ! for he frowned at me, breathing " *Police* you call them ? And do I look to you, Miss Le-strange, like a man who would make an appointment with a relative of yours, and then fail to keep it through fear of such raw meat ? "

" Well, it was my whim to warn you, since——"

He snatched off his cap. " Guess, now, whether I thank you all out, or not ! But can you tell me definitely what sin I am supposed to have committed, to be so insulted ? "

My eyes dropped from his, as I said " You must know that you are supposed to have—taken—or helped to take—my father's casket."

" Yes ! so I begin to gather ! " he cried ; and then he put out his hand and tapped my arm, asking " But guilty or innocent ? "

My eyes lifted then to his ; and like a flood some impulse flew to my head to say to him " innocent." At the same time I felt myself going giddy under his glowing gaze, and, if I had said " innocent," I suppose I should have whispered it in a faint, lip to lip, for I was stretched on a rack of rapture that was stronger than I ; but, in the midst of it, I was conscious of a rush somewhere, and, before one could say " Jack," two of the Cromer men were with us, and had him by the arms. I think they must have spied him from the Piece, as he came on the edge of the Chase, and so shadowed him to the priory.

He glanced down at the one on his left, then deliberately down at the other, as at curiosities ; and then asked them, " What's the racket ? "

One answered that they arrested him for a burglary ; upon which Farrel, with his free fingers, took a watch out of his shirt, glanced at it—it must have been nearly two—and as he put it back, made the remark : " I am innocent."

"I dare say, come along," says the one on his left; but, as that one was saying "along," the other was clamouring out "*Hold him!*", and within three ticks I beheld Farrel rid of them by some rough miracle of his elbows. As they staggered from him, he caught off his cap to me, and took to his heels, up the footpath to The Manor. The two flew after, and disappeared.

I ran most of the way home, ready to cry for distress at what I divined must be happening there. At the brook I saw a pile of bicycles under the oak—the constables'—and Pritchard's pony-and-cart; and when I was some yards from the conservatory steps, out darted Mary with excited eyes to meet me with "They've not got him yet! he's afighting them behind the tump: you can see from the master's room."

"Where's papa?" I asked her.

"On the tump, looking on. Oh, you never did see——"

I ran down the left laurel-path, and saw papa on the tump, the opera-glass hanging in his hand, with Frean, the relieving-officer, and three fishermen, peering. As I ran up the tump, I at once understood how things were: he was in the Little Kiosk, the others trying to get at him; and suddenly the door flew open, and he was out among them, giving and taking. I couldn't look steadily—had never conceived that human beings could be so brutally rude to one another! it was terrible. But he took care not to advance far, and in a minute I got a glimpse of his face, gasping and laughing, as he slipped back into his citadel, and slammed the door.

Papa was quite white with excitement, his lips fixed and spiteful.

"Oh, Papa," I said, crying: "can nothing be done?"

He turned in surprise upon me, saying "Henny, I have to request you to go into the house."

I had to go. . . .

By three o'clock all the village was here. I could hear cheerings, distant shouts. It had then shifted to the woodard's cottage, whither he had manœuvred. At three-forty Mary ran in with the news that they had him at last on his back "*in*" the brook, and would soon conquer him; and at twenty past four I saw him from the south tower-casement flying across the lawn northward, laughing backward at two pursuing him; but just as he got to the Pan, he doubled back upon these two, laid them low with quick business in succession, and fled onward; then the throng of the others rushed into sight, and vanished northward after him.

At about five-fifteen Eliza bounces wildly in with the tidings that he was again grounded, down in the north-west shrubbery. I, for my part, was able to bear the strain no longer, for I thought that he would be done to death; and I ran out, that I might see him, and that he might see me.

I found the crowd peering round him at the shrubbery's edge, three of the policemen's knees on him, the others trampling about him like a crowd scrambling for money. But all in a moment Farrel was half on his legs before they could gasp out "Hold him!", and after some seconds of strain, the mass of them broke from off him, three lay felled, and there he stood free again, with his gasping laughter.

I found myself thinking spitefully " Good, he peppers them well," even as I was pleading at papa's ear : " Papa, for me, can it not be stopped ? "

Papa was then looking steadily at Farrel through the opera-glass—though Farrel was not far from him—did not answer me, but stepped sharply forward, uttering the astonishing words, " Officers, I now have reason to think that the man may be wrongly charged. Perhaps he would be willing to step with you and me into the house."

On this they all laid their heads together ; then Farrel was beckoned, and joined them ; I saw him nod twice ; and all started off for the house by the grass-ride, I following behind with the crowd, the shades of night now falling.

The men trooped by the front into the morning-room. When I, too, entered it, I saw papa opening the gem-casket at the table. He took out the Purchester Instrument, and then, with very evident agitation, pointed toward Farrel's jacket-pocket.

When I looked at that pocket, I saw—just as I had seen it last night—the Purchester Instrument sticking out : it was there—must have been there in the priory visibly, if I had not been too flurried to observe it. But the Purchester Instrument was also in papa's hand ! It had doubled itself.

Papa said to Farrel " Are you willing to mention, Sir, whence you got that document I see in your pocket ? "

" This ?"—Farrel drew it out, all wet—" I picked it up under the cliffs yesterday evening. Why so ? "

" May I just see it ? " papa says, taking it gingerly between thumb and finger ; and, as he opened it on the table, I saw every drop of blood perish from his cheeks, leaving them blanched as death. I heard him murmur " Under the cliffs. . . . "

" If it is yours ", Farrel said—" but, then, it can't well be yours, for I take it to be a paper buried with a body long and merry ago. Makes no matter to me any road, for I did not——"

Papa span round upon him, his eyes wildly alight with excitement, asking " Under what circumstances, Sir, did this come into your hands ? "

" There's no stealing," says Farrel, pacing a little in his " flash " nonchalant way : " was out on the beach at low tide in the gale, gallied about my yacht that was dragging ; and, in coming up again, spotted white paper on a mound of stones, bones, and coffin-fragments that had gone down in the landslide ; took the paper out of a pickle-bottle—looked like a pickle-bottle—and meant to read it later—rather too dark then—but forgot that I had it in all this casket fakement : there's no stealing—take it, if it's any road yours—makes no matter to me."

As he stopped speaking, papa span sharply upon me, to whisper with lips which shivered. " The original Purchester Instrument! . . . not destroyed, but *buried*, by that terrible man in the coffin of Richard Lestrange."

I had to sit down, for I was trembling all over. We had known that the greater part of the Lestrange brick-grave had gone in the landslip ; and this was the outcome : the hammers of the sea had broken open the bars of the door that Robert the Devil had closed.

Papa now suddenly turned to the throng of officers to say "I think, officers, that there has been a mistake. This gentleman is probably—But, then, how, Sir, do you account for the fact of this casket being found at your sleeping-place on Devil's Rock ?"

Farrel, touching his cuts with a red bandana, answered "My good Sir, did you not see me leap your study-window after the three thieves ? Knew they couldn't be far gone, tracked and scragged them crossing the Chase—hence my appointment with you at two, to hand you the casket. But it was purloined from my rock"—he threw me under his eyes a sidelong look, mock-fierce.

"Yes, that was how it was," says papa ; and then, very prettily, offered his hand, saying, "I have to beg your forgiveness, Sir. Many apologies I owe you—and something more than you know. Forgive. Officers, you hear what I say."

On which Farrel ceremoniously bows to papa—too ceremoniously !—and then turns to grasp one of the officers' hand, into which I saw him slip some gold; and he nods to the rest, saying, "Good sport, men. You did well."

I don't think they thought it good sport !—a draggled, mauled lot they all looked. When they bowed themselves out, papa going with them, there was I left with Farrel. It was rather awkward—mountains impended upon me. He said behind me—I was standing within the neuk-window, wistfully interested in what's left of the harvest-moon—"I hope I shall be forgiven for offending your eyes with all this bobbery : I'm afraid I'm weak to the temptation of a flutter." I understood that the remark was unreal, uttered to break a silence ; nor did he say any more, but strolled a little, then stood over me. As the linnet flinching at the hawk's shadow, so was Henny then. He put his hand over mine on the neuk-rail, and I made no sign that I was aware of it. In that still minute I accepted him, "*refering*" and all, and all that weight of Greater British. At the same time I was aware of the two halves of a split sovereign held out to me on his palm, and gathered that I was being invited to take a half, for he is only a big, big, barbarian boy ; and when I hesitated just a little, says he in his touchy independence, "Take it or leave it, as you like" ; so, hearing papa's step, I said "Well, this half with the champion's sword," and had it hidden quick. Are we engaged, then ? this man and a Lestrange? Bush-fashion? I suppose so ! What an "*all-out*" lark ! Has some gaudy gadfly stung me gallivanting ? What do I know of this dandy mastodon, this coxcomb ox ? He may be Crœsus, or a ne'er-do-well, or a bushranger. I may be the seventieth Mrs. Farrel, the other sixty-nine butchered on their beds. But if he slay the seventieth, too, still I'll trust in him, forgiving him till seventy times : for I know what I know—*au fond*. Ralph Farrel, I love you ; I love you, Ralph Farrel ; witness it, earth and heaven. . . .

Then came the new Earl of Purchester in, all smiles, upon me and mine, and I had to pretend to be disengaged. . . .

This story told, the outbreak of tongues discussed it in various senses, the arguments getting to be even warm between those who thought that it cannot have happened and their opponents, both Sir C. Alexander Caxton, the official, and Mr. Killik, the solicitor, exhibiting actual hostility to the hero, having found it impossible to admit to themselves that Britain can be knocked about in that way by Greater Britain; and Mr. Killik, a rather soft, though massive man, showing some red veinlets, like Mars' canals, in his cheeks beyond his region of beard, remarked, " Men sleep in sleeping-bags under the rain when out on the Veldt, not when they can get a Christian bed to snuggle in."

But to this Sir Thomas Ormsby answered " Let us give due weight to the force of habit : a faint taint of staleness indoors may become insupportable to lungs accustomed to the spaces of the Karoo. I persuade Netta to keep this poor sick out-of-doors, inasmuch as the air here is a little fresher—perceptibly to some men, though not to us. Adaptation, Sir—like that man, condemned by the Inquisition to sleep five years on a bed of blunt spikes, who, the five years ended, could sleep on nothing else. In fact, our behaviour is *all* habit—habits of ourselves and of ancestors, two-legged or polyped, the behaviour of the first animal on earth having been determined by the habits of inanimate matter."

Upon which Paul Watts remarked, " Habit decides even the types of fiction that are conceived. In truth, there are only a few stories—so far—a few tunes and paintings, *au fond*. Notice the resemblance between this tale by Shanks, and the first we heard, by Morrissey, called 'The Panel' : in both we have a father who hardly approves of his daughter's choice of a lover, until the lover discovers a document which makes the father rich, and now it is assumed that the old chap can't help excelling the daughter in adoring the lover."

"English fiction, though, is eminently different from French," Sir C. Alexander Caxton remarked—"as a peach differs from an oyster."

And Watts: "Or as a peach differs from an apricot, say: the differences specific, not generic; Greek myth recognizably differing from Hebrew; but the same habits of mind running through; few types: hence two authors' inventions may run on exactly the same rails, and authors—as Dumas—have been charged with plagiarism, to whom such a thing would be impossible; but a Martian author's tale or music would be all foreign to us, like authors of the future doubtless: for when it gets to be recognized that the types are stale, men will stretch themselves to invent fresh types, as Poe invented the detective story—great stuff: for great is to invent and to doubt, and nothing else is great."

"Well said, Watts," came from Sir Thomas Ormsby: "you have a scientist mind, my friend."

"Well, I paint, Sir," Paul Watts answered—"a manual worker like yourself."

"But I think that music of the future, if we could hear it, might interest us," Netta said, "as old music still can: and now comes some from Gerald"—for Gerald Jewson had promised this for that day, and now proceeded to render three pieces, by Purcell, by Milton's father, which the arbour party enjoyed, or wanted to manage to enjoy, before making any move to depart.

CHAPTER V

THE CAT DAY

The next day Greta was taken out as usual to the free air and sun-bath of the arbour, but, as it was Sunday, and no tale, no gathering took place, until the Monday, Mr. Killik's day, when, on the men assembling once more about those eyes of the sick, whose light had died out, it was once more noticed that that " flea," Whipsnade Prince, was not among them ; and when the Rev. Mr. Darrel remarked on it to Mr. Killik, the solicitor answered " Gone off to Genoa " ; at which point Netta, who had gone some way back from the arbour toward the house, thinking to meet Prince coming, and had now come back, happened to move near these two speakers, who, seated with their faces toward the sea, did not see her standing at their backs ; and Mr. Darrel remarked " The co-heir's interest in the tales seems less keen than one would expect."

To this Mr. Killik answered " Gone for an interview at Genoa with Lord Jannock, owner of that yacht yonder—that white one—nice thing she is—screw-schooner by Vickers, two boilers, search-light, ash-ejector, Louis XV saloon—nine hundred tons—forty thousand pound lot : Prince showed me her specification last evening, she being on the agents' lists for sale, and, as he is purposing to purchase in a hurry, wants me to see to the documents for him."

Mr. Darrel frowned, with "Is Prince, then, a man of money?"

On which Mr. Killik shrugged, answering "May be counting his chickens before they're hatched—I don't know. He said that, as that poor Greta may die any day during the fortnight she has been given to live, it would then be cruel for Netta to be left living on in the villa alone: so he is after a yacht, contemplates forming a yachting-party——"

But now, on glancing aside, he spied Netta standing within hearing, and decided to speak of other things, while Netta stood disquieted, knowing that Whip Prince did not own forty thousand pounds. . . . He must, then, be building upon winning in the game of tales; had said that he would probably win, with his customary luck; but it was perplexing that he should be behaving like one who is as sure of winning as if he has already won! And musing on it Netta stood, lost to all the talk about her, till now the music of "Bolero" penetrated, drew her to the strange tale which that tune with differing repetitions tells, and persists in telling differently, its wanderings haunted always by that rolling drum that persists, and will not cease from following whithersoever its wings' fickleness wanders: as some dove, infatuated, may abandon home and all to haunt with mania, fluttering, a seraph's head that, as it wings, hums a thing that no dove's humour has moaned in music; and still the drum rolled fluttering on, growing sometimes madding hot, intolerant, goading the heart to agony of gratitude toward that Granter that already has elaborated men up from apes, from lake-dwellers, to be witnesses of visions so inherent deep, dreamers of dreams so weird, so sweet. But now, too soon, it ceased its dear repeating, and now Mr. Killik tugged his seat nearer the transmitter, to hear, for plugged in his left ear was kept a wad of cotton-wool ; and now the old " This is the national programme from. . . . " " And now for Mr. Matthew Besant's story 'The Flying Cat' " . . . " Mr. Besant. . . . " the habit of the fantasy of whose heart was now unfolded by the rut that he spoke in, by this story that he told :

Mr. Jabez Chambers, on the stroke of midnight, sipped the last of his claret, stood up from his ash-wood fire, listened a little to the raids of the rain on his study-shutters, and muttered, " Well, it *is* a night."

An old fellow, " lean and slippered," living cosy on consols in his nook of Oxfordshire, a male old-maid—fussy ! faddy !—Witness his fussiness in prying with his electric torch to see all tight for the night ; witness his faddiness in the host of scientific toys all about—some of them rather out-of-date !—his Atwood's machine, his hydraulic tourniquet even now wheeling away, air-pumps, puppets which jumped—never was country-house cumbered with rummer lumber. And, surveying his treasures, Mr. Chambers' eyebrows twitch—eyebrows which have a wild and whirling curl upward at their middle, like a spur.

As he was going away from examining the front door, the gale gripped it so like a wrist, that he stood to listen ; and, as he stood, his heart bounded into his mouth at a banging on the door.

Nothing could have been more astounding than

such a thing at that hour at "Ivy House": Mr. Chambers did not doubt that it was a "spirit-phenomenon"; but *this* "manifestation" was so startling, that the banging had to be repeated before he found the power to call at the key-hole "Friend! who are you?"

The answer was in a sweet voice: "Mr. Chambers—please—it is I, Lucy Newcome."

Mr. Chambers made haste to undo the chain, and there tumbled in to him a young lady wrapped in a shawl of old Spanish lace, one lily instep peeping stockingless, her zouave buttoned askew; and instantly she collapsed to the floor, dumb but for the sob that throbbed through her body.

The old gentleman was off—to be soon back with a tumbler of port; and he got some drops between her teeth, which beat a rattle on the glass.

"Now we shall be better," he said, rubbing together palms as soft as pap, as a pad with its stuffing half fluffed out: "Can you come now?"

"Oh, forgive me——!" she began to sob.

"Don't talk! Just come"—and they went, step by step, her head on his shoulder, up into his study, where he placed her in a spacious chair, was away for dry things, then was away afresh to fetch wine and a peeled apple: of which latter he said, rubbing his palms, "Now, I want you to eat me that apple: you don't know—it is wonderful what an apple will do. Ah, the nice fire: that's right!"

By this time Lucy Newcome was sitting with a rug over her petticoat, wrapped in the mass of a camel-hair dressing-gown, between whose collar-flaps her little face peeped with a pitiful stare of scare, her loosened globe of gold-hair hanging down its back. Her shoes, skirt, were drying round the fire, and she looked like a lady in *néglige* in her own home, but for the distress at her intrusion which excruciated her face.

"But, Mr. Chambers," she supplicated in pain, "how *can* you forgive me ?—But if you only knew—I am *so* terrified—I *couldn't* help—*Will* you forgive this infinite——— ?"

"You eat that apple !" the faddist shook his finger at her—"believe me, if people only possessed a little elementary knowledge of Truth, they could escape many an illness by the simple act of eating an apple. Eat the apple, drink the wine, and then we can talk."

He now fussed about a little, flung the curtains together, said "Just hark at the wind!", then seated himself near her, the male in him pleased and purring at the intrusion of this pretty thing, that strangely sat there staring with scared child-eyes and dishevelled hair into his fire, sheltered in his dressing-gown, with one great-toe showing under the rug on her legs. She suddenly covered her face to wail a low "Oh-h-h———!"

"Don't cry," he murmured. . . . "What has gone wrong ? A quarrel with the uncle ?"

"Oh, no quarrel" came through her choking throat. . . . "Oh, what shall I do ? Mr. Chambers, you can't think—it is like hearing every hour the tolling of a bell in one's bosom—my haunted heart—I *can't* stand it any more !"

"Well, I did not think it was so bad," he said. "But has something new happened ?"

"Oh, Mr. Chambers, I have seen it—this night—the flying cat—as Mary said——"

The old gentleman went paler, while those eyes of hers, out of which could sometimes be seen looking the mood of her twelfth year, closed tight, and she rocked her body, moaning.

"How—where—?" Mr. Chambers asked with twitching eyebrows.

"It is too gruesome," she groaned: "you know how poor Davenport went into the book-room that evening—it was a year ago on the 12th. . . .My uncle had told me to fetch him a chemistry-book, and I was going to get it for him, I was almost at the book-room door, when parlour-maid Mary came to call me for something, so I told old Davenport, who happened to be there at the door, to get the book. . . . Mr. Chambers, he had hardly entered the book-room when a short sort of shout sounded from him, as down he dropped; and, as Mary and I span round to him, we saw him on the floor, convulsed, his mouth all crooked . . . dead. . . . Mary must have spun round an instant before I did, and she said she caught sight of a flying cat—of its eyes, she said——"

The old gentleman caught up the wine, presented it to her, and she got down a gulp, then let her head go upon the chair-back, while he patted her hand, saying "Try to compose yourself, Miss Lucy. The phenomenon witnessed by Mary was a spirit-phenomenon—undoubtedly. It may have been the Egyptian cat-goddess, Phthah, with whom a medium of my acquaintance is frequently in communication. And in your own case—where was it you saw it?"

Without opening her eyes, she answered wearily, " I was going to my bedroom—about an hour ago perhaps—later than usual, for I had been writing to —someone ; and, in going along the corridor to my room with my candle and my little Pekingese, Peter, I saw—something—some drapery—like a dressing-gown, I think—which vanished—God knows what it was ! But it did upset me—Pigwell is such a gloomy, ghostly house at night—you can't realize—with only my guardian and me and the four servants in all that desert—Mr. Chambers, I *can't* live there much longer ! "

Again her voice broke so pitifully toward tears, that the old gentleman kissed her hand, saying " Never mind—never mind—tell me of the cat-phenomenon."

" So I entered my room trembling violently, for I am not going to conceal from you, Mr. Chambers, that Uncle Crichton means me no good—I tell you so frankly—no good—Ah, I say it ! It isn't my nerves——"

" Sh-h-h, my dear ! We mustn't harbour such thoughts," Mr. Chambers answered : " Sir Crichton Ritchie may not be regarded by his neighbours as a man of the very greatest amiability, but to imagine that a man of ancient lineage, and a chemist of distinction, would—And with what motive ? To possess himself of your fortune ? Such thoughts are not pretty."

Lucy Newcome stared at the fire till a prolonged uproar of the storm was over, before she remarked " He *would* become possessed of it, if I died before I married, would he not ? That is a fact. God forgive me, if I——"

"I think you do, I think you do. But tell me of this——"

"Well, I went into my room trembling, Mr. Chambers, and for some time I sat at a window, dressed, looking out at the gale, too terrified to go to bed—alone—for you know, Mr. Chambers, that my maid was dismissed some months since, and I have not a friend left now to protect me. But at last when I got cold—for no fire is ever lighted in my room now at night—I began to undress—slowly—for I felt as if something was dragging me back from the bed; till a gust of the gale happened to blow out my light, and I was so frightened then, that I set to undressing hurriedly; in the midst of which my little dog, Peter, made a leap upon the bed—his last leap, Mr. Chambers. He gave out a little half-a-yelp—just audible—so pitiful—and at the same time I sighted the eyes—just a flying flash slightly tinged, sulphurous—and with it that same cat's-spitting that Mary heard—most ominous—and then the little dog dropping dead on the bed—oh, my God——"

"Never mind—don't, don't—it may all have been a sign from the other side——"

"No, a little flash of eyes—and a cat's hiss—Somehow I got on some clothes, then ran, ran, ran——"

Her moan was like the dumb moan that the thunder muttered somewhere in the night. Then silence.

Then Mr. Chambers: "Did you ascertain that the little dog is actually dead?"

"Yes! I ascertained!"

And again silence.

"May I ask, my dear," the old man suddenly said—"is there any question of your marrying?"

A little blush perished in rushing up her throat, as she answered, "I am engaged, Mr. Chambers."

"Well, I didn't know."

"I may as well tell you. . . . It was three weeks ago to-day. I was in Chorleigh Wood one early morning, when someone ventured to observe near my ear 'Don't it sing nice, that bird!'—oh, he is great on grammar, Mr. Chambers!—and it turned out to be Algy Paget—a third cousin of mine—now staying at Castle Chorleigh. So——"

"Uncle know of your engagement?"

"I am not sure: but one morning in the wood both Lieutenant Paget and I became conscious of being watched—my uncle rises very early——"

"Then," the old gentleman said, "what I should do would be to get married secretly and immediately."

She started. "But do you think, Mr. Chambers, that such a thing could be done?"

Yes, Mr. Chambers did—provided he could get his crony, Somerset (the rector), to enter into the scheme of secrecy. Let her first, he said, speak to her sweetheart, and then tell to him, Mr. Chambers, the decision come to, at his north gate the next forenoon. "And now," he concluded, "to bed."

But Lucy insisted upon sitting by the fire until dawn: so he left her there, and did not see her again until noon at his north gate, which is about six hundred yards south of Pigwell house. She was then very flushed, and said in a breathless secrecy at his ear "Lieutenant Paget says 'at once,' and you, Mr. Chambers, will speak to Mr. Somerset—Oh, tell him that it is infinitely secret ! . . . Daren't stay—I think it is known that I slept out, for——"

She stopped, startled by a bang of cannon. . . .

"There goes noon," Mr. Chambers remarked, looking pleased, for the bang came from one of his toys—a sun-dial in his garden, on the sun-dial being mounted a little mortar-gun and a lens, which, focusing the sun's rays, fired the gun at noon.

Lucy looked hurriedly at her wrist-watch, muttering "But, then, my watch is fast"—and was going to alter it when Mr. Chambers, with a reproachful look, said to her, "My dear, I am astonished at your unacquaintance with elementary Truth ; leave your watch alone, I beg of you, and do not add one more to the number of misguided people who surround me. Nearly every clock hereabouts is a quarter of an hour slow because of this gun ! for in vain have I dinned it into the ears of the people that the *solar noon* of the gun and the *mean noon* of their clocks are not, and cannot be, the same things—except on four days of the year. They have got it into their noddles that the gun 'goes off at noon'—and it does ! it does ! in a sense ; but what they *will* not understand——"

"Yes, Mr. Chambers, thanks—I *must* go—You'll write, then, to me"—and her heels went speeding up the gloomy avenue of yews to Pigwell.

An hour later Mr. Chambers was himself on his way through Pigwell Park to the rectory in Alvington Valley.

Now, Lucy Newcome being a minor, it required some talk to win the rector into the plot ; but presently the two friends came to see eye to eye ;

and that night Mr. Chambers wrote to Lucy that all was well in that quarter.

The next forenoon Algy Paget, a young man with a tanned face that made a colour-picture with dark-blue eyes, called at "Ivy House," and he and Mr. Chambers deliberated, Mr. Chambers undertaking to impress upon Mr. Beth, the surrogate, to be utterly mum as regards the granting of the licence, and the taking of the affidavit.

This being settled, Algy Paget went away. He was striding away toward "Ivy House" south gate, when a man stepped out from a tree before him. At the same moment Mr. Chambers' noon-gun banged behind him.

Paget span about, wondering whence the bang came; and when he met the other man, he asked what gun it was that had fired—little thinking that he was asking Sir Crichton Ritchie himself.

Ritchie, a small man in a long frock-coat all rumply at the tails, gazed up into Paget's face, grinning with rings of wrinkles round his mouth, for at his slightest laugh his delicate skin wrinkled and went pink; and there was something wild and ghastly in the glances of his eyes behind his glasses, his teeth showing in a sort of laugh, suggesting a man in the act of strangling a cat, and grinning pink at the effort. He answered to Paget "That is a dial-gun, exploded by the sun at noon."

"Oh, that's it—thanks," Paget said, and went on toward Castle Chorleigh, thinking in himself "Offensive-looking beggar."

By the fourth day everything was arranged for the marriage: and now Lucy Newcome's hands were clasped in one long clasp of anxiety. On that fourth night she did not attempt to sleep, for the next noon she was to take a stroll for St. Agnes—four minutes' walk from Pigwell New Garden—to become a wife—to fly from the old life of gloom to the new of gladness and light.

That dawn came at last ; and at exactly nine minutes past noon Lucy stepped from the porch of the tumble-down north wing of Pigwell. Her soul flew, but slowly her feet paced—through the Old Garden into the New—out by a wicket to the church-path. She had on no hat ; was gowned as usual in sober brown ; and anon she stopped to pick a primrose—ostentatiously—to show her unconcern to heaven and earth.

At a quarter-past twelve—the hour of the rendezvous—she stood at the altar with Mr. Chambers and Mr. Somerset. And they waited for the bridegroom. . . .

But the bridegroom, for his part, was waiting in a shrubbery under the north wall of " Ivy House " grounds. He had been walking toward the church at thirteen minutes past noon, when Mr. Chambers' noon-gun had banged upon his ears : on which he had decided that his watch must have gained, since the sun could hardly be wrong ; and he had said to himself, " I am much too soon, and mustn't be seen about " ; so he had set his watch to noon, and, holding it on his palm, stood hidden within the bush, waiting. A naval lieutenant would have known better ; but Paget was of " the Guards."

At last he started out, cut eastward through Pigwell Park, and got out over a broken bit of park-wall not far from the church-path. But there he stood frozen : for, forty yards off, he saw his bride with Sir Crichton Ritchie by her side—coming from the church, just going to enter a gate of Pigwell New Garden. . . .

Paget recognized that grim grin of the man he had met three days previously ; and Ritchie, too, spied Paget, and eyed him with those spectacles of his.

But the poor bride did not see Paget : her face, bent down, was covered with her hands ; and those sobs that dolefully tolled from her throat reached her lover's ears, and stung him in the eyes.

Before his limbs could move to fly to her, she was gone ; the garden-gate was locked. . . .

He then flew down to the village to telegraph to her—to ask *what* had happened: for she, dreading danger to him, had forbidden him ever to enter Pigwell House.

But no answer came to him from her : she was prostrate in her bed ; nor was she permitted to get his telegram.

"Oh, why were you late ?" Mr. Chambers said to him that night at "Ivy House" : "when she heard her guardian's step coming, and was sure that it was yours, then saw *him*, she—well, it is well for you that you did not see her then."

Paget squeezed his brow between his fists, and groaned.

"It so happens, though," he said, "that I was *not* late. It was she and you who were early."

"Well, we need not argue it now," the old gentleman answered : "what is obvious now is that, somehow or other, you must manage to marry Miss Lucy Newcome at once, or the poor girl will go mad. Let me tell you, Sir, that she seems to be in a situation infected with some elements of tragedy in that house over there"—he wagged his finger toward Pigwell—"and after this attempt, I—have fears. Sir Crichton Ritchie is a singular man—man of distinction—but—a little singular. His eyes—I doubt whether so wild a brightness of the iris is quite normal. Anyway, the Rev. Mr. Somerset and I are both of opinion that a second attempt at marriage should at once be made—not, of course, in the church again, but in Pigwell House itself, where the attempt will be least expected."

"God send that it turn out well this time," Paget muttered, staring.

"Amen," Mr. Chambers said; and though it was then after eleven in the night, Paget was no sooner gone, than Mr. Chambers, full of the new plot, put on scarf and hat, and started out for Pigwell House, to tell Lucy. But he was hardly an ideal conspirator—not a very level head for the tackling of ticklish affairs. He crept with fussy stealth through the park, where no one could see him, but then went tapping at a casement, where he was quite likely to be spied by eyes wide awake. The night, indeed, was dismal and dripping; but still, to a more discreet intellect the thing would have seemed too risky; and he had to tap thrice before a rumpled head over scared eyes was looking out a little above him, asking aloud "*Who is it?*"

He conferred with her a long time there, standing in laurel-bush which flourished lush just under her casement. Anon each sent to the other an anguished "*Sh-h-h . . . !*" But, as he was several feet below her, their talk was hardly inaudible to ears on the *qui vive*.

"But how can he insist that he was in time?" she asked: "he was scandalously late!"

"The poor fellow's sufferings call for your forgiveness," he answered: "his watch may be defective——"

"Then, let it be to-morrow," she whispered, "for, oh, I feel that there is no time to lose. . . . In the Solar-room Gallery let it be—not in the chapel—and ah, Mr. Chambers, let there be no mistakes or wrong watches this time! Tell him it is a matter, not of minutes, but of seconds. Let Mr. Somerset be waiting, exactly at *ten* past twelve, at the little postern opening upon those outside steps of the west wing, and I'll be there to let him in; then, at *twelve* past twelve exactly, let Algy be on that door-step where the Dancing Faun is in the laurels at the end of the Long Corridor, and I'll be there to let him in—*twelve* past. There is an ogive hole in the portal at the end of the Long Corridor, let him look in through that, then I shall see that he is there, and open the portal. And now good night—my whole heart thanks you——"

The old gentleman stretched up to whisper "Seen nothing more of the flying——?"

"Nothing more—give him my love—good night."

Mr. Chambers then made his way back to "Ivy House"; then, late as it was, drove to the rectory; and thence in the opposite direction to Castle Chorleigh, to impress the details upon the rector and upon Paget.

Unfortunately, much that had been said under Lucy's window had probably been overheard; and, anyway, that sub-agitation in Lucy's face the next morning must have told its tale to such an eye as Sir Crichton Ritchie's. . . .

Certain it is that at half-past eleven the baronet was in the Long Corridor—a ground-floor corridor—very sombre—in that deserted south part of the house, a corridor whose muteness the echo of a foot scarcely ever disturbed.

The great length of the corridor was divided up by a series of doorways, one telescoped within the other to an eye looking down the corridor—small doorways with old oak doors ; so that, if the doors had been closed, the corridor would have become a succession of rooms.

At one of the doorways, in the darkest part of the corridor, Sir Crichton Ritchie laid down a box—a mahogany box with brass handles. It had a hole in its lid, out of which stuck a wire-end ; to this wire-end he fastened a piece of fine wire, led this up one side of the doorway, twisted it round a tin-tack which he pressed into the door-frame, and then bent the wire, so that it lay half across the doorway.

He then tied another piece of fine wire to the box-handle, led that up the other side of the doorway, and bent it across—doing all this with rubber gloves on his hands.

The ends of the two wires now pointed at each other across the doorway, a foot apart ; so that Lucy, or anyone, passing through the doorway, could scarcely escape touching the wires with the breast, so making " contact " between them : through that breast a mortal shock would then pass.

Ritchie then stepped backward a little to inspect the thing—to satisfy himself that the fine wires were unnoticeable till one was quite up to them, and that the box was well hidden behind the door ; then, diving under the wires, he went wildly away inward, his eyes alight.

Before noon struck he flew out, wild with excitement, into the park in front of his ballooning coat-tails, eager to spy the arrival of Paget. . . .

He was concealed among the laurels close to the portal of the Long Corridor at twelve past noon—the time appointed for Paget to be at the portal ; and, lurking there, grinning like a strangler, glancing at his watch, he said to himself, " At about this moment she drops a corpse."

And, in truth, Lucy *was* at that instant tripping with a wild face through the doorways down the length of the Long Corridor, to unlock the portal for her lover—was not at that instant five yards from those wires of death.

A minute later Ritchie said to himself, " He is late "—for Algy Paget had not come.

In his malice, Ritchie was there to watch the dismay of the lover when he came to that door to be wedded, and no door opened to him ; but after waiting three, four minutes, and still Paget did not come, Ritchie sprang up to be looking after himself—to remove at once from that doorway in the corridor the box and wires, which, if once seen, would reveal the reason why a dead body lay there.

First he peeped through the ogive-hole in the portal to assure himself, to *see* the body—could see nothing for some seconds, the corridor was so dim ; but then, his eyes becoming accustomed to the dimness, he duly saw the body of Lucy prostrate on the floor near the door of the wires ; and he turned to run round into the house to remove quickly the box and wires.

Meantime, Paget had been waiting near Mr. Chambers' north gate ; and, on hearing the noon-gun hoot near, he had glanced at his watch, which he had set by the noon-gun the day before ; and he had said to himself " Exactly right "—thinking that he had twelve minutes more to wait ; but three seconds later Mr. Chambers had come running up to him, pale, breathless, saying. " My good Lieutenant Paget ! Why in Heaven's name are you now here ? "

" I have still twelve minutes ! " Paget had exclaimed : " the gun has only just gone off ! "

" Oh, my, my, my," Mr. Chambers had mourned in deep distress : " really, I am astonished, Sir, at your unacquaintance with elementary Truth. Surely at this time of the year the solar time *must* be behind the mean time ? Pray, pray——"

No more had Paget waited to hear, but with all his long legs, had fled down the avenue to Pigwell : and so it was that just as Ritchie turned from peering through the ogive at the body of Lucy prostrate, he found himself face to face with Paget.

Ritchie had then a wild face : there was that in it which shocked Paget more than ever the thud of guns had shocked him. " What a wild beast ! " the lieutenant breathed ; and instantly he understood that the whole scheme had somehow miscarried. But *this* time he had come for a bride, and meant to have her anyway—to drag her from that place and that man. At that ghastly grin of Ritchie his eyes flashed, wrathful blood rushed to his brow, and he began to bang at the portal with a heavy oak stick, as a preliminary to entering, somehow, that house.

"Beware," Ritchie cried out, "lest you dare to attempt to enter my house!"

"I'll show you 'beware'," Paget grimly muttered, springing up to catch the ledge of one of two Gothic windows beside the portal, both more or less open.

On which Ritchie's face became the colour of death: there was that box, those wires in there, beside the body!

He had to be at that box before Paget, whose masterful attitude had not been reckoned on; so, springing like a wild cat upon Paget's back, as Paget struggled into the window, he clawed him down in an intense silence.

Paget dropped back, sitting, to the ground; and instantly Ritchie was dashing to the other window, into which he clambered with an ecstatic agility, and was dropping into the Long Corridor almost before Paget could pick himself up.

Ritchie thus got some start, though Paget was soon after him: and down the length of the Long Corridor Ritchie raced, with wild eyes and flying hair, through doorway after doorway, aware of Paget chasing behind.

There in the dimness, close beyond a doorway, lay Lucy before Ritchie's eyes. . . .

That doorway was not, however, the doorway of the wires, but the one next inward; nor was she dead, as Ritchie imagined—had only fainted.

For, on tripping down the corridor to unlock the door to Paget, she had paused on not seeing Paget's face looking in through the ogive, as arranged. She had not wished to open the portal until he was actually there : and he was late—again, *again*. No face was there : she could see the sunlight framed in the ogive. . . .

One minute, two, she had paused, waiting with shivering knees for his face to appear ; and, if it had appeared, how she would have rushed to him—and perished !

But the noon-gun had made him late—and saved her.

Then, as she had stood waiting in anguish, a face *had* appeared . . . but not his . . . ! Ritchie had peered in through the ogive to *see* her body before coming to remove the box and wires ; and she, seeing, instead of her lover's face, those glittering glasses, had sunk down fainting. When his eyes had become accustomed to the dimness, he had seen her prostrate. . . .

Now, however, as Ritchie pelted toward her, she was coming to herself ; and, as the two men came racing down the corridor, Ritchie well in front, Paget after him, Lucy's eyes opened. The next instant a shriek from her pierced the house : "*The flying cat !*", as afresh she fainted.

She had seen the flying light—heard the cat's-hiss : for Ritchie, in the wildness of his flight to find the box and wires, had rushed upon the wires, being certain that they must be at that door were Lucy lay, being unable to see the wires until quite near, and, anyway, not caring if he touched them now, since he was sure that the electricity in them had been discharged through Lucy's body ; and, as he touched them, and made contact, Lucy saw the flash of the electric spark, heard the hiss of the discharge, and, even as she shrieked, fainted.

At her shriek Mr. Somerset flew from another part of the house to look for her, and found her in Paget's arms. . . .

As Paget bore her to a settee, her lips stirred, he heard her murmur the word " Late " . . .

Then the two men ran to Ritchie, to see him all gripped together, grinning, electrocuted. . . .

Algy Paget whispered in a hurry of agitation, " We mustn't let her see this ! "

But Lucy had soon stood up from the settee where he had laid her, and had crept near to crane her neck and peer. She breathed in a daft sort of way " It was the flying——"

" Here is what did it ! " Mr. Somerset suddenly cried out, sighting the wires, and then the box behind the door ; and when the box was opened, within was discovered a battery of condensers, enough to shock three men dead. . . .

Meantime, all overwrought, Lucy was laughing and sobbing at once, uttering wild words, charging Algy Paget with being the cause of the death, through being late !

" Dear," he said to her, " try not to be too agitated. Of course I was not late—not by the noon-gun——"

" Noon-gun ! " she cried, sobbing in her laughing levity : " but, my dear, I am astonished at your unacquaintance with elementary Truth ! "—Mr. Chambers' words to *her*.

" Through his lateness," Mr. Somerset said to her, " you have been rescued from—let us not think what ! Come away, my child "—he led her sobbing and laughing by the hand.

This tale ended, Netta switched-off, and, with eyebrows on high, twisted round to ask Mr. Killik: "Well? what is the verdict, Herbert? Can it have happened?"

"Never," the solicitor answered: "flying cat? cock-and-a-bull yarn."

"Or cat-and-a-bird," Gerald Jewson suggested.

And the little Mr. Coward: "Well, I would have bet seven-to-three that that uncle would come to a convulsive end: his mug had a grinning expression."

And now Netta, twisting round to Sir Thomas Ormsby: "Can it have happened?"

"May be"—from Sir Thomas—"I doubt it."

"What do you say, Paul?"

"No"—from Paul Watts—"cannot have happened, I think. The incidents, yes, perhaps, but not the character of the uncle: there cannot be a scientist who is a murderer."

"Dear me, you say that, Paul?"—this from Gerald Jewson—"haven't several scientists been like that—a doctor named Palmer, who poisoned everyone?"

But Watts: "Doctors aren't scientists, most of them—not in England, anyway. A scientist is a person whose chief interest is in science; if his chief interest is in fees, he's a common workingman. A scientist mayn't know half as much science as that Dr. Palmer—may be a crossing-sweeper whose chief interest is in metal-work; and this interest removes his mood a thousand furlongs from the murderer's mood: he lives in a universe, a universe consists of things, so he is thinking of things, forgetting himself; the murderer lives in a village, a village consists of persons, so he is thinking of persons, especially of himself. So little his interest in anything else, that his egoism festers, and, if gashed, or lashed, may flash into killing. A scientist, too, does sometimes kill, but then it is ever himself that he kills, eager in his forgetfulness of the importance of persons, of himself, in his interest in things, to win one glimmer more of truth for humankind, as when Chervin drank black-vomit, when Garré gave himself glanders, Lola tetanus—hosts of them: holy, holy, holy."

Stillness now two seconds, until now Netta: "But, Paul, mayn't someone have been a scientist at one time of his life, then his interest in things may have so died out, that he acquires an interest in persons as tiny-minded as a murderer's, as this Sir Crichton Ritchie appears——" but at this point the thoughts of all were drawn off to a great dish of delf-ware, its shape a truncated cone, which was now approaching, this containing "floating-island," which Netta and Lady Dale-Eldon had passed half the day in preparing, battering guava-jelly with a clapper till it evolved from ruby to blanched, then incorporating with the mass many egg-whites, with rose-water, then setting its snow-mountain afloat in a yellow sea of milk mixed with eggs; of which grub-poem the Rev. Mr. Darrel remarked "Of such food the angels eat," and with assiduity he continued to eat and to eat of it, keeping streaked with white his fiery moustache, until he was visited with a feeling of sickness, through not being already an angel, so that he went away in haste rather before the rest made any move to break up for that day the arbour party.

CHAPTER VI

THE LION DAY

AND anew on the Tuesday, which was Gerald Jewson's day, the men met eleven-less-one, " Whip " Prince not appearing.

That morning, indeed, Netta had had a note—from Genoa—saying that he would soon be looking in ; but nothing that day could console the woe of Netta, for during the night her sick had refused any food, and now lay with eyes quite closed, even Sir Thomas Ormsby not knowing if the sleeping beauty was asleep, or had perhaps relapsed into a coma destined to forerun death ; so that mum sat Netta over that silence, a world of yearning in those yearning eyes of hers, hearing, but answering only with a smile of sadness, Gerald Jewson's speech, who, seated a little behind, was breathing near her ear " You are grieving—don't you grieve, dear Netta. Nice day, after all, the sun bright, the sea bright blue, the whole thing singing, and—listen—they are rendering Liszt's 'Campanella.' But, then, as Paul Watts says, the interest of us little people is in persons, not in things ; and it is this, one can see, that is the cause of sorrow : for the truth of things would set us free of every pain, as already it has set us free of the pains of cavemen. In some minutes we shall be hearing of the pain of some person in a tale ; but in the future, no doubt, interest will be wholly in things—no tales then—fiction will die out to make room for science and music, whose theme is things, implicit in music being some mood or other of the universe of things. No, don't you grieve. This is my day, I shall be winning the competition, and I know men who will direct me how to lay out the money just as Greta wished; then my sister, Minna, you know, has a place near Loch Ness, and when what we apprehend has dropped upon us, we three will be off North for a holiday—" but now the piano's twitterings of "Campanella" went dumb; in some moments a voice born of a mother that was blueness, and its father was vastness, was announcing: "This is the national. . . . " "And now for Sir Llewellyn Arthur, the traveller, in his story 'The Lion'" . . . "Sir Llewellyn Arthur" . . . whose habit of being and speaking was now revealed, as he began to give this story:

A land in hilly France as flat as Lincolnshire—land of vineyards, and pine-woods, and calm stretches of rushes, marsh-reeds, whose plumed heads move in waves under the winter's winds. . . .

I had come for a week's shooting in the marshes of Little Camargue, but the north-wind had driven the birds further up toward the submerged vineyards about St. Laurent d'Aigouze, and from St. Laurent a friend had telegraphed me, "Plenty of snipe, come at once." I had then set out from Sylveréal in a cart with the *garde champêtre*, Prosper, whose horse would break into little gallopings, as if whipped by the nor'wester which lashed our faces, and crystallized our moustaches.

St. Laurent was twenty-five kilometres away: and along the hard white road we jogged, jolted, through that land of monotony and solitude—no one within the horizon, not a vehicle on the clear ribbon of road; only, here or there, little twists of sand and dust dancing to the whim of the winds. I pulled my cap over my eyes and closed them, hiding my hands in my coat, not troubling to wipe my tears at the cold which froze on my cheeks.

Then suddenly, when we had passed the cross-roads of Aigues-Mortes, and had just turned to the right toward St. Laurent, the voice of my Prosper roused me: "Hullo! What's that? Bohemians, perhaps."

Twenty paces away was a caravan standing still; between its shafts a white horse with skeleton spine, fleshless haunches; and before him, in tandem, a little African she-ass with a hanging head, hairless rat-tail; while a man in an overcoat once black, his cap on the back of his head, fussed round the ship-wrecked vehicle—a bulky fellow, with a rosy nose, a moustache which ended in two brushes.

The horse's hames had got broken, and the man was poking angrily about, rattling the harness.

Toward the back of the caravan a little girl of ten or eleven stood looking on, visibly shivering in a cotton dress and a piece of wool "comforter," which was hardly, any longer, bluer than her hands which held it crossed on her breast.

Prosper pulled up and questioned the man, who in some grumpy words explained his mishap. He was from Aigues-Mortes—was on the way to St. Laurent—was the showman of a menagerie—just a few beasts that were coming by train in the afternoon to St. Laurent—he now going to take charge of them.

I, too, had got down from our cart, and while my Prosper helped the man to tie the hames together again, I went and spoke with the little girl. She had fixed upon me her dark, bright eyes, inherited probably from some daughter of Spain, or Algeria, or from some *gitane*, such as one sees smoking a pipe in the bivouac on summer sunsets—a pipe which her eyes might have lighted.

" That your papa ? " I asked her.

" Yes, Sir," she said.

" What is his name ? "

" He is called Rachilde."

" And you ? "

She smiled. " Mica."

" And you are alone, you two ? "

" Yes, Sir. . . . My mama is dead. She was ill in the hospital at Avignon."

" Was that long ago ? "

" I can hardly say."

She shrugged her shoulders—did not seem very timid. I felt that it needed little to put her at her ease.

" So you are alone with your papa ? " I said.

" Sometimes there is also Merki, the clown, who is now in the train with the beasts."

" Is he good, this Merki ? "

" Oh, he never says anything. And, then, we change them often, the clowns."

" Well, you seem to have a nice little caravan there. Have you a nice little bed in it for yourself ? "

" I have the mattress."

I had stepped backwards, could now see into the

interior by a doorway through which Rachilde had been taking out his repairing tools, and saw a sordid den that gave out the smell of a smack's cabin, mixed with old odours of tobacco and tallow-candles. In England the interior of even the Cumberland gipsies' caravans is much neater, more ashamed of naked indigence. A bottomless chair, crockery long broken, a mattress—the relics of a mattress—a box without a cover containing tinsels and coloured clothes, a pair of shoes with tassels, a tamer's-whip hanging from a nail in the roof. . . .

While my eyes rested on it, Mica stood silent.

" And the beasts," I said, " how many ? "

" There is the jackal whose name is Demon, and there is the hyena, Zoe, then there are the two monkeys, Pirouette and Pierrot, and there is Apollyon."

Her eyes brightened at this name.

" And who is this Apollyon ? " I asked.

She replied with a certain pride, " He is the lion."

" Those, then, are all the beasts ? "

" Well, there is the boa, the great snake . . . he is in there in a box with paddings of wool. He does not go by the train, he—he goes with us in the waggon."

" Why does he ? "

" In order to be warmer."

" Do you love the boa ? "

" No."

" Which of them do you love the best ? "

" Apollyon. I call him Pol."

" Does Pol know you ? "

" Oh ! Yes ! "

" Do you ever go into his cage ? "

"Yes, with papa, since last July 14th; it is that which brings in the money."

I looked at her, not without a pang at heart: eleven years old at the most; no mother; no home but that vagabond waggon, with that mattress for her resting-place; her only friend a wild beast; sole reason for existence—"to bring in the money"; and, wishing to know—hoping to find something consoling in this destiny—I asked her, "And your papa, do you love him, too?"

For the first time she seemed embarrassed, and said "Yes" very feebly—like a sigh.

"And he? He loves you, too? He is good?"

The timid underlook which she stole at her father was very revealing. But again, very feebly, she whispered "Yes."

I stood silent, while she crossed her bit of scarf on her breast, then, with a gesture already very feminine, tucked under it with her finger-tips a lock of hair which the wind had swept across her forehead.

At the same time a rough voice called "Mica!"

For the harness, by Prosper's help, was now mended.

"Quick! Mount!" Rachilde shouted; and Mica made haste to scale the wheel to her seat.

But before they moved off, Rachilde said in answer to my question that he would "work" at St. Laurent at least two days, then might not set out on his travels again for three days more; and I then said to Mica, "Then, we shall meet again!"

She replied with a faint smile, a silent stirring of the lips; and the caravan started.

Meantime, Prosper had taken the reins of our

cart, and we two were off at a trot, at once leaving Rachilde behind. When I glanced backwards I could see the old bag of bones, which the nag was, dragging away at the caravan, aided by the little African ass, which was hauling with all her force, somewhat slantwise, with petty precipitate steps. And behind the seat where Rachilde sat cracking his whip, I could half see, half divine with my eyes, the faded blue of the scarf of Mica, my new friend.

I arrived at St. Laurent about two o'clock ; and in returning to it late in the afternoon from a shoot, caught sight of Rachilde's tent already up, and of a square of paper stuck on the wall of the *Café du Canard Blanc*, on which the show was advertised in pencil.

The next evening I heard the sound of the drum, the yelping of the hyena within the gaudily-daubed canvas which the wind shook, the " Come in, m'sieurs et 'dames " which Merki, the clown, in a green wig, howled outside the tent—" Come in and see Rachilde, the famous tamer ! " while Rachilde himself sat at the pay-box, receiving the " fifty centimes for adults, thirty centimes only for children."

Then the drum was done ; the clown ceased from troubling ; little by little the tent had filled ; Rachilde was within in his flesh-coloured tights, tasselled shoes, Mephisto hat, and a horse-whip which he cracked at the jackal and the two ironical monkeys from Morocco ; and, after an awkward salute to the audience, he began " to work."

The man, of course, was as uninteresting to me as his lean beasts, or the boa which he was soon rolling round his throat ; but I had come to see

Mica in her actual environment, and meantime kept my eyes on her friend, that "Apollyon," whose name she had mentioned with a caress of her voice, and a light of affection in her eyes.

Certainly, "Pol" was meanly thin, his hair and mane much worn away by continual friction against the front of his cage. He now lay with his head erect, his tongue-tip showing a little between his teeth, statuesque and disdainful in his captive sadness, probably foreknowing the approach of his gaoler—the being with the whip and steel-shod stick, who had humiliated, enslaved and subdued his youth—not without revolts! but the sticks and pricks, the weariness and grief, of the everlasting prison had gradually ground down the great beast to a growling resignation—though even now, as I was to hear, on his "bad days" of spleen he still showed his blood, refused to leap the steel-shod stick, threw out rough thunder, and for some moments the fire in those eyes of fallen royalty awed once more.

Apollyon was in such a mood that evening, as was evident from the moment Rachilde entered the cage. The creature squatted in a corner, and would not leave it, even showing Rachilde that he would not permit any close approach; and soon the public were asking themselves if the man would dare to persist in such perilous play.

He did not long persist: after two or three minutes of it, he retired to the back of the cage, half opened the door, whistled: and at once Mica, brisk and liberated, flippant with the light carelessness to danger of childhood, slipped into the cage.

The door slammed behind her with a clang.

Some of the people were visibly outraged ; some too excited at the mere spectacle to have any other sensation ; all sat dumb in an utter stillness. Then what we saw was so extraordinary, that there commenced to arise cries of surprise, sighs of admiration, throughout the tent.

For the little girl had no sooner entered the cage, than the expression of enmity on the brute's face underwent a change. He had lately been half-erect on his front paws to confront the tamer ; but now, stretching forth, one after the other, his great paws, he lay down, tame and yawning ; then his lids half-shut themselves with a soft and sheepish meaning ; but when she advanced and grasped a rag of his mane, he reopened his eyes, to fix on her a quiet look.

Most of us who saw shuddered ; some few clapped. . . .

Meantime, Rachilde, irritated perhaps at his own lack of mastery, struck the floor savagely with the stick—the "have a care, you !" of the tyrant gaoler. But Apollyon no longer resisted doing his share of the show, seemed to wish to avoid a broil before the little one, and buoyantly vaulted the vaulting-barrier, Mica's thin little voice calling out to him at each leap "*Up ! Up !*"

And after each leap the vaulting-barrier was raised. Apollyon continued patiently to obey ; until, all at once, Rachilde, through some bravado perhaps—at any rate, without apparent reason—cracked the whip before the lion's nose : and at once the lion stood still and roared.

The tamer then seized the steel-shod stick to shake it menacingly in the lion's face ; the lion struck it away; and a sort of contest then commenced—the man darting the stick, the lion striking it off with his strong paw; till at last, seizing the stick between its teeth, the lion commenced to shake it in a rage, to wrench it from the tamer.

The thing became highly exciting; but almost before one had time to be frightened, the child had sprung forward, crying "Apollyon! Will you let go?"

At the same time she struck the lion twice on the nose—frail blows that must have seemed to the brute like caresses; at any rate, he gave up, and turned away blinking from that little hand. In a moment more, however, her arms were suddenly flung round his neck, protecting him from the whip of vengeance which Rachilde, full of fury, held raised. "Oh no! don't beat him!" Mica cried, flinching meantime, as if she expected the cut to come upon her, flinching, trembling, not at the brute, but at the human brute whose bottom-jaw grinned above her.

And now the crowd, whose emotions had become painful, intervened; cries of "Enough!" began to arise; and then Rachilde turned and bowed to us; Mica left her friend; the door behind opened and closed upon her and her father; and the lion was left alone, to lie with crossed paws, his head held high, sculptural in his pride.

Five minutes later when I went out, I caught sight of a solitary little figure propped against the canvas in the tent's shadow: and I recognized Mica. Her head was bare. She was rubbing her eyes. I heard her sob. But as I moved toward her, she made off—with a limp in her gait, it seemed to me—gained her caravan back of the tent, disappeared into it ; nor did I see her more during the three days that I remained at St. Laurent.

I therefore had no personal knowledge of the sombre drama that transacted itself in that caravan and that tent on the third night thence ; but I have constructed it with some certainty from the police-reports, and from the statements of some men who knew Rachilde, among them Merki, the clown.

It seems that during the two following days the Rachilde show went on without any incident of importance. Apollyon was in a better temper, and Mica charmed her public, who rained sous into the wooden bowl which she bore round, repeating in her paltry voice that falsehood long learnt by heart : " Please, m'sieurs et 'dames, do not forget my own private little benefit."

That little benefit went in alcohol.

Rachilde was a drunkard, a true and sinister drunkard, who drank solitary and long, until all was up with him. In St. Laurent it was the *Café du Canard Blanc* which was his resort, and there, after each show, he was known to toss off a long series of drinks, ending always in neat absinthe.

Evidence was given by several witnesses that on that third night he left the *cabaret* at an early hour, already well on the way to inebriety, saying that he was tired, and would be better " at home," where he would drink the litre of brandy which he had bought in the morning. Strange to say, however, he went back to the *cabaret* half-an-hour afterwards, not more drunk, but gnashing his teeth, hissing, raging inwardly at something or other. He then sat at one of the little tables and drank steadily until the place closed, going away with a step so heavy, that the *cabaretier*, in getting him into the street, had wondered if the man would be able to get home.

Did Rachilde go straight to the caravan, or only reach it near morning, after having slept in the open somewhere? This was never known.

What is known is that, after the show, the little Mica had remained alone in the caravan, had then dined on a stale stew and bread, and, as the end of candle was short, she, not daring to use it all, had put it out. Her meal was thus finished in the dark; she proceeded to undress in the dark; and so it happened that, in groping about that narrow space, she struck against the bottle of brandy, which dropped and broke. What followed one can divine: the coming home of her father, who lights the candle, looks round for the bottle, discovers the disaster, and understands that the culprit is that poor child who cringes and stares, her hands wringing together in vain supplication.

Then—an alcoholic hurricane—deaf rage—blasphemies—blows—almost murder. After which the man steps down from the caravan to go back to the *cabaret*, without even closing the door, leaving the little girl exposed to the cold in a faint on the floor among the broken glass, her head a chaos of calamities, her body of pains.

How long did she remain there? Without doubt until the hour when the cold roused her. Stabbed then by terrible memories, she shrinks from the still more drunken coming back of her father; and presently, appalled by that solitude, cold, darkness, slowly she succeeds in raising herself, and in creeping out of the caravan, gashing hands and knees on the fragments of glass.

But outside are winds whistling, she shivers under her petticoat, wishes herself back under shelter. Anything, however, rather than go back into the grim waggon ! So at last, after roaming some time in the open, moving about in a nightmare of pain, she remembers that in the tent yonder are lives that do not hate her, that Apollyon, the lion, is fond of her, and that close to their vitalness the cold may be less cutting. . . .

When she entered the menagerie, as she knew the means of doing, the animals must have recognized her in the dark, and made no movement ; she may have gone to the cage of Apollyon, leant on his bars, spoken to him. But still it must have been so cold ! and at last she moved round to the back, managed to slip the crazy fastening, crept into the cage, and quite simply went to lie down beside the lion, craving of him some rays of comfort for her poor bruised frame, making of him a bed for her heavy head.

And under the half-closed guardian eye of the lion, amid saw-dust and that acrid odour of the animals, she fell into a sleep of weariness, and death.

Very soon after Rachilde began to hunt for her the next morning, he found her there, lying in white slumber beside the lion.

Catching up the steel-shod stick, he dashed to the back of the cage—instantly sobered ; opened the door, made a step into the cage : but Apollyon had sprung up, and, with one paw placed on the body, gave out such a grumble, accompanied by such a look, that the man skedaddled out quicker than he had come in.

He flew to get help. People came ; and, on seeing Mica's face, which looked quite puny and white, understood that she was dead.

As there was blood from her bruises on her, they supposed that Apollyon had killed her ; but then from time to time they saw him lick her face. And there was no separating those two : every effort was made in vain ; mayor and gendarmes there with the crowd. Finally they had to decide to kill the lion : near noon the rifle was aimed, the trigger drawn ; and the haughty head dropped upon its little friend.

The story of the drama was told me on my return from shooting that evening. I saw the doctor who had to make the medico-legal report, and he told me that he was convinced that it was injuries inflicted by the father which had caused the death. But eventually Rachilde was released—not enough evidence.

Afterwards the man's fatherhood awoke, for he bought Mica a grave, over which a cross now stands in the cemetery of St. Laurent d'Aigouze, the sale of Apollyon's skin having gone towards defraying the expense.

This tale was the occasion of no little discussion among the men as to whether the thing can have happened, as to whether the alleged behaviour of the lion was like lions, of the father was like fathers—a difference of view that was a gulf as big as the globe's width appearing between the Rev. Mr. Darrel and Sir Thomas Ormsby, Mr. Darrel saying that the lion's behaviour was too intelligent, Sir Thomas saying that it was not intelligent enough ; and some little heat, it must be admitted, was generated.

"The animals have no consciousness, Sir," the reverend gentleman remarked in his sharp manner, having now fully recovered from his too much of "floating-island" of the Monday.

"'The animals'," Sir Thomas repeated : "who are 'the animals' ? Hasn't Man consciousness ?"

And Mr. Darrel : "Man is not called an animal, Sir."

"Dear me, surprising," Sir Thomas muttered. . . . "But I assure you, Sir, that Man *is* called an animal by some people, for I have heard them, people who divide Life into two kinds, plants and animals, and know that any life that is not a plant, like a fly, a man, is an animal."

"Well, call him an animal, if that pleases you"—with a flush which enriched red to redder.

"Thanks for the permission"—Sir Thomas bowed—"I will, then. So Man has consciousness, but not the other animals ? Is that it ?"

"No self-consciousness, anyway. A cow does not say to itself 'I am I'."

Twice now Sir Thomas bowed sardonic, with "Dear me, I did not know that : thanks for telling me. . . . You state it, Sir, as roundly as if you had this minute come from being a cow, and remember what a cow says to herself : hence I do not ask '*How do you know ?*'—you may not be accustomed to be asked that question. But suppose the cow is right in not saying 'I am I,' while you are suffering under a delusion in saying 'I am I' ? Suppose it is one person who says the first 'I,' and another person of the same name who says the second 'I,' billions of changes having occurred in 'you' between the two 'I's,' so that at the second 'I' you, having changed, are different : a different thing can't be the same thing, you know. . . . But the truth, it appears, is that cows have, not less, but more, self-consciousness than men : with the lowest animals—amœbæ—it is all self, self, they can care for nothing else ; then when sex was evolved, there was some bothering by the mother about her offspring, though, if the father got at it, he'd gobble it up ; then the father, too, began to bother about something other than himself ; then they began to bother about neighbours, until it got to 'love thy neighbour as thyself' ; then, lately, it has got to bothering about a world, until now you see scientists immolating themselves in experiments, world-Christs, poisoning their bodies, not for 'neighbours,' not for Tom or Mary, but for a cosmos, with scarcely any consciousness of self."

Now Mr. Darrel, his legs crossed, agitated up and up one red sock, watched by Watts, Netta, Jewson, Harry Ransom, who had paused in their talk to hearken to this argument; and he answered, "I am not careful to dispute all that, lest I make more 'round statements.' The prophets and the seers made round statements. . . . But will anyone say that that lion, Apollyon, was not much more intelligent than animals are ?"

"Yes, Sir," Sir Thomas answered : "I, for one, say that he was even less intelligent. When, the child lying dead in his cage, he'd let no one touch her, the tale suggests that he did not know that she was dead ; but how could he not ? doesn't a cat know if a rat is, or is not, dead ? Ah ! the vanity of Man—to make a cat laugh. Far less now our vanity is than that vast vanity of savages and of the ancients, for whom there was joy in all the solar systems if village Jim did something or other : but still we are laughing-stocks in our estimate of our intelligence as compared with other animals'. It is only the fact that we have hands with long thumbs, and flexible mouth-muscles, which gives us the pull, and makes us as gods above dogs—not intelligence. Those Elberfeld horses knew vastly more mathematics than Mons. Maeterlinck, and some shepherd-dogs, I know, are more intelligent than some shepherds. Only lately a case in point came to my knowledge : a shepherd and his dog were taking a mob of sheep through Horsham in Sussex, when the sheep blundered into a corner between two walls, and there got jammed in a mass —no advancing, no withdrawing, trapped, the silly things standing panting, all at a loss, waiting for Providence to extricate them, the shepherd scratching his nut, not knowing what in the world to do now ; but the dog did : after some reflection, he—invents : leaps upon a sheep, walks along the mass of backs to the corner, leaps down, and now proceeds to bark them out of the impasse. Had *he* 'consciousness' ? or not ? I'd rather have his consciousness than a bishop's, or an Oxford don's."

Mr. Darrel laughed. " I would rather have a bishop's."

" Well—more remunerative, certainly."

" Just what I was thinking, Sir—more remunerative, and more respected by most people. But it is not only the lion's character which I still consider exaggerated, but the father's. Surely 'as a father pitieth his children' is more or less true in every case ; but in this——"

"Not in every case, Sir, I think"—from Sir Thomas : "ask the Society for the Prevention of Cruelty to Children. Animals and plants do as their chemistry does in them, and when a man's blood is super-saturated with alcohol, nothing good is true of him, his psychology is wrenched all through—alcohol is the devil. It is odd how we civilized use for enjoyment the two most evil poisons known, alcohol and tobacco—nicotine being *the* most mortal of all poisons, one drop killing within fifteen minutes. Some pharmacists do compare prussic acid with it, but all other poisons are harmless in comparison. Two smugglers bound some tobacco-leaves about their bodies, and started walking from the beach for a cottage not far off ; but they sweated on the way, and never reached—dead. So when a ploughman at an inn tipped the juice of his pipe-stem into a mate's ale—in fun ! he went home alone that night : mate dead within some minutes. The little mote of it that smokers imbibe into the blood may be good—mighty heart-stimulant—as a little alcohol, or arsenic, or strychnine, may be good ; but there is a fixed quantity of each beyond which the two are about equally lethal, nicotine to the body and also to the mind, alcohol to the mind and also to the body. If you say that that father would have pitied—" but at this point three spinster ladies from Villefranche entered to drink English "tea," and this called off attention, modified the composition of the conclave.

CHAPTER VII

THE PLACE OF PAIN DAY

THEN afresh on the Wednesday, which was Mr. Coward's day, that little person whose nature was all a suggestion of jockeys and "the turf," the concourse attained to eleven—or to twelve, counting a visitor, a Miss Routledge—Mr. Whipsnade Prince again appearing, gracefully fingering a cigarette. And says Netta to him, as he passed into the arbour, "You are come, then. I got your note from Genoa: you were good to write, and good to come back"—she being in a mood less downcast this afternoon, since two spoonfuls of nutriment had been successfully got into the moribund Greta a little before; and Prince replied, "'Good,' 'good': don't be so—None is good, save One, who's a girl."

"An old girl: your grandmother."

"I wish you *were* related to me in some way."

"Then perhaps you would explain to me the motives of your flights."

"Always business, some penny-farthing matter—raising the wind to ward off the whirlwind."

This was not frank; nothing about raising the wind to sail a yacht: so she was silent awhile, to see if silence would urge him to blurt it, but in those moments up comes Mr. Coward, saying "Hello, Whip, back again. This is my day, my boy: I take you seven-to-five that my tale's so all-out impossible, that I win the fakement."

Prince glanced sharply at him with "What makes you so sure?"

And Coward: "No sureness; but the minute I entered the arbour Mr. Darrel said to Sir Alexander Caxton 'Impossible, Sir!' which put me in a betting mood. Are you for taking me?"

"Done!" leapt from Prince: "seven thousand to five it is."

"Right O"—coolly from Coward, now moving off, while astonished stood Netta at the bigness of the stakes, as if Prince had heard somebody say "Possible, Sir!", and was still more certain of possible than Coward of impossible. But rhythms of Rimsky Korsakov, the king of Rhythm, that were sounding, came now to an end, and now some mouth is announcing out of some town of cloudland "This is the national . . ." "And now for Professor Oliver Currie's story 'The Place of Pain'" . . . "Professor Currie" . . . who now made known his voice and point-of-view, telling this tale:

Though my theme is about the place of evil, and about how the Rev. Thomas Podd saw it, it is rather a case of evil in heaven: for I think British Columbia very like heaven, or like what *I* shall like my heaven to be, if ever I arrive so high—one mass of mountains, with mirrors of water mixed up with them, torrents and forests, and roaring Rhones.

It was at Small Forks that it happened, where I went to pass a fortnight—and stayed five years; and how the place changed and developed in that short time is really incredible, for at first Small Forks was the distributing centre of only three mining-camps, and I am sure that not one quarter of the district's two million tons of ore of to-day was then thought of.

At the so-called Scatchereen Lode, three miles from the lake, there was one copper smelter, but not one silver-lead mine within fifty miles, and no brewery, no machine-shop, no brick plant. Nor had Harper Falls as yet been thought of as a source of power.

It was Harper Falls that proved to be the undoing of Pastor Thomas Podd, as you are to hear ; and I alone have known that it was so, and why it was so.

I think I saw Podd in my very first week at Small Forks—one evening on the Embankment.

(You may know that Small Forks runs along the shore of an arm of Lake Sakoonay, embowered in bush at the foot of its mountains—really very like a nook in Paradise, to my mind.)

Podd that evening was walking with another parson on the Embankment, and the effect of him upon me was the raising of a smile, my eye at that time being unaccustomed to the sight of black men in parsons' collars and frocks. But Podd was rather brown than black—a meagre little man of fifty, with prominent cheek bones, hollow cheeks, a scraggy rag of beard, a cocky carriage, and a forehead really intellectual, though his eyes did strike me as rather wild and scatter-brained.

He was a man of established standing in all Small Forks, where a colony of some forty coloured persons worked at the lumber-mills. To these Podd preached in a corrugated chapel at the top of Peel Street.

He held prayer-meetings on Monday nights, and one Monday night, when I had been in Small

Forks a month or so, I stepped into his conventicle, on coming home from a tramp, and heard the praying—or, rather, the demanding, for those darkies banged the pew-backs and shook them irritably.

When it was over and I was going out, I felt a tap on my back, and it was the reverend gentleman, who had raced after the stranger. Out he pops his pompous paw, and then, with a smile, asked if I was "thinking of joining us." I was not doing that, but I said that I had been "interested," and left him.

Soon after this he called to see me, and twice in three months he had tea with me—in the hope of a convert, perhaps. He did not succeed in this, but he did succeed in interesting me.

The man had several sciences at his finger-ends ; I discovered that he had a genuine passion for Nature ; and I gathered—from himself, or from others, I can't now remember—that it was his habit ever and anon to cut himself off from humankind, so as to lose himself for a few days in that maze of mountains in which the Sakoonay district towers toward the moon.

No pressure of business, no consideration or care, could keep Podd tame and quiet in Small Forks when this call of the wild enticed him off. It seems to have been long a known thing about the town, this trick of his character, and to have been condoned and pardoned as part of the man. He had been born within forty miles of Small Forks, and seemed to me to know Columbia as a farmer knows his two-acre meadow.

Well, some two weeks after that second visit of his to me the news suddenly reached me that something had gone wrong in the Rev. Thomas Podd's head—could not help reaching me, for the thing was the gossip and laugh of the district far outside Small Forks.

It appears that late on the Saturday evening the reverend gentleman had come home from one of his vast tramps and truant interviews with Nature; then, on the Sunday morning, he had entered the meeting-house scandalously late, and had reeled with the feet of some moon-struck creature into the pulpit—without his coat! without his collar! his braces hanging down!—and then, leaning his two elbows on the pulpit Bible, he had looked steadily, mockingly, at his flock of black sheep, and had proceeded to jeer and sneer at them.

He had called them frankly a pack of apes, a band of black and babbling babies; said that he could pity them from his heart, they were *so* benighted, *so* lost in darkness; that what they knew in their woolly nuts was just nothing; that no one knew, save him, Podd; that he alone of men knew what he knew, and had seen what he had seen. . . .

Well, he had been so much respected for his intellectual parts, his eloquence, his apparent sincerity as a Christian man, that his congregation seem to have taken this gracelessness with a great deal of toleration, hoping perhaps that it might be only an aberration which would pass; but when the reverend gentleman immediately afterwards took himself off anew into his mountains, to disappear for weeks—no one knew where—that was too much. So when he came back at last, it was to see another dark parson filling his place.

From that moment his social degeneration was rapid. He abandoned himself to poverty and tatters. His wife and two daughters shook the dust of him from off their shoes, and left Small Forks—to find a livelihood for themselves somewhere, I suppose. But Podd remained, or, at any rate, was often to be met in Small Forks, when he condescended to descend from his lofty walks.

Once I saw him intoxicated on the Embankment, his braces down, his hat in tatters—though I am certain that he never became a drunkard. Anyway, the thin veneer of respectability came off him like wet paint, and he slipped happily back into savagery. On what he lived I don't know.

I met him one afternoon by the new shipbuilding yard which the Canadian Pacific Railway was running up half a mile out of Small Forks. He sat there on a pile of axed pine-trunks lying by the roadside, his chest and one shin showing through his rags, his eyes gloating on the sky, in which a daylight moon was swooning ; but, on catching sight of me, he showed his fine rows of teeth, crying out flippantly in French : " Ah, monsieur, ça va bien ? "—in French, because negroes are given to a species of frivolity in speech which expresses itself in that way.

I stopped to speak to him, asking " What has it been all about, Podd—the sudden collapse from sanctity to naughtiness ? "

" Ah, now you are asking something ! " he answered flippantly, with a wink at me.

I saw that he had become woefully emaciated and saffron, his cheek-bones seeming to be near appearing through their sere skin, and his eyes had in them the fire of a man living a life of some continual exaltation or excitement.

I wished, if I could, to help him; and I said "Something must have gone wrong inside or out; better make a clean breast of it, and then something may be done."

On this he suddenly became fretful, saying "Oh, you all think a blame lot of yourselves, and you are nothing but a lot of silly little babies fumbling in the dark!"

"That is so," I answered; "but since you are wise, why not tell us the secret, and then we shall all be wise?"

"I tell you what"—shaking his head up and down, his lips turned down—"I doubt if some of them could stand the sight; turn their hairs white!"

"Which sight?" I asked.

"The sight of Hell!" he sighed, throwing up his hand a little.

After a little silence I said "Now, that's rot, Podd."

"Yes, sure to be, Sir, since you say so," he answered quietly in a dejected way. "That, of course, is what they said to Galileo when he told them that this globe moves."

With as grave a face as I could maintain, I looked at him, asking "Have you seen Hell, Podd?"

"I may have," he answered; and he added "And so have you, by the way. You have probably seen it since you started out on this walk you are taking, and haven't known."

"Well, it can't be very terrible, can it," I said, "if one can see it and not know? But is Hell in Small Forks? For I'm straight from there."

At this he threw up his head with a rather bitter

laugh saying " Yes, that's beautiful, that the ignorant should make game of those who know, and the worse be judges of the better ! But, then, that's how it generally is." And now, all at once, whatever blood he had rushed into his face, and he pointed upward : " You see that world there ? "

" The moon ? " I said, looking up.

" The souls in that place live in pain," I heard him murmur, his chin suddenly sunken to his chest.

" So there are people on the moon, Podd ? " I asked. " Surely you know that there is no air there ? Or do you mean to imply that the moon is Hell ? "

He looked up, smiling. " My, goodness, you'd give a lot to know, wouldn't you ? Well, look here, I'll say this, and it's the truth : that I've had a liking for you from the first, and I'll make you a business proposition, as it's you. You agree to give me three dollars a week so long as I live, and when I'm dying I'll tell you what I know, and how, teaching you the whole trick. Or I'll put it in writing in a sealed envelope, which you shall have on my death."

" Dear me," I said, " what a pity I can't afford it ! "

" You can afford it well enough," was his answer, " but the truth is that you don't believe a word of what I say : you think I'm moonstruck. And so I am, a bit ! By Heaven, that's true enough ! "

He sighed and was silent some time, looking at the moon in a most abstracted manner, apparently forgetting my presence.

But presently he went on to say " Still, as a spec., you might risk it. The payments wouldn't be for long, for I've developed consumption, I see—the curse of us coloured folks—had a hæmorrhage only yesterday. And then, as a charity, you might, for I'm mostly hungry—my own fault ; but I couldn't keep on gassing to those big-lipped niggers, after seeing what I have seen. If you won't give me the three dollars a week, give me one."

Well, to this I consented—not, of course, in any expectation of ever hearing any "secret," but I saw that the man had become quite unworldly, unfit to earn his living, I considered him more or less insane—still consider so, though I am convinced now that he was not nearly so insane as I conceived : so I promised him that he might draw a weekly dollar from my bank while I was in Small Forks.

Sometimes Podd drew his dollar, but often he did not, though he was aware that arrears would not be paid, if he failed to present himself any week. And so it went on for over four years, during which he became more and more emaciated, and a savage.

Meantime, Small Forks and the Sakoonay district had ceased to laugh at the name of Podd, as at a stale joke, and the fact of his rags and degradation had become a local institution, like the Mounted Police or the sawdust mill—too familiar a thing in the eye to excite any kind of emotion in the mind.

But at the end of those four years Small Forks, like one man, rose against Podd.

It happened in this way : at that date the Sakoonay district was sending an annual cut of some four hundred million feet of lumber to the Prairie Provinces ; the mining and smelter companies had increased to four—big concerns, treating three to four thousand tons of ore a day ; in which condition of things all through the district had arisen the cry : " Electricity ! Electricity! "

Hence the appearance in Small Forks of the Provincial Mineralogist with a pondering and responsible forehead ; hence his report to the Columbian Government that Harper Falls were capable of developing 97,000 horse-power ; hence a simmering of interest through the district ; and hence the decision of the Small Forks Town Council to inaugurate a municipal power-plant at Harper Falls.

But Podd objected !

He thought—this is what I found out afterwards—that Harper Falls were *his* ; and he did not wish to have them messed with, or people coming anywhere near them.

However, he said nothing ; the new works were commenced—so far as the accumulation of material was concerned ; and the first hint of a hitch in the business was given one midnight at the beginning of May—a night I'll ever remember—when the mass of the municipality's material was burnt to cinders.

The blaze made a fine display five miles out of Small Forks, and I witnessed it in the thick of a great crowd of the townspeople.

It was assumed that the thing had been deliberately done by someone, since there was no other explanation. But the mystery as to who had done it !—for there was no one to suspect. And, like a spider whose web has been torn, the municipality started once more to collect materials for the plant.

Then, at the end of June, occurred the second blaze.

But this time there were night-watchmen with

open eyes, and one of them deposed that he believed that he had seen Podd suspiciously near the scene of the mischief.

The town was very irritated about it, since the power-plant was expected to do great things for everybody.

At any rate, when Podd was captured and questioned, he did not exactly deny.

"It *might* have been I," was his answer; and "what if it *was* I?"

And this answer was a proof to me that he was innocent, for I took it to be actuated by vanity or insanity. The authorities must have thought so, too, for the man was dismissed as a ninny.

The town, however, was indignant at his dismissal; and three days later I came upon him in the midst of a crowd, from which I doubt that he would have come out alive, but for me, for he was now nothing but a bundle of bones, lighted up by two eyes. Indeed, my interference was rather plucky of me, for there present was a North-West policeman lending his countenance to the hustling of the poor outcast, a real-estate agent, the sawdust-mill manager, reeking of turpentine, and others, whose place it was to have interfered. Anyhow, I howled a little speech, pledging myself that the man was innocent; and my éclat as a Briton, perhaps, helped me to get him gasping out of their grasp.

When he found himself alone with me on the road outside the town, down he suddenly knelt, and, grasping my legs, began to sob to me in a paroxysm of gratitude.

"You have been everything to me—you, a

stranger. God reward you—I have not long to live, but you shall know what I know, and see what I have seen."

"Podd," I said, "you have heard me pledge my word that you are innocent. Let me hear from you this instant that it was not you who committed those outrages."

With the coolest insolence he stood up, looked in my face, and said, "Of course I committed them. Who else?"

I had to laugh. But then I sternly observed "Well, but you confess yourself a felon, that's all."

"Look here," he answered, "let's not quarrel. We see from different standpoints—let's not quarrel. What I say is, that during the few weeks or months I have to live no plant is going to be set up at Harper Falls—afterwards, yes. You don't know what I know about the Falls. They are the eye of this world; that's it—the eye of this world. But you shall know and see"—he looked up at the westering quarter-moon, thought a little, and continued: "Meet me here at nine on Friday night. You've done a lot for me."

The man's manner was so convincing, that I undertook to meet him, though some minutes afterwards I laughed at myself for being so impressed by his pratings.

Anyway, two nights thence, at nine, I met Podd, and we began a tramp and climb of some seven miles which I shall ever remember.

If I could but give some vaguest impression of that bewitched adventure, I should begin to think well of my power of expression; but the reality of it would still be far from pictured.

That little dying Podd had still the foot of a goat, and we climbed spots which, but for his aid, I could scarcely have negotiated—ghostly gullies, woods of spruce and dreary old cedar droning, the crags of Garroway Pass, where a throng of torrents awe one's ear, and tarns asleep in the dark of forests of larch, of hemlock, of white and yellow pine.

We were struggling upward through a gullock of Garroway Pass when Podd stopped short ; and when I groped for him—for one could see nothing there—I discovered him with his forehead leant against the crag.

To my question, "Anything wrong?" he answered "Wait a little—there's blood in my mouth."

And he added "I think I am going to have a hæmorrhage."

"We had better go back," I said.

But he presently brightened up, saying "It will be all right. Come."

We stumbled on.

Half an hour afterwards we came out upon a platform about eight hundred yards square, surrounded by cliffs of pine on three sides. A torrent dropped down the back cliff, ran over most of the platform in a rather broad river, lacerated by rocks, and dropped frothing in a cataract over the front of the platform.

"Here we are," Podd said, seating himself on a rock, dropping his forehead to his knees.

"Podd, you are in trouble," I said, standing over him.

He made no answer, but presently raised himself with an effort, to look at the moon with eyes that were themselves like moons—the satellite, about half-full, then waxing ; and now in her setting quadrant.

"Now, look you," Podd said with pantings and tremblings, so that I had to bend down to hear him in that row of the waters, "I have brought you here because I love you a lot. You are about to see things that no mortal's eye but mine ever wept salt water at——"

As he uttered those words, I, for the first time, with a kind of shock, realized that I was really about to see something boundless, for I could no longer doubt that those pantings had the accent of truth; in fact, I suddenly knew that they were true, and my heart began to beat faster.

"But how will you take the sight ?" he went on. "Am I really doing you a service ? You see the effect it has had on me—to think that What made us—our own—should bring forth such bitterness ! No, you shan't see it all, not the worst bit : I'll stop the view there. You see that fall rushing down at our feet ? I have the power, by placing a certain rock in a certain position in this river, to change that mass of froth into a mass of glass—two masses of glass—immense lenses, double-convex. Discovered it by accident one night five years since—night of my life. No, I am not well to-night. But never mind. You go down the face of the rock at the side here—easy going—till you come to the cave. Go into the cave ; then climb by the notches which you'll find in the wall, till you come to a ledge, one edge of which is about two feet behind the inner eyepiece. The moon should begin to come within your view within four minutes from now ; and I give you a five-minutes' sight—no more. You'll see her some three hundred yards from you tearing across your brain like ten trillion trains. But never you tell any man what you see on her. Go, go ! Not very well to-night."

He stood up with an effort so painful, that I said to him "But are you going into the river, Podd, and trembling like that already ? Why not show me how to place the rock for you ?"

"No," he muttered, "you shan't know ; you shan't ! It's all right ; I'll manage ; you go. Keep moving your eye at first till you get the focus-length. There's a lot of prismatic and spherical aberration, iridescent fringes, and the yellow line of the spectrum of sodium bothers everywhere—the fault of the inside eyepiece, this iridescence, for the object-glass is so big and so thin, that it hardly seems at all to decompose light. Never mind, you'll see well—upside down, of course—dioptric-telescope images. Go, go ; don't waste time ; I'll manage with the stone. And you must always say—I paid you back—full measure—for all your love."

At every third word of all this his breast gave up a gasp, and his eyes were most wild with excitement or the fever of disease. He pushed and led me to the spot where I was to descend. And "There she comes," his tongue stuttered, with a nod at the moon, as he flew from me, while I went feeling my way with my feet, the cataract at my right, down a cliff-side that was nearly perpendicular, but so rugged and shrub-grown, that the descent was easy.

When I was six feet down I lifted my chin to the ledge, and saw Podd stooping within some bush at the foot of the platform-cliff to my left, where he had evidently hidden the talisman-rock ; and I saw him lift the rock, and go tottering under its weight toward the river.

But the thought came to me that it was hardly quite fair to spy upon him, and when he was still some yards from the river I went on down—a long way—until I came to the floor of a cave in the cliff-face, a pretty roomy cavern, fretted with spray from the cataract in front of it.

I went in and climbed to the ledge, as he had said ; and there in the dark I lay waiting, wet through, and, I must confess, trembling, hearing my heart knocking upon my ribs through that solemn oratory of the torrent dropping in froth in front of me. And presently through the froth I thought I saw a luminous something that must have been the moon, moving by me.

But the transformation of the froth into the lenses which I awaited did not come.

At last I lifted my voice to howl " Hurry up, Podd ! "—though I doubted if he could hear.

Anyway, no answer reached my ear, and I waited on.

It must have been twenty minutes before I decided to climb down ; I then scrambled out, clambered up again, disgusted and angry, though I don't think that I ever believed that Podd had wilfully made a fool of me. I thought that he had somehow failed to place the rock.

But when I got to the top I saw that the poor man was dead.

He lay with his feet in the river, his body on the bank, his rock clasped in his arms. The weight had proved too much for him : on the rock was blood from his lungs.

Two days later I buried him up there with my own hands by his river's brink, within the noise of the song of his waterfall, his stupendous telescope—his " eye of this world."

And then for three months, day after day, I was endeavouring in that solitude up there so to place the rock in the river as to transform the froths of the waterfall into frothless water. But I never managed. The secret is buried with the one man whom destiny intended, maybe for centuries to come, to know what paths are trodden, and what tapestries are wrought, on another orb.

This tale ended, Mr. Coward broke the muteness of some moments that ensued with the exclamation, " Bravo !—there you are—I said it would be impossible ! "

" No, Sir," the Rev. Mr. Darrel answered : " I assure you, I have myself had that very notion—ha ! curious—that the moon may be Hell."

" I should say the sun," Sir Thomas Ormsby grumbled—" being hot. Moon's frozen with cold."

" Has a sad light, Sir "—from Mr. Darrel : " Milton considered that ' those argent fields more likely habitants translated saints or middle-spirits hold ' ; but *I* say holds the damned."

" Or the blasted, say "—from Paul Watts—" being frozen."

And Sir Thomas Ormsby : " But for how long, Mr. Darrel, are these damned damned ? "

" For ever, Sir ! "—sharply from the reverend gentleman.

"Well, but," Sir Thomas said, "isn't Hell in the universe? Must be, since 'universe' means 'all that exists.' But it is a law of the universe that pain is not long-lasting: animals in pain either (1) die, or (2) adapt themselves to the universe, so that the pain is evaded: as when cold men become covered with fur-coats, as cats become when put to live in the cold-storage holds of ships, their kittens coming thickly furnished with fur."

"Yes, yes," Mr. Darrel answered, "that is natural, Hell is supernatural."

And Sir Thomas: "Can't be on the moon, then, which is natural, nor can be anywhere in the universe, which is natural. But 'universe' means 'all that exists': do you say, then, that something exists which is not included in 'all that exists'? Doesn't seem to hang quite right together."

Now Mr. Darrel flushed. "We don't know everything, Sir. Do you know that the whole of the universe is natural? Parts of it may be supernatural."

"Its secret parts"—from Paul Watts: "it is bashful about the supernatural."

"But the point is"—from Mr. Coward—"that the fakement's impossible. Sir Thomas says so, and he's a host in himself."

"No, no, no"—quickly from Whipsnade Prince—"Sir Thomas doesn't say that it can't have happened: he says——"

"Yes, Prince"—from Sir Thomas—"I do say that it can't have happened. Its science is awry, man. The moon has an orbital velocity eastward of some thirty-three miles a minute; relative to an observer on the earth—rotating eastward, too—

her velocity is some seventeen miles a minute: so, if lenses could be made that brought small objects on her into visibility, their speed also would be brought into visibility, and they'd be seen as streaks streaming like meteors—faint streaks—no details. That Rev. Mr. Podd was excitable——"

"Had Hell on the brain," Paul Watts remarked, "hence brain on fire."

"Oh, but as a tale," Lady Dale-Eldon now said—"great, I thought, so gripping. Novelists can't be expected to know all that about the moon's doings."

"Shouldn't writers of moonshine have the moon at their fingers' ends?" Gerald Jewson suggested.

"Then they'd be cold-fingered," Paul Watts said, "and write with writers'-cramp, more fact than fiction, more moon than money."

And Sir C. Alexander Caxton: "To me, I confess, the tale seemed too sincere to be fictitious."

"And to me"—from Mr. Killik.

"Right, Sir!"—from Mr. Darrel.

And from Whipsnade Prince: "You see, Coward, you're nowhere—voting's going against you."

But before Coward could protest as to this, a Miss Routledge, of the Conservatoire, spending that day with Netta, rose, as promised, to recite "The Celestial Pilate," and the drum's hum and tremolo of that evolved voice was now the point, pronouncing strong

> *. . . fa, fa, che le ginocchia cali,*
> *Ecco l'angel di Dio, piega le mani,*
> *Ormai vedrai di siffatti ufficiali.*

CHAPTER VIII

THE VENGEANCE DAY

THEN on the Thursday Mr. Paul Watts, whose day Thursday was, brought with him, as promised, a fellow-craftsman, a Mr. Bristow, a conjuror, to lend to his day some trick of luck, Bristow chancing to be then at Villefranche, and bringing a packet of the paraphernalia of his craft he came. Only Whipsnade Prince was absent up to three minutes before the story was due to begin ; but Netta, happening to glance over the sea, saw him coming in a dinghy from the yacht in the offing called *The Roe* ; and when he had been deposited at the bottom of the villa-steps, which the wash and wobbling of the water's liquidity slobbers always with kissing, and had stepped into the arbour with his pressing way of stepping, Netta remarked to him " Nearly late," to which he made the strange answer " Yet I came pelting."

" Pelting ? " says she : " aren't you from that yacht yonder ? "

" Ah, you saw me coming," he answered—" on the look-out for me. . . . The boat came pelting."

" Oh ? I should say pelted—by the waves. So who is the yacht's owner ? friend of yours ? "

" Not exactly. I was looking over her for someone whom I know."

Now a little stillness, filled by a lung that roared

Handel's "Oh, ruddier than the cherry," until she muttered "Someone whom you know. . . . The sage says 'Know thyself.' Do you pretend to know yourself?"

This affected him with some shyness, his lids fell a little, and before ever he could reply the roaring lung left off; now a voice is announcing "This is the national . . . " "And now for Mr. Frank Newton, specialist in Society in the 'nineties, in his tale named 'Vengeance'" . . . "Mr. Newton" . . . and now out of the bowels of the profound of space a voice was born to relate this tale:

The Rev. Stanton Jones was going up Piccadilly one afternoon of November fog when he met Ivor St. Aubyn, for five years lost to him.

And, contemplating that jolly face, still rosy-and-white like a girl's, Jones said "Well, I seem to know you; the beard may be an effect of the fog."

"Yes, and I seem to know you," Ivor said, "for, like November, you will never be a day over thirty. What became of you? I meant to write you at—St. Something."

"That was St. Jude's, Hackney; I've been transferred to St. Anne's, Lambeth: rise of three-pun-ten: a superior brand of 'bacca——"

"Same old Jones. . . . Talking of 'bacca, Netherclift—you used to know Nethercliſt—has brought home the weirdest little things, made by Chinese emigrants in Antigua—opium, I think—seductive—a box at the club: you come—make one of the old nights of it."

Now, the outcast about St. Anne's, Lambeth, had tales to tell of the Good Samaritan that dwelt within that narrow coat of Stanton Jones ; and he had other merits : but to resist following whither that witching wildness of Ivor invited had never been in Jones from the age of seventeen. So they were off in a taxi, Ivor, who was all chatter and memories of Cambridge, not noticing that Jones was a little odd, looking anon as if he wanted to say something, but checking himself. . . .

They got out at a club in Hanover Square, by which time the darkness of night was mingling with the darkness of the fog ; and that quickened activity of taxis, cars, which precedes the dinner and theatre hour was at work within the murk and turmoil of the streets. Still, it was a little early to dine ; they sat awhile in a lounge, sipping byrrh for apéritif ; and presently, all at once, Jones found himself in the act of disclosure.

" Ivor," he said, " I have to tell it ; perhaps, after all, I ought——"

" Well ? "

" Well, then, your uncle is going to be married, Ivor."

Ivor laughed—a rather ghast laugh—asking " Which uncle ? Attenborough ? "

But Jones, his eyes on the floor, said " It's true " : and suddenly now those roses of Ivor died.

" I was doubtful whether it was well to tell," Jones muttered, staring at nothing : " for it is more or less a thing committed to me—not expressly committed, that's true. Anyway, the cat's out of the bag now, and—it's a fact."

" How can you know ? "—from Ivor : " I saw him a fortnight ago——"

" Ivor, he wants to keep it dark—at least, I

suppose he does, since he picks out a little hole-and-corner church like St. Anne's——"

"Oh, I see—it's *you* who are to marry him. . . . Well! So when does this wild wedding take place?"

"To-morrow—eleven. And don't think, Ivor, that I haven't burned to tell you: it was a hope of running across you somewhere in your haunts that brought me West to-night, for the third time lately. But I wouldn't exactly seek you out, go to you—I wanted to, and didn't want. He came to me not knowing that you and I are friends, and I wasn't sure that it was quite the dainty thing, don't you know—conscience of the priest."

"Quite so, I don't blame you," the other muttered: "simply my little fate. . . . Know anything of the lady?"

"Found that out. Spanish. Her name's Salvadora—a mouthful; her father a certain Don Carlos de Miraflores. City-King—once; he and Sir Bernard in business-friendship up East for years. Daughter British-born. But lately the father gone bankrupt; and Sir Bernard marries the daughter—out of pity, or something."

"Oh, that's not it. One of two things—either his motive is simple spleen against me, or he has been tricked by these people into this."

"Quite possibly tricked," Jones said: "girl a beauty, I gather—one of the 'divinely tall'—the sort of being that will bring down the grey hairs——"

Here "dinner served" intervened, they stood up, and Ivor pulled himself together with a tug: a big tug, for now things looked black. He did not "understand the City," how to get underwriting godsends—understood Newmarket, and so anon turned an honest penny; but anon had stared, and been low-spirited; and anon had had to raise the wind in ways recondite and devious.

But on the prospect of £22,000 a year he had made gay debts, having it on doctor's authority that his uncle was due to die. However, the main items of the St. Aubyn estate only verted to Ivor, if Sir Bernard was unmarried at death: so that his dinner-chat now was only a mask over that stare that stared within him, in spite of more wine than happy wights quaff.

When he presented a cigarette to Jones at the "punch Romaine," Jones remembered the Antigua cigars, craved to taste one, and picked from Ivor's case a slim stick of pallid tobacco. Then Ivor arranged through the bureau-telephone for a box at musical comedy; and they left the club in a cab.

All was now fog: even the nearest street-lamps appeared like eyes in tears; all the dark barked with coughings. Nevertheless, Ivor, peering through the creeping taxi-window, happened to spy someone on a pavement, cried out "Hullo, Dyson!", and stopped to talk to Dyson, one of the wildest boys about town; and now, instead of going on to the comedy, they were off with the new man to some chambers in St. James', where a very merry set were met together to the accompaniment of popping corks. There Jones, after a brief struggle between dare-to-be-a-Daniel and let's-all-be-jolly, had to give in to the spirit of the thing, Ivor being his syren; and when at half-past ten the party sallied out to pay a flying visit to a music-hall, Jones uttered praise of Netherclift's cigars, craving yet another cigar—his third.

At this Ivor looked at Jones—hesitated—but then held out his case.

Jones smoked that third one in the music-hall ; he lit a fourth on entering a Soho club ; on finishing a fifth, the dancers there seemed to him dream-unrealities reeling through air.

He left that place pressing upon Ivor's arm ; and, says he " I do feel fantastical somehow. Take me home, Ivor, take me home."

It was then 2 a.m. ; and, as Ivor knew that at 11 a.m. Jones had to join Miss Salvadora de Miraflores to his uncle, he had a hazy notion that it was his duty to take Jones straight to Jones' home in the wilderness beyond the river. When a taxi-driver demanded " Where to ? " Ivor hesitated ; but so small a matter as his ignorance of Jones' address solved his doubt : for Jones was already dozing ; and, as a matter of fact, slept that night, not in Lambeth, but in Mayfair.

Now, about two hours before he left that club, a young lady of eighteen was seated at the knees of an old man, who kept patting her head with his soft palm—the scene a lodging-house to which they had migrated from a mansion in Belgravia. The lady's hair, her strong point like Samson's, still unscissored, was hanging down her back, making a black mat on the carpet and the old man was saying to her " It is only lately that I realize the sacrifice that you are making, Salva : for I am just as surely immolating you as Jephthah when he plunged the weapon into his darling's heart."

" Now, what a comparison," the girl murmured.

" Then, why this new drooping, those red eyes ? Isn't it because you see that you are casting away your youth to rescue my remaining days from those hardships to which Jehovah has seen fit to submit me ? "

" But am not I poor, too, Daddy ? " the girl asked, raising the glory of her gaze to the old man's face : " it is to make myself rich that I am marrying ! "

He shook his finger at her. " Now, that's a story—that's a story. No such motive is in your head. You understand that you have youth, brains, a bountiful dower of beauty, with which somehow you could make your way. Let us be frank. You are doing it for me."

" And if I am ? " she asked. " Let us be frank. My beauty, etcetera, are from you. . . . Oh, but what's the use of talking now ? The die is cast—ah yes ! " A sob trembled through her body.

" Girl ! Girl ! " the old man cried, " this is not the destiny you had a right to expect ! " And suddenly he lowered his outcry to a grumble to add " But, then, your married life may not be long——"

" But that's the worst ! " she cried out : " don't you see ? The constant temptation—*since* he is infirm—to wish—how hideous ! " Now she hid her face away, frankly sobbing ; on which he sprang up to stamp about, bent now and palsied, his head thatched with a mass of hair as absolutely blanched as Salva's was black.

" It is not too late ! " he exclaimed : " you shan't be butchered ! If I have to go back to the old place in Spain, and beg my bread——"

Now she stood up to put her arm about him, standing half-a-head the taller, saying " Time for bed—your toddy "—and tripping to a spirit-lamp, she concocted toddy, saw him sip it, then kissed each cheek of his, he each of hers, in the foreign manner, he groaning each time " Good girl ! Good girl ! "

Her own room was higher, lit by a little lamp which showed fair hair on the pillows—hair of a certain Gertrude Stokes, who had refused to be sent away when Salva became poor. And now her loyalty was to be rewarded with new wealth, new excursions into that Continental life which she liked, there in her head as she slept being a vision of Paris prattling in a whirl where nobody works but Worth.

Salvadora looked down on her with a dreary smile ; then looked round the room, and saw all in order for the morrow—necklaces on that common table, tissue-paper, a Rue de la Paix creation. . . .

Then, for the last time, Salvadora Micaela Arbos de Miraflores knelt at that bedside, crossed herself, pressed a kiss upon her thumb-nail, *pour faire ses prières*.

As she rose, tears now streaming down her cheek, she heard the sleeper murmur the word " to-morrow " ; and " Yes," she muttered " to-morrow."

But that to-morrow was not certain : for, first of all, when Ivor St. Aubyn opened his eyes he was going to sleep again, believing it still night ; but just then at his head a little clock's gong gave out ten hushed clashes, and he called " Magennis ! "

A man of soft foot looked in.

" Is it morning or not ? " Ivor demanded.

" It is morning, Sir."

" I see—fog, is it ? But what a fog ! . . . By the way, what about Mr. Jones ? "

" Mr. Jones is asleep, Sir."

Some minutes of stillness, filled with someone's meditations ; and suddenly the master muttered to the man " Better go and have a look at him. Tell him it's ten o'clock—that is, if he has awaked. But—perhaps—no, better not wake him."

" Yes, Sir."

Magennis went to " have a look," as commanded, at Jones—a mere formality, since Jones was making no secret of the fact that he believed himself in Antigua : and the man went back with this fact to the master.

Ivor then got up, a wrinkle of perplexity on his forehead. What his motive was in practically holding Jones from going to celebrate the marriage he did not himself analyse : for, if the ceremony failed that day, Sir Bernard could make it take place the next ; but there was the feeling in him that, since the old man was playing him a nasty trick, it was only in human nature if he played the old man another, the chance having offered itself : for he had not tied nor drugged Jones. . . . Yet his conscience smote him. Sequences more serious than he could foresee might result ; and he hurried out, half dressed, to rouse the parson.

But outside he stopped. " No," he said : " why should I ? Not my business to get my uncle married ! " And he went back.

By a quarter-past eleven he had breakfasted, had given fresh instructions to Magennis not to wake Jones, and had got into a taxi for " St. Anne's, Lambeth," to see the fun.

On alighting before the church, he could see the St. Aubyn arms on one of two cars waiting there, so that the wedding-party was still within—must now have been waiting half an hour. He listened, could hear no sound but a coughing, and peeped warily in, feeling now against his uncle all the spleen which his uncle had always shown against him, pierced too with a stitch of fun at the joke of an old uncle waiting there for Jones, while Jones, with a note of challenge, was snoring praise of Netherclift's cigars in St. James'.

The nave was clogged grey with fog-mist, through which vaguely glared six or eight gas-jets, so that Ivor could just discern five persons down by the chancel, one of them tramping agitatedly about, clad in sacristan black, while the other four sat mum in a front row. No Jones. And anon the echoing of a coughing haunted all the hollow of the edifice as with goblin guffawing—the barking of the baronet : for the fog was dank and grasping.

Presently Sir Bernard called the verger to recommend him to hurry in one of the carriages to the clergyman's house : so now the verger was off trotting ; and afresh they waited, the bride sitting quite a white thing, but smiling, while her father, all in a tremor, kept drawing on and off his left glove, anon patting Salva's hand, as to say " All's quite well, he'll come."

But no one spoke ; they were as at a funeral ; Miss Gertrude Stokes had begun to feel that she was destined to see no France that day ; and ever the echoes of the baronet's coughing sounded like applause of goblins in the vault of fog—he a pigmy being, his eyes goggle and sloppy, which anon he wiped dry with a spotted bandana, elaborately.

But as Jones' home was near, within some minutes the verger returned with a very pestered expression, with the news that Jones' housekeeper was also at a loss. Aware that a wedding was on, she had sent to all likely places to find him—in vain.

What, then, was to be done? Sir Bernard felt certain that no other clergyman would officiate in Mr. Jones' church, in which the marriage was bound to take place, this being the church of the banns. At a registrar's notice was necessary.

At last the baronet stood up, saying with vindictive lips " Well, we will see whether some punishment cannot be discovered for this clergyman commensurate with his worthlessness. Come, Carlos; come, ladies; let us be going "—he took his bride on his arm with no little distinction, though she, walking down the aisle by his side, seemed an archangel in veils leading some poor mortal.

She had nearly reached the door when she chanced to catch sight of a man seated solitary in a far corner of one of the regions of pews—Ivor—but fog and distance hid their faces from each other.

Now they were outside, where Sir Bernard insisted that, if the wedding was spoiled for a day, their luncheon need not be: so the party started for the Langham Hotel.

They were moving over Westminster Bridge when the baronet said to Salvadora " My good and patient Salva! What, not a word of complaint? But I will avenge you. I am not too sure, by the way, that there is not some kind of foul play here."

" By whom? " Salva asked quickly.

" One must not be rash in suspecting," the

baronet got out, bent with coughing—" rash, I say, in suspecting. But who could have any motive? Only my nephew, Ivor."

"But surely——" she began; then suddenly: "What is he like, this Ivor?"

"Stalwart young fellow, fair, fresh face. Often up to mischief, I know; inveterately wrong in tendency—from the mother—from the mother. But, then, I can't think how—he's not even aware that I am to be married."

"He *may* be," leapt to Salva's lips to say, as a suspicion sprang up in her that *he* may have been the man whom she had seen in the church; but she checked herself to ask "Why, though, should he desire you not to marry?"

But now the baronet was all occupied with coughing, until with blanched lips he got out, panting, "This fog, Salvadora, will be the death of a score of people in London alone—yes, a score. His motive? I don't see that he has any motive, except ill-will, an innate tendency to devilry—though, of course, you understand, dear child, that the instrument by which I settle upon you my all is void by a tail, until we marry."

"Why settle upon me 'all,'" she demanded, "when you have a near relative?"

"His mother—I dislike him! But, dear child, I hope you are not going to argue the point, since everything is already fixed."

And now stillness, they moving now up the Haymarket within a cavern of damp, and gradually a lamp would move to them out of gloom, glow close, move into gloom again—a funeral thing. In which other cavern of damp the other car with de Miraflores and Miss Stokes was they did not know. Salvadora shuddered ; and once more the old man, coughing, remarked " Yes, the death of a score. We must leave London——"

He stopped ; but she, occupied with her own woeful thoughts, was not noticing him. At Oxford Circus, though, conscious of a sigh at her side, the girl glanced round, saw an ashen face, and all in a scare shook his arm. But the baronet's head dropped backward ; and now she cried out upon the ways of Heaven, as she found herself in the presence of death.

That death, she was to find, robbed her of all. Since she was not a wife, the one lawyer whom her father consulted advised against the making of any claim ; and none was made. . . . Gertrude Stokes went off to a ladies' school in Kent ; the income from the sale of Salvadora's jewels did not amount to fifty pounds a year ; she went with her father from Camden Town to still cheaper lodgings in Barnsbury.

Now, Don Carlos was at that age at which sick men are given to groan and grumble ; and, although he was aware of the pain which a groan gave, he had to groan, his crabbedness being heightened by a cataract which he was acquiring in the right eye : so that the lessons on the piano which Salva gave to three girls set him nearly frantic ; and to her, conscious of this fact, " practices " were passions on the rack.

Then after seven months de Miraflores fell ill with pneumonia. . . .

Salvadora called in the greatest specialist in London : and when expenses increased upon her, went to a broker, a friend of old days. He warned her that big interest means thin ice; but she "plunged"; and within two months had lost much of her little fund.

Not a syllable did she breathe of it to de Miraflores: but the mere fact that they had to flit to still meaner lodgings, even while he was very ill, was revealing. She then confessed, expecting him to groan and grumble; but he lay calm. It was, in fact, his death-blow and last straw: a week later he ceased to live.

In the evening dusk before his burial-day she was seated by his coffin, her red gaze resting on her dead with a tearless grief, when a woman entered to say "A letter for your father."

It came late. . . .

She read:

"Sir,—We are instructed by our client, Sir Ivor St. Aubyn, to inform you that, taking into consideration the evident intentions of his uncle, the late Sir Bernard St. Aubyn, in respect of your daughter, he is prepared to make over to your daughter out of the estate a life-annuity of £500 (five hundred pounds), this to devolve upon you till your death, should your daughter's death antedate yours, and to be considered as dating from the date of Sir Bernard's death. We should have communicated with you some time ago but for our difficulty in discovering your address.

"Hoping that this proposal may prove agreeable to your views,

"We are, Sir, yours truly,

"EDGAR & GRACE."

From beneath her lowered eyelids proceeded a piercing ray, as Salvadora sat meditating this letter ; and presently she was hissing " Thief ! Thief ! "

Had her dead been alive, she would no doubt have trampled her Spanish pride underfoot, have accepted for his sake ; but he lay there dead, and craved no bread ; so that night, with fire in her eyes, she wrote :

" Sirs,—My father being dead, I have opened your communication to him on behalf of Sir Ivor St. Aubyn. Be good enough to inform that man that I cannot accept the gratuity he proffers me, nor any gratuity less than the entire estate of the late Sir Bernard St. Aubyn. It may be of interest to your client to be informed that I am not all in the dark in regard to the fact that the fiasco in St. Anne's on the day when I was to have become the wife of the late baronet was the result of some device of the present baronet. The Rev. Stanton Jones, who should have performed the ceremony but was kept away, is a *friend* of Sir Ivor St. Aubyn, and was in his company the previous evening : I have found out. He is guilty : this proffer of his being but the offspring of the stings of his guilt.

" Sir Ivor St. Aubyn, I fancy, might find the publication of these facts of some social inconvenience. But pray assure him that he has nothing to dread from me : I should not be at the pains to punish a man of his stamp.

" I am, Sirs, sincerely,

" Salvadora de Miraflores."

On her home-coming the next day from her father's grave, it was impossible for her to escape a sense of relief—the old man had been such a load ; and at once she set to think of grappling with things-as-they-are.

She chose to be a teacher—was a violinist, could skirt-dance, talk, had beauty, four languages by nature, a manner, a social past—would hardly starve.

First she learned from Gertrude Stokes about scholastic agencies, how one gets " places," and in two weeks was in a lord's family in Derbyshire in her middle names of " Micaela Arbos " : for " Salvadora de Miraflores " had been eminent socially, and now cried aloud for burial.

During two happy years there she had the pleasure of " declining the hand " of a viscount of fifty—indeed, she had very rashly promised that irascible old man, her father, shortly before his death, never to marry an Englishman of the titled class, of the class of that Ivor St. Aubyn who had wronged her.

But after two years the wife of her employer died ; she had now to fly from his eyes, which followed her ; and found herself in London anew, seeking a " place."

At the same time it happened that Gertrude Stokes was doing the same thing : and the two friends slept in the same bed in Bloomsbury.

Both soon got " places " ; but, before parting, they went one day together to Brompton with a little wreath to lay on Sir Bernard's grave, and had just laid it, when a third lady came up with a big wreath, and entered into talk with them. Without revealing who she was, Salva told that she had known the baronet intimately, while the other told that she was Sir Bernard's niece, a Mrs. Garry, and, seeming to have fallen in love with Salva at first sight, invited her and Gertrude to a conversazione. Three days later she was begging Salva to become the governess of her daughter, Aimée.

It is said that every girl is at heart an adventuress; and though Salva had some trouble in withdrawing from the appointment she already had, she managed: for this new thing drew her.

Now, at this date, four years after the late baronet's heart-failure, Sir Ivor St. Aubyn was a different man from the larky Ivor of Piccadilly—clean-shaven, broader of build, rural, down on the brown rat and on Socialists, having his model village down where the clover ended and the corn commenced, apprehensive now in his head on his bed for his mouse-coloured cows of Kerry. "Money for money's sake," moreover, had come to be among his motives. Hence, with three of the *débutantes* of a season, and the county's femaledom, seeking after him, he was still single, through thinking of other things.

However, seated one evening on a seat that surrounded a yew-tree, he was watching a young woman with unusual suspense and abstraction—this yew-tree being on a domain named The Glen, to which one came down through the Hall-park, The Glen's tenant being Ivor's widow-sister, Mrs. Garry, who paid him rent; and the young woman was his sister's "governess-companion," who was playing tennis.

Here was a waist which swayed with such an ease as if each wind wielded it, he regarding her with a sort of farmer's interest, from the standpoint of pedigree, as horse-fanciers regard a filly expanding the elastic of her limbs in a winter morning's scamper. And said he in bidding her good-bye "You know that we are near neighbours, Miss Arbos—no getting out of meeting rather often."

On which she flashed a glance at him, and he had a sense of an arrogance compellingly grand in these black flambeaux that glanced. It was with his eyes on the ground that he added "My sister will bring you over—old place—good-bye."

Four days later Mrs. Garry did take her "over," or up, at five o'clock; and Sir Ivor, seeing her stroll away from the groups on the terraces, went busily after, to say with a hollowness of mock awe "Now's your chance for the haunted tower—if you are interested."

"Yes, I am interested in Waveney," she answered.

So, with her Aimée, they went up to the second floor of a tower, to look along a gallery in which a ghost rose each New Year; and it was when they were descending that Aimée, who was nothing but a tongue hung on stilts, said that her Uncle Ivor must be liking Micaela, since he was going to The Glen so oddly often....

The fellow flew red to the roots of his hair; but Salvadora took it coldly. "Get a bit of it clipped off," she muttered with a nod at Aimée; and they descended in silence, till down at the door he, with a fresh rush of his roses, dared, saying "I wonder if it is true?"

"That——?"

"I go to The Glen——"

"No, don't believe all you hear," she just

muttered, and called his attention to sunset on the lake.

But there was truth in it ; and the thing got to be like fire, not to be ignored, though Salvadora seemed to be constantly on the watch to give him no chance to speak with her.

However, about Hallowmass, when damps begin, and leaves drizzle down from trees, he waylaid her one evening in a lane. It was at a country-house a good way from Waveney, and she had taken the habit of rambling rather far in the night there among those mountainous boundaries of Monmouth. This evening it was blowing great guns, she holding-on her toque from the wind, and so, blind on the right side, did not see anybody under a tree, till, in opening a gate, she saw him run to help her—and her heart started.

" Well, you," she said: " how are you—here ?

He attempted to laugh. " Came by a train."

" Not of thoughts. You startle."

" Meaning that you were not thinking of me ? "

" You hit it. The only man I was thinking of is the man in the moon : he seems to have been stealing, and is fleeing with a leer, like Tom, Tom. But you come as a guest at the house ? "

" No, just for the ride—partly. A keeper told me that you had gone this way, and I thought I might as well meet you."

" Well, you have. Isn't it a nice high wind ? . . . I am now going back to the house, and you may come."

" No, not to the house. . . . To be frank, I—only came in the vague hope of seeing you."

"Seeing *me*?"—her voice sang falsetto, she pointing to her innocent chest.

"Who else is there?"

Quick she curtseyed: "*Merci!*"

"But don't jest, if you are kind," he said dejectedly; "to tell the truth, I am rather miserable, for you have not been very favourable, and, heaven knows, I do intensely——"

"Want my favour? That has been said to me, so I know it's coming. You *were* going to say that?"

"As far as words——"

But all at once the very expression of pride arrested him—Semiramis-eyes! She went "*You*" at him with the pulled nose of contempt.

With a poignancy now in his voice, gazing boylike on the ground, he began to say "I was going to say that, as far as words——"

But again she stopped him—with a chuckle, bitter still, but cold now. "No, we must be more serious, really. Look here, if ever you speak to me in that sense again, I go, and then you can look out for your sister's tongue. Also, I ask you to leave me now."

Up leapt the hat, he moved, hankered back a moment, and now was gone. And presently a groan came from between his ground teeth "God, she don't like me; what dog's-luck!"

After that he took care to keep clear of The Glen, trying to return to his late self of work and landlord interests, sitting long in the saddle, hunting three days a week, planning with woodard, architect, land-steward. Only from his pew on Sundays did he see her, till trees were bare, when they met one day in the rectory lane. He would not have stopped, but her smile seemed good, and he asked "Am I supportable to-day?"

"You know on what condition," she answered: "I am going down to the rectory, and you may come."

He was with her two hours, and at the good-bye at The Glen gate said "I am going home now to sit and live over again everything that you have said, and every goddess glance——"

"Goddess," she muttered: "don't begin again."

"Be *good*, Micaela."

"'Arbos' is more sonorous, please. Supposing I was disposed to be 'good,' I couldn't."

"'Couldn't'—how?"

"Shall I tell you, I wonder?"

"Well?"

"The reason, then—the exterior reason, I mean—is that I am under an obligation. . . . It is like this: I have a friend—awfully near and dear—who four years ago suffered a wrong of a man. Spanish girl; her father a merchant who got poor—my guardian; and she, to rescue him from penury, consented to marry an old man. Well, for a lass of that sort—born free and spirited—rich—this was a sacrifice—racking! But she went gamely through with it—that is, she tholed the subjection and despair of it; but then whatever compensation was going was dashed from her hand."

"Ah?" Ivor went, going gradually haggard.

"Yes"—with spite: "the old man, having no relative whom he liked, settled everything upon his bride: so a nephew of his devised some devilry by which the parson to marry her was kept away; and that same day the old man, who had long been dying, died. My friend's father, too, soon died—heart-broken."

In a wholly new tone, hard and hoarse, he remarked "Surely the heir offered the girl a portion——"

"Yes, I think—a little portion ; but then Salva—her name's Salvadora—said that the man had no rights (except in 'law')—was utterly 'out of it.' Don't you agree ? "

"No. What is the 'obligation' you referred to ? "

"I'll tell you. Salva's father, my guardian, when almost dying, made—us—vow at his bedside—Andalusian—lusty, oldtime folk, with blood in their veins, who make vows, and keep them, Sir Ivor."

"Well, the vow ? "

"It was never to marry an Englishman of what in his last days my guardian called 'the false class'—meaning the landed class. Since then two men of that class have been rather eager to marry Salvadora, but she considers herself bound, as I consider myself—unless, perhaps, every penny and rood of the stolen property be restored to its owner."

"I don't know if you or she imagines that that could be done" came in harsh sarcasm from the other's throat.

"Couldn't it ? " she asked.

"No—how ? "

"Heaven knows ! Aren't there such things as deeds-of-gift, and so on ? "

A flush of resentment rushed to Ivor's forehead. "Out of the question. The girl has no conception of the immensity of what she asks."

"Of what *she* asks? But she asks nothing! She seems serenely content to let the man go on enjoying her property. She asks nothing."

She heard him hiss to himself "Vile mess!", and she said "You couldn't think how *she*, that poor ousted girl, suffered."

"Oh," he tossed back quarrelsomely, "I don't doubt that the ouster considered that his kinsman had been tricked into wedlock by a pretty wench, and, on the whole, thought that he had as good a right to the property of his race as anyone—when the law gave it him."

"Salvadora regarded him as rather a rogue," she coldly muttered.

And he stood there haggard, two braziers of angry resentment in his eyes, like the hot eyes of the cat besieged by the dog—pestered by her gaze, tugged between impulses as big and liberal as the sea, and impulses niggardly and hard-headed; and, suddenly spinning upon her, he bitterly cried out "But do you mean to stand there and tell me that you, living with the girl, never heard the name of the estate, or of the heir who was 'regarded as rather a rogue'?"

Her eyes fell. "There were several estates——"

"Oh, you know perfectly well that it was I—as a matter of course: I can see it in your eyes."

"You have looked too often into my eyes, I'm afraid, Sir Ivor."

"I will look into them until I die! If they drive me lunatic, I will look, and look, and look, and own them!" he bullyingly said, spinning again upon her.

"You shan't," she coldly answered.

"Meaning that you never intend to forgive me for the law of the land?"

"Oh, I," she said with a shrug, "till seventy times; but the daughter of Don Carlos de Miraflores, I'm afraid——"

"I care nothing about the daughter of Don Carlos de Miraflores! But supposing—I say supposing——" He paused, appalled at his own thought, and began again: "Supposing I gave back all—only, it is too stupendous a thing! I'm not sure that it could be done! Still, I say 'supposing': would you, in that case, undertake——"

"Oh, no, no, no!" she put in quickly: "understand that I undertake nothing, nothing. Though—possibly—I don't know—in that case, what is now moonshine—wild-goose lunacy—might begin to be—a little—thinkable."

"God," he muttered, tossing up his palms, and was suddenly gone, full of madness and folly; and she had to press her hand on her heart, it beat so, as she breathed "He is going to! He *is*! Oh, Daddy, if you had lived to see the getting back of our own again!"

And in truth during the next few days Ivor, for his part, passed through the finest fight of his life, that now staggered to the negative south pole, and now was away at the positive north. What added to the war and storm of it was that he had once floundered in shallows and miseries, and remembered well; and then she had promised nothing, perhaps meant nothing, intending to avenge her friend to his very undoing: for he knew that the Spanish can be savagely inhuman to dumb animals and to man; and, although he had moments of hope and trust in her, somewhere in him he utterly mistrusted, suspected, and hissed enmity at her.

However, the battle was not long: there came an hour when, like a man blind and wild, without allowing himself to think one other instant, he sprang into a car, and was away for London.

And presently she, aware that he had vanished from Waveney, was counting all the hours of the days. But he was long away. Sometimes her heart sank and sickened.

Then one night after nine, when Mrs. Garry was absent, and Salvadora dozing over a piano, moaning " La Paloma " to her soul, and Spring so far advanced, that the French windows stood open to a wind which dented waves down the valenciennes, and wafted-in scents of hawthorn off the lawn—then he came. Suddenly, to her heart, she was conscious of a presence behind her, span round with startled eyebrows, and it was he.

At once, on touching her hand, he dropped upon a sofa, tossed something upon a card-table, and said with the sigh of one very tired " There's what I've brought you, since you wanted it "—an oblong document, engrossed.

" And this is ? " she breathed.

" Conveyance: everything directly inherited from my uncle; made over to Salvadora de Miraflores—good while I live, till the tail begins again."

" *Got it!* " she thought, and all her loveliness stood radiant. For some time she remained with her face slightly raised, triumphing, dilated.

" So you've done it ? " says she, glancing down from her height, a little smile curving her lips downward.

" There it is," he said: " I thought I would, and I did."

Suddenly now she caught up the document to carry it off to a corner, like a cat carrying off stolen food, to sit with it and examine it. Silence reigned. Then she came again to him to say " But you bring it—to me ? "

" No one seems to know whereabouts the girl is," he answered wearily : " *you* had better give it her, I suppose."

" All right. I'll run over to Mrs. Garry at Singleton, tell her, and start in the morning for London—that's how I'll do it. And now I'll say, on behalf of Salva, that I think this pretty of you."

" Oh, not much prettiness, I'm afraid," he muttered—" no sense of duty—nothing of that sort—it simply means that to my particular fantasy there's more heaven and Turkish delight in you than in Waveney."

" But if you get neither ? " she asked, her eyes musing coldly on him, watching the colour go slowly out of his cheeks.

And, as hate is next door to love, venom was on his lips, as he glanced up to her with " Who ever bought at such a price ? "

The irony of her chuckle gashed him to the heart with razors of despair. " Am I bought ? *I ?* The priceless for a price ? Oh, you mistake ! After all, you have only done the duty of a man of honour. . . . But, then, I can't stop to argue : must go—pack. So say good-bye; and I hope we shall meet—some day—again."

He rose, saying stiffly " I—hope so."

" Yes, we will," she said. " Very likely I shall write, asking you to meet me—that is, *if you like* "—

arming her eyes with an underglance of coquettish fire—" and my friend, ' the girl,' shall be there to see you. Will you ? "

He bent his head, saying " Thank you," but inaudibly, because of the lump of sentimental self-pity and pathos that plugged-up his gullet ; and when she said again " So till 'some day'—good-bye, Sir Ivor," he wrung her hand hard, and swerved away out from her with a feeling that nothing was left anywhere, his earth turned turtle.

She stood and watched his form pass shadowy across the lawn, till the Hall-park swallowed him ; then went to the hearthplace, where for a long time she stood musing, with something very dejected now and powerless in her manner by reaction, the precious parchment hanging in her languid fingers. But presently her lips smiled a little wistfully, whispering " He's a pet ; he's a pet " ; adding a minute afterwards " Because women are simple little pigeons, you see, Sir Ivor " ; and still a minute later she was shrugging, muttering " No, it isn't much good struggling against " ; and now she held the paper, gained with so much pains, to the blaze, and watched its ashes crack from black to grey in the grate, two tears now streaming down her cheeks at the surrender of her girlhood.

But then again came a reaction, a throe of pride, fixed teeth, a light in her eye. " To be brought down like a rocketer, first shot ? *I ?* Thank you, no. To be purchased like a *fille ?* Six months hard for him first—six months on the rack of doubt, of care, of excruciation ! "

But one month saw it over. . . .

In consequence of a letter received, Ivor went to

London, and one misty day stood waiting eight or ten minutes before a house in a mean street, amazed at the mysterious caprice that had brought him there. He looked anew at the letter : " Wait before the door of 12 Lollard Street, S.W." : and this was it.

And soon she duly drove up in a saloon-car in a robe of ivory satin, and with her another lady, who, too, was in white. . . . When he had run to her, and was handing her down, he moaned in a low and heartfelt tone at her ear, " I see you again "; and she, seeing his face careworn and paled, closed her fingers in a pressure on his.

But she was rather breathless, flurried, the peach of her cheeks flushed now almost to rose, her eyes as alight as his ; and at once, as her shoe touched the slush, she pushed an orchid from a bunch which she had into his coat-lapel, and curtseyed.

He, all in a maze in Paradise, said, " This is extremely——"

" Come," says she.

" Your friend—this isn't Miss de Miraflores—'the girl' ? " he asked.

" She'll be inside presently. Miss Gertrude Stokes—Sir Ivor St. Aubyn. Come, let's go in."

" 'In' ? Where ? "

She nodded toward a little church just opposite. " Come."

Ivor's heart started to knock at his ribs at a thrilling foreboding that rose in him ; but even when they were " in," he was still at sea, until his eyes lifted from her to the sight of a parson in his robes at the altar. Yes—Jones ! Dry Jones with the old dry smile which anon he wetted with wine—no other—and suddenly Ivor remembered and knew: this was St. Anne's, Lambeth.

"It's all right, Ivor," Jones whispered to him: "everything arranged by her and me—take the ring; don't be foreign and nervous, *I* am with you."

And Jones married them with a proper solemnness.

It was only when they moved into the vestry to sign the book that Ivor knew his bride's full name; and then there rushed through his brain the memory of just such a day four years before. Salvadora's robe, it was the same; the building; the dim day; Jones there smiling, not snoring this time; Miss Stokes there, as before, with her "Continent" veritably in prospect now; all the wrong drawn right—and in Ivor's knee a wish to dip to worship the girl who had made him the victim of this angelic vengeance.

No sooner was this tale told than, in the moments of dumbness that ensued, Lady Dale-Eldon muttered "beautiful!" on a sigh of her breast, wiping her eye; upon which Sir C. Alexander Caxton remarked, "It cannot, I think, have happened! or we may say that it cannot, the indecorousness of an English cleric being intoxicated is so extraordinary."

"Well, yes," Lady Dale-Eldon answered, "I didn't quite like that bit; it was the rest——"

"But!" exclaims Mons. Makla Pascal, of Jones, Pedrick, Pascal & Co., champagne-merchants, Mincing Lane—a foursquare skull, bulky for his small body, looking a solid block of acumen—"shall we say 'cannot,' Sir, when we mean 'does not'?

Nor can we know 'does not,' since, if a cleric becomes drunk, no statistics record it."

And now the Rev. Mr. Darrel : " We know more than is in statistics, Sir: we know of a general level of moral conduct in which drunkenness is remote from entering."

" 'Moral' simply means 'customary'," Pascal answered : " does not mean 'right,' but what is considered right locally ; and each man decides for his private self whether what is customary or moral about him is, in fact, right ; nor, without statistics can you tell how many in private decide that to be drunk is not wrong. It is only lately, in some countries, that to be drunk is even immoral—considered wrong ; in your Bible you know how the old worthies—Lot, Noah—are asserted without any note of censure to have been drunk ; staid old gentlemen like Socrates, St. Paul, were often drunk——"

" *Who ?* Paul ? "—Mr. Darrel started.

" Does it not seem so to you, too ? " Pascal asked with that French lack of humour which is the result of the hard-headedness of French intelligence —" nothing at all immoral in it, Sir—then and there : a little falling short, that is all : hence in his lists of spiritual excellencies that preacher never omits to mention 'temperance,' which to you and me is no achievement, but to him seemed an achievement ; and when he speaks of a weakness of his, 'a thorn in the flesh, a messenger of Satan,' this seems to mean a liking for wine, for you know how, dropping down on a road, he saw two suns—a light in the sky other than the sun ; also he had that notion which topers acquire that wine is a medicine—'take a *leetle* wine for your stomach's good' he hints as with a leer of complicity, as a toper once said to me 'but for brandy I should have been dead years ago'—toper's superstition!"

"But surely, Makla," Netta said with an underlook, "a saint who drinks is a grotesqueness."

And Harry Ransom, who was bent over Greta, threw behind him "Try reading it again, Pascal!"

And the Rev. Mr. Darrel sharply: "Apostles are not topers, Sir!"

And Sir Thomas Ormsby sardonically: "Believe the statements you hear, Mons. Pascal!"

And Pascal, all astonished: "But are not facts facts? Times change, and our notions change with them. Will you not say that the founder of Christianity was a saint, Netta? and was not he commonly upbraided by puritans for being a drinker? Is he not said to have changed a quantity of water into wine for men already 'well drunken' to drink? So it stands written—facts are facts: why should I read it again, my good Ransom, if I have already read it with attention, and if there is no ambiguity in the phrases used? And, after all, what is it to get drunk? Really, one cannot *get* drunk, one being already drunk before one drinks, since to live is to see, and to see is illusion. One of the English dramatists when going to tea-parties takes in his waistcoat a pinch of cocoa, which, on pouring water upon it, he drinks, then to the others who have drunk tea he says 'Now you are all drunk'—imagining perhaps that he has uttered something sage, but he has uttered something shallow: for they were as drunk in one mood before drinking tea as in another mood after, as drunk as he was before drinking cocoa, and after. A life must see the universe in some mood, through eyes of some kind of hue ; but the universe itself is absolute, not of any mood ; the moon is no more of the mood and emotion with which the poet views her than of the mood in which the broker, the opium-smoker, the whiskey-drinker, views her, each view being an illusion, a different mood of drunkenness—meaning by 'drunkenness' any mental state due to the circumstances of the moment, due to having drunk brandy, or due to not having drunk brandy : and every mental state is such. One who has drunk deep will sometimes say to a 'sober' companion 'Oh, you *are* drunk, old man,' while the 'sober' will consider that it is the drinker who is drunk : which is right ? Both are equally right here : for though, in general, the conclusions of the 'sober' are truer than the conclusions of the drinker, a mental state of intelligence is no less due to the circumstances of the moment than any other state : most men must be 'sober' to be intelligent, others require to be tight with wine that their intelligence may be at its brightest. If the poet views the moon with a 'God-drunken' emotion, but the broker with no emotion, this broker 'level-headedness' is *his* eye-queerness, the fantasy of *his* dream, *his* mood of drunkenness, which would undergo modification if he was feverish, was sleepy, was a goat, an eagle, a Martian, an archangel, if he was under cocaine, under champagne, under soda-water —or under 'floating-island,' as Mr. Darrel was when visited with qualms of the stomach on Monday. The reverend gentleman will admit that he was in one of the states of drunkenness then, and it needs little perception, I think, to perceive that he was as drunken previously, and since."

"But *will* Mr. Darrel admit——?" Sir Thomas Ormsby began to say, but now the discussion was broken into by the brisk wrist-business of Bristow, the trickster, who, standing at a table at the arbour's sea-brink, proceeded to bring forth out of emptiness ribbons, flowers, by that same dower of trickery and victory that out of the void of Being brought forth those radio voices.

CHAPTER IX

THE VENETIAN DAY

On that bright Friday which was Mons. Makla Pascal's day a breeze was blowing fresh when, about noon, they were bringing the invalid's stretcher into the arbour, and Sir Thomas Ormsby, walking alongside her, was watching the harbour-waters all choppy that morning, millions of little billows jigging, tickled to " numberless giggling," as by the gusts' and the sun's tickling, all the gilt sea wriggling like Sirius with vigorousness, when all at once Harry Ransom, stepping by the stretcher, called out " Oh, look ! she has smiled ! "

" Harry ! " leapt from Netta.

And from Sir Thomas: " My good fellow! Are you sure ? "

" Well, I wouldn't swear "—from Ransom—" but her lips certainly stirred."

Sir Thomas bent close over ; then : " Stay, I have it : it is the wind—loosened those few hairs, moved them over her epidermis with a tickling effect—the 'smile' a reflex : that was it. We might try that on artificially——"

But when this was experimented with, no reflex came—the wind may have tickled with a friskiness more exquisite in skill than fingers ; and that gay wind soon lulled, before the eleven began to gather, so that now the waves lay quieted to a waste of wine,

" wine-dark," *oinopos*, every hour now fresh wines and changes of taste, fancy after fancy, dyes of Tyre, violets, lilacs, which half-mixed their porphyrines in patches with the vat of waters, dyeing them : at which the eyelids lower with love. And when Rubenstein's staccato study drew to an end, into the mixed bruit of tongues that prattled broke out of Utopia the announcement, " This is the national programme from London " . . . " And now for Mr. Stephen Duke, the historical novelist's, tale 'A Night in Venice' " . . . " Mr. Duke " . . . who now addressed himself, invisible to invisible in Limbo-land, as one among the dead may address a numberless assembly met in realms of the dead, they wondering " Is he anywhere ? ", he wondering " Are they anywhere ? ", while he related this tale :

To Brand, making the grand tour, the bustling world was a keen interest ; his eyes were brisk ; his way of dashing back his hair characteristic of him : but Woman, somehow, had engaged little of his interest, until, one third day of Carnival, he saw a chin between the draperies of a gondola-cabin : and this he followed.

Venice, the mysterious ! By Giovedi Grasso (Shrove Thursday) he had already brushed the lips above that chin, and was told that he did it in peril of his life. That was a great carnival night—revelry gone crazy—he at eleven being at the old Procurazie Palace, where a municipal masque was dancing mad, By twelve he had left the roulette-room, had crept down a stair, and in a dim corridor found himself alone—with her.

Her bosom heaved, her eyes looking two black

moonlights behind her maschera. . . . " Listen ! I was *foolish*, you see ! These tassels may be ears——"

To him it was so incredible, that he only smiled, admiring the dash and curve of her, as she stood with one slipper advanced, the other hip supporting her palm, her figure clasped in a trainless skirt of canary silk, a " tabura " (black mantilla) drooping from her head.

" But, Beatrice, why agitate yourself ? "—with a tenderness new to his voice. " What I say is this : here am I summoned back to England—will you let me go alone ? If you are beset with dangers——"

" But not to *me*—Harold "—her fan touched his arm. " He dare not hurt me, you see. But you ! You cannot guess the number of Mauro Bellini's emissaries——"

" Dear love ! What emissaries ? "

She whispered : " Members of *The Banda* . . . Is it not the design of his life to revive the old majesty of the Doges ? enthrone himself in the Ducal chair ? Hence *the League* ! He knows that I know of it, and secretly fears me—guesses that I, too, have friends, servants—I ! But he will not be lightly balked in his life-work by our love—Harold."

" But I have no desire to balk this old gentleman in anything whatever ! Personally——"

" It is a question of money, you *see*. You know that my wealth is much ? No, you did not know ; it is for myself only—*good* you are. But it is in his hands—dear—till I marry ; and he will destroy a thousand lovers, as he can—Look there, that tapestry stirring ! At One, meet me—Santa Maria della Salute—under the arch——"

Now, in fact, a tapestry parted not far off, and Beatrice started away from Brand, as a gallant, very smartly garbed, strolled up, to bow profoundly to Beatrice, as he passed ; on which she held up a finger to Brand, her lips shaped to "One," and walked after the stranger out of the corridor.

When Brand again went up to the halls the throng had formed a lane of bent heads, down which was pacing an old man, gorgeous in cramoisy velvet, the blaze of candlelight lighting up his network of wrinkles, his lips inclining inward to a crevice ; but on that bald brow of Mauro Bellini sat power—some grand priest he seemed rather than a civil dignitary. With eyes that dwelt on the ground, with sideward under-looks, he stepped ; but at one point of his progress his head deliberately turned to direct a gaze on Brand's face, conspicuous there by its rosiness—a gaze which Brand, surprised, returned with a frown of the coolest insolence, and eyes that measured the great man's length.

Then, impatient for the rendezvous at One, Brand loitered through the rooms ; but before the stroke of One two men were lurking behind a buttress of Santa Maria della Salute—one of them a black, a squat ox, called Ali, the other Manfredi, the signore of the profound bow in the corridor where Beatrice and Brand had been spied upon : for, low-voiced as had been her making of the rendezvous, ears had been near ; and she, having reason soon after to believe that the rendezvous had been heard, had returned to the corridor, looking in agonized concern for Brand ; but he was gone ; and, despairing of finding him quickly in all that swarming of the halls, she had darted out into the piazza, reached the Merceria, and, turning into a lane, uttered a kind of yodel : whereupon a door opened, and, within, a tall old woman, with dishevelled hair, stood shading a lamp, a diamond, in contrast with her poverty, glittering on her finger—a gift of Beatrice ; and now Beatrice's breath : "Brescia, quick ! I told the Englishman to meet me at Santa Maria at One, and, I think, was overheard by Manfredi : something brewing this night, some plot—Be there before the Inglese—warn him away—force him away—keep sharp *eyes*, will you ? Mauro Bellini has looked at me queerly this night. And, Brescia, at Two be back with news : I shall be here."

Upon which Brescia covered her head with her skirt behind, took up a stick, and was off with rather a hobble of the right hip through mazes of *calli*, many little bridges, northward to the Rialto, and now westward, southward ; and ever, as she went with stick and hobble in a rhythm, she was muttering to herself, uttering often that name "Mauro Bellini."

On reaching Santa Maria just before One, she lurked in the deep dark of the church-portal, awaiting Brand.

But, as she had come, the black Ali, had run to Manfredi behind a buttress of the church to whisper "He's come ! "

"Saw him, did you ? "

"Yes, Signore, saw a figure go under the middle portal."

"It isn't the signorina ? "

"No, Signore, the Inglese : heard his stick , figure too big for the signorina."

Now Manfredi, dagger in hand, glided out ; in some moments his cloaked stalk was doubling round the corner of the deeply recessed portal ; and, conscious of the deeper black of a form in there, he struck, half a cry starting up in the instant before he struck. In the instant after, a sound of feet tripping near reached his ear, upon which he dashed off to his gondola at the quay-corner, plunged in, and at once Ali was at the oar.

Those tripping feet were Brand's, arrived a minute late, and he came prying to see Beatrice, peering into the portal's recess ; seeing something, nothing ; hearing, however, a moan ; and now he tumbled upon his hands over Brascia, as " What the mischief ? " came from him ; then he half lifted the body toward the porch-pillars—no moon, but the vault all a swarm of stars, which just showed the wound ; while, hanging heavily upon him, the old woman groaned brokenly " Mauro Bellini did it—hurt my life—a girl—then shut me in the cells ; I meant to get even with him—God give my spirit power—Oh ! "

Brand said " Dead, I think " ; and at the same time that he noticed his palms all red noticed, too, a measured tread coming, echoing footfalls of a squad of six of the City *sbirri* (police) ; whereupon the probability of a night in the cells, anyway of a visit to them that would cause him to miss Beatrice, brought from him a " No, thank you " ; and, depositing the body, he took to running.

Half laughing—at first ; after one minute not laughing : for he had run too late, the *sbirri* having already caught sight of the body ; and, as those narrow *calli*, slab-paved, have an echo which guides a pursuer, they tracked him close, while Brand's heels went flying through an intricacy of twists and twines, over little bridges, in a rage to be free ; but his pursuers, intimate with the maze, were quite his equals—one was winning upon him.

At last, hearing the foot-beats near round a corner, he sprang down three steps into a patch of deepest shadow, and, seizing a ring in a quay-wall, let himself into the water to his neck ; whereupon one of the *sbirri*, rushing down to the water-side, halted astonished, then trotted to and fro, looking for him.

And not less interested in him than they at that moment was Mauro Bellini, walking alone in an oval apartment, all columns, statuary, mirrors, his hands behind him, his ample sleeves ending tight at the wrist in the fine lace named "merletu" ; till presently there entered one of five who waited outside behind the hangings of five doors : and now the quiet walking ceased, while the rheumy eyes moved over the note that the man had brought : "The affair of Brand is ended. He lies for the present where you know. Manfredi."

"Where is the Lady Beatrice ?"—in a voice deep and strong, contrasting with the senility of his hollow cheeks.

"The lady is not in the palace, Eccellenza."

"I know. Where is she ?"

"I cannot tell you, Eccellenza."

"Send me Dandolo."

He resumed his walk, till Dandolo, a big swaggerer in a velvet jacket, one-armed, stood before him.

"Who knows the whereabouts of the Signorina Beatrice ?" he demands.

"Orseolo, Ronaldo, and Marco, Vostra Signoria."

"Where is she?"

"I cannot tell you. Ronaldo should be here when there is anything to report."

"Send me Antonello."

He resumed his walk, till Antonello, a waterman, timid, diminutive, stood before him; whereupon he paced to a table which beamed like a mirror beneath the dreary vigil of a chandelier, and there, selecting one sheet from a heap of official sheets, he held it up to read through a magnifying glass.

"It appears, Antonello"—speaking with a strong distinctness—"that a pauper lunatic at the Asylum of San Giorgio has lately died."

Antonello ducked nervously.

"I see from this schedule that a relative has been persuaded to undertake the burial, the Asylum providing, as usual, a coffin; and the lunatic's number is L. 385. Say L. 3, 8, 5."

"L, 3, 8, 5"—with a duck of one dodging a blow at the nape.

"Very good. Is there now at the water-gate a swift gondola waiting?"

"One, Eccellenza—that of the Signorina Beatrice."

"Take that; and take with you this signed mandamus for the delivery of the body of No. L. 3, 8, 5. You will obtain his relative's address at the Asylum, and to that address you will convey the coffin."

Antonello began to retire.

"Stay! I happen to know, Antonello, that you are a fellow capable of driving a neat nail. Take, then, with you some nails, a hammer, a screw-driver, also some lead or stones, with some string; and, when in the middle of the Giudecca, you will unscrew the lid of the coffin given you, you will attach the weights to the body, and you will consign it to the waters. I think you comprehend me."

"Right, Eccellenza!"

"I may as well tell you something of my reason, Antonello"—with a toss of the hand: "a poor youth has been killed in a quarrel, and it is to the interests of *The Banda* that his body be secreted. If cast into the canal, there is a chance that it may some day confront us, bearing its wound; whereas, in the case of No. L. 3, 8, 5, the body of such as he, recovered from the water, would be unknown. I propose, then, that we have the slain youth buried according to ordinary forms in the coffin of L. 3, 8, 5. You will, therefore, lay the youth's body, which you will find at the façade of Santa Maria della Salute, in the lunatic's coffin; *nail* the lid; then convey it to the relative undertaking burial. A man of his class will little desire, I think, to look upon the face of the lunatic; and, even so, your nails will have put the gratification of such an inclination beyond his convenience. Be sure, then, Antonello, and swift."

Within ten minutes Antonello was hastening toward the islet of San Giorgio; within thirty, on the Giudecca, he had drawn the body from its shell, an oblong box, not coffin-shaped, such as are still used in southern Italy, Sicily; and he stood in the lampless cabin staring at it.

"Body of the Madonna," he whispered, "he is blacker than an ebon Christ!"

And now a thought tickled him. " It is that camel (cammello) of an Ali's father ! He did, I think, have a father in the asylum, the black ! Well, but, then, the house I am going to must be his Excellency's Red Palace ! "

He struck steel to flint, looked at the slip received at the asylum-gate, and on it, in truth, was the name of Ali, the address of the Red Palace—one of the three palazzi of the Bellini, Byzantine-Gothic, which had long stood empty, gloomy, save that in it Ali and some few of Bellini's henchmen now had their quarters.

And presently the weighted body rolled over to disappear into the deep, sending up a belch of phosphorescences. In some minutes more Antonello was bending over Brescia.

" But is this the ' poor youth '," he said in wonder, " that his Excellency spoke of ? Or was that his Excellency's deep way of speaking merely ? Yes ! he's deep ! "—a finger tapped his knowing nut—" does not blab every meaning as a marketman does ; one must put together his hints, and obey ! "

As he bore the body to the gondola, a glitter of the diamond on its finger caught his eyes, widened them ; and they were wider still in the throes of temptation to take the diamond when he placed the dead in the shell—an eye of him ogling at the abandoned gondola of the *sbirri*, just astern, with the Cross of San Marco on its prow. He thought it an ill omen to see a sbirri-boat just then, and crossed himself. Just in front of him, too, behind a corner, lay Brand's abandoned gondola.

At this time Brand was again in flight. One of the *sbirri* had stood over him at the water-side, but, failing to discern his head, had spurted further; then Brand had continued to cling to the ring, until a shivering had seized him; then, drawing himself out of the water, had started back toward Santa Maria, on the chance of even now meeting Beatrice.

But when near Santa Maria, in crossing an open quay, where he recognized his gondola, again pretty close behind him he heard a hushed call: "Come! here he is!"—the *sbirri*, who, too, were returning to their boat; whereupon Brand ran madly to spring upon his deck, to whisper his barcaiuoli to fly for life, then to plunge into his cabin amidships. But as his boat moved out, he could see the *sbirri* furiously oaring after him; and, hardly ten yards ahead, Antonello's boat.

At that moment Antonello, bending over the coffin, with one blind drawn up, had nail and hammer in hand, when the temptation of the diamond again overcame him. The little man hesitated—believed in the omniscience of his Excellency, and since the diamond had formed no part of his instructions, the little rat-eyes blinked quick, he thinking of it, slowly meantime sliding the lid footward; and all at once found himself in the act of taking.

But he hardly had the diamond when he was aware of the two boats behind—of a sbirri-boat racing, chasing—ominous stuff—chasing the middle boat? or chasing *him*?

And just then, his boat passing under a lamp, Brand, now close behind him, recognized, as he pried forth, the luxurious gondola of Beatrice, its liveried cabin of black and gold: on which his heart leapt at the probability that she was within it, going away from the rendezvous at Santa Maria; and it leapt, too, at the prospect that, if he could secretly board her, that would mean safety for himself; so he crept out to his men, pressing them to overtake quickly the boat in front, a double prickly-heat of haste within him at the peril behind, at the hope before; while Antonello, too, guilty, aghast, darted, bent down, forward, begging his gondoliers to get her going in his Excellency's name; whereat the three slim skiffs went skimming like swifts athwart the fretted water.

Venice, the mute! The Canalazzo's lonesomeness seemed to reach to the zodiac, its hush unbroken, save when the boats' wakes waved away to their lazy slap against some old palace, or when at a corner some gondolier gave warning of his coming in their wawling way; and, far yonder in the dark, a gondola-lamp might dart like a meteor and disappear.

The foremost of the three boats had gone winding like a thing of life into an intricacy of canals absolutely black, except where some corner-lamp caused rivulets and lizards of crimson to wobble upon the water's ink; near one of which lamps Brand, who had been crouching ready at his prow, sprang soft upon the poop before him, just as the little Antonello, in a flurry of apprehension, had the dead hand in his to restore the ring to its finger; and, at the little concussion of Brand's spring, the guilty fellow, dropping the hand, was gone through the cabin window into the canal, feeling that either the *sbirri* or the fiends were at him.

And so featly and easily did he slip away, that his gondolieri, both for'ard, rowing erect with their backs to him, had no suspicion that he was gone, as they had none of Brand's entrance, hidden as it was by the hearse-shape of the cabin from them, they supposing the concussion of his jump due to some moving of the coffin by Antonello ; but Brand's own men, watching for his jump, stopped, and were overtaken by the *sbirri*.

Brand, meantime, had slipped into Beatrice's cabin, more sanguine of seeing her than he had good reason to be, and saw instead—Brescia ; recognized her, on bending close : that body again confronting him, as if he was, in truth, her murderer. And in Beatrice's boat. . . . This rather horrified him, the idea that she might be mixed up ever so little in the dark deeds of her uncle.

Little time, however, was given him for thinking : the boat was then running past a brown old house, without any opening in its frontage, save one row of round windows up under the roof ; round a corner of which the gondola shot ; stopped at a portal ; and now Brand, springing up, found himself confronted with three men at the portal, and with the two gondolieri, who had come to the cabin to help Antonello with the coffin.

And one of these two, when they had stared in amaze at him, raised the cry, " Why, he is a foreigner —Has he killed the little Antonello ? See there, the gore on him ! "

" Oh, go along——" Brand began, but stopped, seeing a *galante*, whom he recognized, appear at the doorway—Manfredi, who, even as he started at this apparition of Brand, still living, bowed, saying " Does she (i.e., Brand's signorship) enter ? "

" No, thank you "—from Brand ; and now at

once Manfredi whispered the others near him, who instantly rushed to drag Brand to the landing-steps ; whereupon Brand's British fists went flying ; but by the time the scuffle had reached the doorway he was on his face, and was being dragged to a near apartment, where he was left behind a locked door.

The two gondolieri, meantime, had gone into the cabin to take up the coffin, which Brand had covered with its lid ; and, knowing from Antonello that it was for Ali, they stumbled with it up to Ali's quarters, a room near the palace-top, so dark, that though the lid had slipped a little in the ascent, they did not see the dead face, nor see that they deposited the coffin partly on a mattress that lay on the floor by the door : tossing the bore of it off them, they were gone.

As they re-entered the gondola, Manfredi handed them a note ; and at half-past two Mauro Bellini, still pacing, stopped to read this note : Brand was alive, but in his power at the Red Palace ; and Manfredi awaited instructions in these new circumstances.

At which the old face flushed with anger. " These bunglers ! " he muttered ; and, after twice pacing the chamber, thinking, he scribbled " The Torture of Fear till four ; then I will myself come to the Red Palace."

Half-past two ! And Beatrice, pale as death, waited within Brescia's door, palm on supple hip, watching.

" She does not *come*," she said. Then, all sudden energy, she was running, till at a dark water-side she stepped into a hired gondola for Santa Maria. There in the porch she saw blood—Brescia's ? his ?

She leaned there, faint ; then, with her forward, high-heeled walk, went back to her boat, flew to Brand's hotel. Not there ! "I have to *find* him ! " she said.

She stood later in a squalid apartment, a hump-backed man before her, saying " You must *find* him, Paolo—you have *wit* enough, I should think. He is either dead or in great *danger*, you see. . . . Send out all my friends and yours, let them search, search. I am going to the Palazzo Calvo—send everyone to me with news."

In twenty minutes twenty men were dissecting Venice for Brand. . . .

But the Torture of Fear—that ordeal awaited Brand, who, seeing resistance useless, permitted his arms to be tied together behind him, and walked, as bidden, with perfect contempt, before three men, one of whom bore a tin lamp, from his prison to an upper floor.

There he was locked into a large round chamber, after the three had paused over Brescia's white face, and scratched their puzzled heads, and gone laughing, leaving on the thickness of a round window-sill the little lamp, which just revealed walls that seemed of tarnished old copper—it had been a torture-chamber of the Inquisition—and three old boots on the floor, some wine-flasks, the mattress by the door—nothing else ; and half over the mattress, once more, Brescia : she was his fate, she chased him, and got from him a look of reproach : for the coffin-end was angry with the tangle of her grey hair ; and, pushing the lid with his leg, he once more covered her. . . .

As he turned from her, he heard a clack somewhere, saw a part of the flooring disappear, and his heart started. . . .

At that hour Beatrice at the Palazzo Calvo was receiving messenger after messenger, announcing the failure of their search for him.

By half-past three she was hastening from the Calvo to the Bellini Palace, having another gondola with hers containing seven men with weapons; and from a Bellini Palace ante-room she sent in a request to see Mauro Bellini.

On which the old man summoned Dandolo, almost ran to whisper him something; then, bidding him admit the signorina, sat at a table.

To which table she in her amber dress, still masked, walked with her brisk step, placed one palm upon it, placed the other upon her waist, and said "Mauro Bellini—the Englishman, Brand!"

Those tumble-down eyes of Bellini looked up with a mild fatherliness at her.

"Am I to take this as an open defiance, then?" he asked.

"As you like."

"It is the first time, Beatrice."

"Is there not *cause*?"

"You most not suppose, my child, that you can defy me with impunity."

"You think I *care?* The Englishman, Brand—tell me where he is, or by to-morrow, sunset, everyone of the Ghibillini leaders knows of *The Banda!*"

"I fancy three of them know already. That is a vain threat, my child. But I will tell you, if you like."

"I *like*, of course."

"You may regret it, if I tell you."

" You fancy I *care*, Uncle ? There is not a thing in this whole world I care for but him. So you *know* now. I will ruin you, and Venice, and I care not what, if you dare harm him. Tell me, will you, where he is ? "—her table hand shifted to her hip, and her hip hand to the table.

" I will tell you ; but I think that you will regret it."

" You are not *trifling* with me, surely ? *Let* me regret it."

" He is in the chamber of the Torture of Fear at the Palazzo Rosso."

Now her hands met wringing. Then, without a word, she walked away to a door ; but, Bellini having twice struck a bell, she found the door fastened. Three more she found fastened ; the fifth opened upon a corridor leading to Bellini's chamber, from which there was no other egress.

" I am a *prisoner*, then—— ? "

Bellini, reading a document, did not answer ; when he presently walked out to prepare for his visit to the Red Palace, Beatrice had thrown herself, sobbing, upon a couch.

It was now nearly four o'clock—a moment when Brand, for his part, was dancing—had long been dancing : for the flooring contained many small pieces, two and three feet square, and, under these, joists must have been cut away, for these were dropping out of sight, one by one, at irregular intervals, then deliberately rising again—with every drop a clack ; and gradually their movement had grown rapid, incalculable, and the clacking an uproar ; here, then there, then here, in endless change, gaped the sudden patch of blacker in black, Brand now going through the antics of a strange jig, treading upon terror, every nerve stretched to detect the first tendency to yielding beneath his feet, sweat raining over his face ; and frantically he tore at the rope that held his elbows tight behind his back, as he dodged and dashed himself all over the hall, like some solitary mad dancer stung by the tarantula, dancing to a music whose tumult clacked, and lacked all musicalness.

At one point he thought of the coffin—that possibly *it* lay safe on two joists, thought of flying to lie on it ; but when he next had time to dart a glance that way, he saw that it had slipped footward into a patch, and now lay aslant—that dead face, *twice* covered by him, *again* uncovered ; and all through the rest of his dance he had a sort of consciousness of her there, watching it, half sitting up.

For the patch into which the coffin-foot had dipped did not fill up again like the others, the droppings being worked by hand—by the withdrawal of pins that passed through tubes and through rods within the tubes—and the hand did not trouble to relift the coffin's weight.

But the danger to life was hardly real, the lower floor being only ten feet lower—(though the victims of this " torture of fear " never knew this) : so it is probable that Mauro Bellini had now decided that it would be better not to kill Brand, but to rack him with terrors, to have him ready to consent to quit Venice instantly.

It was now a little past four, and Beatrice, who did not long lie sobbing, lifted her eyes, saw that her uncle had left the room, stood up, commenced to pace : and " Can I do nothing ? " she asked herself:

"am I a ninny, *born* like that?" Suddenly she stood still—had noticed Bellini's discarded red robe on a chair, his four-cornered biretta; and now, darting to the table for a pair of scissors, she clipped off the fringe of an antimacassar; then cast away her mask; and with swift art at a mirror arranged the white fringe round her hair under Bellini's cap; then arrayed herself in his robe; touched a bell; and retired to the remotest shades of the chamber.

When someone entered she, with her head half-turned, said carelessly in the very voice of Bellini "The signorina has retired to my chamber; you may now undo the doors, Dandolo."

In a minute she was flying through the palace toward the water-gate; in a minute Bellini, returning ready for the Red Palace, had discovered her ruse, and with a stamp of his foot bade five men follow him. As the clocks of Venice chimed a quarter-past four, the three gondolas—Beatrice's first, her seven next, Bellini in urgent wrath behind—went churning in wildest chase over the whitening Canalazzo.

And presently Brand, lying spent near the circumference of the room farthest from the door, the torture of the droppings now over, heard a footstep without, and sat up alert, as a key turned; then someone entered, lurched, tottered on the edge of the opening in the floor, just rescued himself, and stood staring in stupid amaze at the hole, grumbling "What's all this?"

Brand could dimly see a great curly head, a black face—Ali, returned to bed from the trattoria, drunk, swaying on his bow-legs, his eyes straining to be open.

And soon, noticing the coffin tilted there, with its lid slipped, half over his mattress, "Hello," he grumbled, "are you (tu) my cursed father? That's all right!"

Then, after sage reflection, with a pointed finger: "But *you* are not my cursed father! Do they turn so pale, then?—with long hair——?"

He went a step nearer to gaze and meditate on it, his arms akimbo; and, standing so, he commenced to shake with merriment. . . .

"Ho! Poor boy's gone white. Is *that* the way they do, then——?"

Suddenly, though, he was grave; then gradually angry.

"Now, look you," he said to Brescia, "I want no fathers here; besides, *you* are not my cursed father."

And in a minute more, grinning murderously, his under-jaw projecting beyond his upper-lip, bull-dog like, "Here, get out of this, you!" he cried; "where do you reckon I am to sleep?"

Now he stooped, got his great arms round the coffin, and, staggering, with "Out, I tell you——", managed to get to a window, where coffin and Brescia shot crashing through the glass.

Ten seconds more, and Beatrice bounded in, gazing wildly round, sighted Brand, pounced upon him, dragged him out.

"Quick! Ah! so *weak*? He will be here instantly, meaning nothing but death, I think!"

Out in the corridors they could hear sounds, echoes of shoutings, of feet hurrying about the palace; and she: "They are after us—you *hear*? Oh! for God's sake, try——"

As fast as he could he ran by her side, breathless, still with bound arms, through a number of dark halls, down stairs, she seeming to know the place well ; but in one passage they heard a tramp of feet in front of them, and she stopped, baffled, turned back, ran down a side-corridor, another, lost her way : and the footsteps seemed to follow. " In here, then ! " she panted, and they slipped into a room, which, though she did not know it in the dark, was the State bed-chamber. As the footsteps still approached, she sprang to the door, bolted it ; and, as the steps stopped outside the door, " I will *die* with you ! " she whispered.

Someone on the outside tried the handle—there seemed to follow a consultation—then shoulders were pressing at the door ; then blow on blow from crowbars rained on it, till it cracked, flew inward ; and Brand and Beatrice stood at bay in a room now full of lamplight.

But the throng of men, their faces very grave, scarcely looked at them.

" Lay him on the bed," Manfredi said; and three men shuffled toward the bed, bearing a body, whose skull had been crushed—Mauro Bellini, brought to this by Brescia, whose coffin had crashed upon him, as he had passed in chase under the palace windows. . . .

Beatrice's face lay buried on Brand's breast, till he said " Come " ; and presently, as they glided together from the Red Palace, dawn was all in the sky and on the waters.

This story told, a discussion ensued of the question whether it can have happened, within the general discussion being a special between the artists, Paul Watts and Gerald Jewson, as to the artistry of the author, Watts saying "I think it good tragedy," and Jewson, "I don't call it tragedy: calamity is not tragedy; tragedy is calamity pitiably brought upon one by one's own fault, by the mode of one's own constitution."

"Quite so," Watts said, "as here. It was the dead woman, Brescia, who was the undoing of the old fellow, she whom his youthful debauchery had wronged, whose death now was caused by his ambition and pitiless politics: all his ruin brought upon him by his own fault."

And Jewson: "Yes, yes, that's so: but in real tragedy it must be the hero who is the faulty one, he mustn't be a rascal, but a faulty good man struggling in vain in the grip of Fate. Tragedy has no 'villain,' or it has ever the same 'villain'—Fate: Fate persistently using the idiosyncrasy of the hero's disposition to undo him, and so evoking that pang of 'pity' which is the characteristic of tragedy: *Othello*, then, is not tragedy—no Iago in tragedy; *Macbeth* is not tragedy—hero mustn't be a criminal; *Hamlet* is, *Romeo and Juliet*, *Mayor of Casterbridge*. Tragedy is difficult to do: *Ghosts* for example, is far from being tragedy, the undoing there being brought on by someone else's fault."

To this Watts answered: "Yes, I agree, but not as to Macbeth: the one crime that he committed was itself due to Fate, to the incitement of the witches: the reader forgives and pities. And the crimes of this old man of the tale were due to the Fate of his environment; so I call it tragedy, and 'good,' because it ends happily, as I think that every tragedy should, after the tragedy—like *Romeo and Juliet*, say—if it is to be true to Life, whose history is a series of happy endings. But the tale, if good, is not best, its tragic suggestion not rich in effect : if the author had been more knowing, the old boy would have been *warned* not to follow his nose, not to start out on that last voyage of his, and he would have paused, forefeeling, hearing a whisper of Fate within, but still persisting——" But now Netta, leaving off speaking with Whipsnade Prince at the cliff-brink, came saying, " Now, Paul of the chalks," whereupon Watts, who that afternoon had to draw caricatures of all in the arbour, sprang up to his easel, to cast the party into fits of laughter with that ease and rapid wrist of his practised hand.

CHAPTER X

THE FUTURE DAY

On the Saturday, Whipsnade Prince's day, an added sense of tension in everyone was manifested, he himself entering the arbour with perhaps half-a-shade of pallor showing about the nose and under-lids. In shaking hands, Netta's eyes dwelt steadily some time on him before she said "This, then, is *der Tag*, Mr. Whip : still confident of whipping all competitors ?"

"No, by Jove," Prince answered—"am rather in despair."

"Why the change ?"

"Why, just the name of the tale—'Course of True Love'—doesn't sound wildly impossible : one knows beforehand that it never does run smooth."

She smiled upon him. "But it winds somewhere safe to sea."

"It does ? Thanks for saying that. Thanks !" Then irritably: "But I'm afraid——"

"Well ?"

"I'm rather a sinner, not good enough for you : I lie, I feign, I——"

"Only 'a little,' I think"—eyeing him mildly, with that tiny smile of a mouth that every moment seemed about to tremble under the teeming of some emotion of humour : "and, if we confess our sins, Whip——"

" You dear ! Thanks for that. Thanks ! "

As he was pressingly whispering this, the radio's variations on a theme by Rosenbaum ceased ; but when now everyone took his seat to hear, and now the announcement sounded, " This is the National . . . ", there happened what had never yet happened, for it was not the tale scheduled in the *Radio Times* which was announced, but " Mr. Keith Richards, regarded as the most prophetic of our romanticists, has considered it well to substitute for his tale named ' The Course of True Love ' another tale named ' In 2073 A.D. ' " . . . " Mr. Richards " . . . whose voice now arose out of Nowhere upon the consciousness to recount this story :

My Clarence,

Here is the inner history of the incident as to which your letter pumps me. But it is for ever secret between us. *Remember !*

Linda and I had set out early in the morning from Bakersville, purposing to make some purchases for her mother at New London, then to spend the day with friends at New Brighton. But from the first I observed in her a certain stillness and fixity of the lip.

Now, our Bakersville, you know, is only a mid-Atlantic townlet, that drinks distilled sea-water ; yet it boasts a Hindoo girl, who finds it amusing to be called a *palmiste* : and this girl, Maya, had prophesied that, if I travelled far during the next six days, I should fall, and be killed. It was at my sister, Cicily's ; Linda had been present : so I wondered now, as we flew over the Azores, whether that twittering could have anything to do with her tendency to stillness; and, to test it, I said " Suppose, Linda, we tumble this minute into the sea ? "

" Well, suppose," says she, looking away eastward at Venus waning within prairies of crimson and primrose.

" You and I together—nice," I said : " pity such things don't happen."

" They *may*," she answered with singular gravity, her brow bent over that worm-and-pinion of the tiller—she being captain and crew, I doing nothing but adjust the stove, if it got hot, lying at my length on the deck, my eyes fixed on those lines of Linda's chin and cheeks which deliciously peeped between the chinchilla of her jacket and the chinchilla of her cap.

" How may they happen ? " I asked, puzzled at her that morning.

She looked me suddenly in the face to say "Not ten years ago a whole village dropped to the ground in Hungary, and three people were killed. Remember Maya, the *palmiste's*, prophecy yesterday."

Her eyes twinkled now a little on me, killing me with desire to kiss them. I reached my lips forward to touch that sea-shell sheen of her toe-nail, saying " Maya's ancestry was of the gnats! No such luck to go tumbling in your company. I suppose that in the Hungary case the drop was due to some stoppage of the dynamos at the works——"

"Your supposition hits it! " she cried with laughter in her throat thrown back ; but then bent quickly toward me to ask " But you are not sure, really, Aubrey, to what it must have been due ? "

" No, let me be frank," I answered : " I don't know—I don't care. That's old me ; I can't be made into an engineer. I only care about one mechanism, and that's the divine dynamo that lights your eyes."

This, I could see, scandalized Linda rather seriously; and presently she answered with some offence "And I only care about the children I am to bear."

"But, Linda," I said, "my sisters both say that you and I should have quite nice children!"

At this she looked at me under her eyes, studying me, while a passenger-boat dashed past above us, showering down over us a momentary shout of singing, band music, and that slap of bare feet dancing—lasting so long as when one lifts one's palms from one's ears in some clamour, and claps them back, after having heard a burst of hubbub, like a bung that bursts out.

Then Linda said "Nice children do not depend only upon the beauty and well-being of their parents, Aubrey, but also upon the intensity of electrical resonance between them. I love your sisters; I have a liking for your idle, idle society: hence—perhaps—am here. But I am a child of the twenty-first century, *not* of the tenth, *not* of the twentieth; and, like other people, I more or less despise a girl who yields her maternity to a man not of a scientist type. I was wondering last night—suppose you were cast on a desert island: could you make an air-boat?"

"No, couldn't," I answered. "Forgive! This comes of being born myself. *You* could, of course, Linda, I know——"

"Why, what could prevent one—given fuel, iron-ore, time, and some insulator or other? But this is laughable ! Why should you be different from everybody ? They say you write rhymes ! "

" There's old England," I remarked evasively, chancing to catch sight of low coast at the ocean's edge.

" I saw England two minutes ago," she said ; then, bending to stare quizzingly with wide eyes into my eyes, she added " But about the rhymes ? "

" I may have scribbled some rhymes," I replied : " they were about your chin and toes."

I thought that she might have smiled a little at this : but she bit her lip, and was grave.

" And if your children write rhymes, too ? " she dryly asked.

" Linda, they won't," I answered. " Let's have 'em, Linda, and trust to luck. Even if they do a little, there have been ages, I assure you, when people who wrote rhymes were even highly respected."

" Yes, I know, poor people "—a shadow of pity touched her expression, for Linda, I think, has the tenderest heart in her. She added " I have been looking through a book of the early twentieth century, a kind of make-believe narrative of events—*novel* was the technical name of such books—and, oh, they must have been sad ! not positively sad, I mean, but negatively, in their lack of hilarity—no hozanna apparently, no pang of rapture at this spectacle of heaven : it is not strange if they spent time in writing rhymes, to pretend to themselves that they had the song that they lacked. Pretty grumpy folk : as late as 1960 they still thought it a natural thing to live (without respirators !) down there in the dust of the earth. Why they didn't all die one doesn't know—hereditary immunity, I suppose. But, of course, they never knew what health is—never suspected : when they felt no pain anywhere they considered themselves healthy. Yet they could fly, you know—on a kind of kite, the name of which was *aeroplane*, a kite upheld by an oil-engine, instead of by the tension in a string : but they looked upon the air as a place to make excursions into, then return to earth ; it was always *the earth* that they considered their fated place of residence."

"Funny," I said. "But, then, that is very ancient—ten years ago is ancient now, with such increasing speed does the fashion of the world pass away. Those, look, are some of their works down there."

I had seen a town eastward above us, about which hosts of boats were flitting, the sun being now up ; and now through the choroscope I saw, below the town, wharves and warehouses, docks with ships of steel still sleeping on the sea within them, some walls of a city still standing amid cornfields, and in the cornfields labourers, whose respirator-masks I could detect.

"That's New Southampton, that town there," Linda said, glancing at the chart-frame—"you see the double-pharos, largest in the world, and the——" she stopped to chirp "*sweet*" to a bird which, astray in migrating, had perched atop of the stern-magnet, and was gravely gazing sideward with alternate eyes at her and me.

"Little cheeky !" she went, leaning toward it, her face flung up : "is it free, free, and built for bliss ?"

She then turned to say to me " Birds ! To think that that little one's ancestors were lizards that ran up trees from enemies, and in the end *flew* up ! and now, if you put one of her feathers as a pen to paper, of itself it might write ' Triumph ! ' : for to-day, after their many, many, millennia of pain and effort, they are safe in the millennium of Heaven : we can hear the screaming madrigals of glee and victory with which God has crammed their maw and enchanted the thrush's tongue, and we witness within the winds the levity of their blessed wings, such is the working of the eternal Urger, and the milk of His Kingdom. . . . It is strange that birds did not suggest to earlier men that the air is men's destined dwelling-place, since the sea is evidently for footless things, the land for four-square quadrupeds, the air for bipeds—birds and men ; and did they never run in March-wind and forefeel then in their happiness the passion of worship which this world reserved for her children of the wind ? "

Linda seemed to be forgetting a little now whatever it was that had kept her taciturn, and I loved the noise of her voice in the air, raised to struggle against the hundred tongues of the draught, that wrangled at our irruption's rush with a gabblement of bad language, shaming her face to a rosebud burning out of a bower of furs ; so, though I had little interest in ancient men, I said, to keep her speaking, " Even if they had foreknown, Linda, about living in the air, they'd know little of magnetism——"

" Who didn't ? " she put in : " no, don't be fantastic. So they had no lamps ? No transformers, economy-coils. . . . ? They knew the mathematics of magnetism as we do—almost : knew, for example that magnetism can sustain a city in the air at a cost of one seventh fewer watts than are required to light the city. But they don't seem to have imagined that this marvellous minister of man was of much use *in itself* : whenever they used it, as in their generators, meters, it was for the sake of electricity, their only direct use of magnetism being for such little things as trembling-bells, relays, indicators, carrying plates in machine-shops !—just think."

"Perhaps they didn't know how to make vacuums," I said.

"Who? Oh, Aubrey, you *are* ignorant!"—with a laugh, and an underlook of reproach that was not without some fondness and indulgence, I thought: "fancy twentieth-century men not knowing—then, how did they make X-rays, glow-lamps—? Aubrey, you *are*——"

As she spoke, the air about us had become populous with boats of all sorts, we now passing over fields of corn, sheep and oxen, old cathedrals, museums: so I now said to Linda "Well, I suppose I am very ignorant; but here we are at New London, and"—I drew nearer her foot—"to speak of our more pressing selves——"

At once I could see her expression change to gravity again; but I went on to say "You know, Linda, that I am looking forward to a happy day, and who says 'Yes' betimes says 'Yes' twice. Bless me before we enter New London, and I'll give you a kiss."

Her answer was: "Kissing rhymes with missing; and mess, as well as bless, with yes. You who make rhymes should know."

"I am done with rhyme for all time!" I cried,

rhyming : " I'll go in for high atomic science, and become the model of a father of engineers."

" One must *be*," says she : " for though a father of engineers need not—perhaps—be himself an engineer, he must have the stamina of a Man—be innately efficient, strong-brained, strong-breasted, ready and steady at the threat of death——"

" 'Pon my soul, Linda," I said, with a laugh, " I believe I am something of all that."

" Are you ? " says she. " You *may* be—underneath somewhere. I hope you are."

" Believe that I am, and answer now ! "

She held her face to the gale, gazing skyward, smiling ; then, very low : " Not now. Some time—perhaps to-day."

We could now hear going on, like trembling-bells rattling, that so-called " chattering " of vacuum-covers in their stuffing-boxes rattling the " multiplyers " at the magnet-ends, which " chattering " grows to a species of little roaring in the neighbourhood of great cities. In another second Linda had knocked a hundred knots off our speed, and we were running through a suburb named Bayswater.

Early as the hour was, it was a most alert and teeming scene that we had burst into, for, though that street must be three hundred metres broad, both it and the intervals between the buildings were brisk and buzzing with a rushing of boats, which brushed each other, a huge rumour of music and brabbling of draughts pervading the air—the host of cables overhead, by their echoing, adding to the whole a tone of the harp.

Moreover, in this town each class of Council-hawker announces itself by sounds of music in a conventional way : those who sell milk or *yaghourt* sing out a yodelling, the newsvendor uses a flute, the fruit-vendor blows a bugle, as they draw up at the mansions, which here are built on platforms of cedar, have verandahs, and are mainly frames, with over-sailing verge-roofs to take the rain, like bungalows : we could see people at table, ladies doing their hair, fingers, toes, they are so public here. These London erections strike one as quite elegant, their pillars elaborate, in etched steel or ebony, each magnet gay with statuary, many of the dwellings having gardens, or "vulcanea," as they call them, the marl being covered with vulcaneum, like our own Bakersville park —a perforated rubber, with little cones within the perforations, to prevent the rising of dust containing the microbes of nitrification and putrefaction.

But these people, I think, are hardly very well-bred. Several times I had to breathe to Linda "Take care ! ", for each one seems to fly harum-scarum about, as if there was no one in the air but himself, so that I wondered that there are not some accidents—in fact, I actually saw an omnibus bump upon a barge's poop ; but nobody took much notice.

Linda boarded the boat of a boy to enquire the way to a Council-store called "Whiteley's," for we both chanced to know more of New Peking than of New London, which is a huge place, occupying, they say, an area of some sixteen hundred square kilometres ; and this boy, who lay on his face playing a fife in an environment of potatoes, instead of replying, held up a little pink foot—to bid us wait, I suppose, until he had finished a phrase of his hymn. This put Linda to pushing up her lips into a pettish temptation of the flesh, and to steering the boat toward a traffic-officer, who sat with his feet hung over his boat's beam, drawing conics : so she called to him "Tell us, will you, the way to Whiteley's," and—there was no reply ! There he sat abstracted over his curves, as if alone in the world. Such is London.

When he at last consented to direct us, we passed onward by a park called, I was informed, High Park, a vast place, in which we saw a brigade running at morning-drill, the men naked to the waist, the ladies in a merino flimsy—a crowd of thousands, and the pat, pat, of their soles tapping on vulcaneum reached our ears before we could see them through shrubbery : then we saw the mass of them darting out and drawing back their arms in a rhythmic mood to their band-music, some of them so drunk and ruddy with hilarity, that they ran with their throats thrown quite back, like Bacchants, laughing and clamouring their thanks to the skies.

In this High Park is also a lake or length of water, with diving-platforms along it, and we saw throngs of men and ladies taking headers into the lake, which at that height and time must be icy, these diving-platforms standing among a procession of great magnets which resemble triumphal arches, every one having statuary at its summit—the London magnets being wound with four bobbins, two opposing the other two at break, so that there is never any sparking at break, since there is no real break. Our Bakersville magnets have breaks, and only two bobbins, but with a system of condensers to take the break, the largest being excited by alternating current at a frequency of 120—so the gossips say : I know little of it.

From the park it was not far to Whiteley's—a great place, with a disembarking-quay hundreds of metres long. There Linda left me amid a host of boats, saying "fifteen minutes," and vanished into the shop. On which I, seeing wireless near within, fastened the boat, and went to ask my sister, Thea, at Bakersville, how she did, for seven days before this she had given birth to a son.

She answered that she was well ; then she put to me this question: "You haven't had any accident ?"

"*Accident?*" I said. "What, Thea, makes you put to me so *outré* a query ?"

Her answer was : "I thought I would ask."

"But you must have some *reason* !" I insisted. "Be good enough, Thea, to tell me what it is."

"It is nothing," she answered with some abashment. "In any case, be brave ! be brave ! . . . Good-bye——"

Before I could say more she shut me off, leaving me astonished. I supposed that she must have heard from my sister, Cicily, what the *palmiste* girl had prophesied me ; but it was incomprehensible to me that that babble should have attracted all this attention !

I then went back to the boat, and sat looking at all the swarm and buzz of the coming and going. The London girls are certainly beguiling with their baggy gauzes, bright to gaudiness, and their hands and feet—making one think of Greek dancers.

It is said that since the bigness of the great toe began to be regarded as a trait of beauty, the toe has markedly grown in bigness, as the thumb in length ;

and these ladies do not forget to display their graces in these respects—though I cannot say that I noticed among them any bigger toe than Linda's or my sisters'. It is astonishing, after all, how much expression—of archness, lovableness—can ambush within one wee foot, like a lily mother, nude, blushing at her lily brood of three, who blush, and then the baby ; anyway, these ladies know their way : their feet are feats. They have on ebonite anklets hanging nickel bells, that click and babble. And how they laugh in the face of heaven ! at every gust, with all their gums and gullets, they laugh.

One of them, passing by, said to me " Well, Pensieroso, thinking of her ? "—and laughed ! and threw a rosebud backward into my boat. I saw throngs of them in a high white tea-house opposite Whiteley's, a place with four floors ; on the first and third was dancing, and from every opening poured an uproar of merriment.

Then came Linda with a commissionaire bearing her parcels ; and we started off for New Brighton.

She was now again grave ; and I said, to say something, " Got your mother's things ? The crêpe ? "

She said yes with her eyes—pensive.

" The bulbs ? " I asked.

Again she closed her eyes, and inclined her head —pensive, serious.

" The turkey-eggs ? " I asked.

To this no answer ; and, to get her, I suppose, to say something to one, I asked again " Did you get the eggs ? "

" No, I did not get the eggs," she now said.

" What, forgot ? "

Her answer was not a direct answer. What she said was: "I will get those at New Brighton, probably."

I thought this odd: but before I could say more, I noticed that New London looked a long way below us; and I put to Linda the question: "Why are we rising so high?"

She bent forward to fix her eyes on the barometer, but did not reply; and it seemed to me that she was somewhat pale, somewhat moved somehow. A terror of I knew not what all at once struck to my heart. I could see that we continued to rise—*why* I could not divine; Linda, speechless, was staring at the barometer.

Suddenly, with a swift twist of her waist, she was gazing over the gunwale earthwards, and down she kept staring twenty, thirty seconds; then, with an action as busy and quick as a conjurer's wrist, she dragged open the inlet-valve of the poop-vacuum, dragged at a lever of the engine, and instantly was poring anew at the aneroid.

The boat now stopped moving forward, but continued to soar rapidly, the little helicopter over the front magnet now spinning invisible. Not a word from her; and I could not now doubt—Linda was pale, her lips fixed like nickel. With my heart in my mouth I called to her "*Linda!* is something wrong?"

Blanched, with a shriek, she sprang to her feet: "*Aubrey!* The dynamo! *We are falling!*"

I heard a click of something or other, then dumbness: the dumbness of the little engine below; the dumbness of the little dynamo's hum; then, in an instant, not dumbness, but wind—wind whistling upward past us, wind wrangling, wind growling round us like tigresses crowding to grind us. . . . I caught Linda round the waist, I propped my back, sitting tight against the fore-magnet ; then I snatched from my pocket a self-igniting cigarette, and commenced to smoke. . . .

Our fall must have lasted from fourteen to sixteen seconds ; and I think that before we were half down my puffing had lit the spark-cigarette, and I was comfortably propped. . . .

The boat struck ground in a mid-field. . . .

We two were tossed a foot upward ; bumped back upon the deck.

Linda was staring at me, dreadfully pale, shocked, breathless, and her laugh had a sob in it. As for me, I was shocked, but I do not think that I was pale at all.

She was the first to laugh, but I the first to speak.

" Well ! " I said, " it doesn't seem that we are dead ! Now, what a fraud ! "

She had antiseptic respirators ready, for, as I spoke, she poked the prongs of one up my nostrils, another up her own ; which done, her first words were a cry of delight : " Aubrey, you are smoking ! "

"Yes," I said, " I thought I'd have one last——"

" *Brave* ! " she hissed, staring close into my eyes.

" Is that so ? " I said : " I can't say that I see anything—One may as well die comfortable and smoking."

She looked at me under her eyes, and said "Well, I like that."

" I am delighted that you like it," I said ; and I added " Does this mean, by the way, that I am in permanent favour ? "

She flashed a shy eye at me.

"Have I merited marriage?" I asked.

She impulsively held up her lips to me, upon which, snatching out the respirator-prongs, I took her in a passion to kiss her from top to toe, letting her go with her palm over her eyes.

"But why aren't we dead?" I then said: "I don't quite see."

"I did not think that you would!" she gaily cried, "though it is a guessable thing, Aubrey, that boats would be made to withstand drops. Always a little danger, that's true. If this one had dropped sixty metres more, or sixty less, than just a thousand, we might have been injured. Boats' bottoms are concave a little, aren't they?—parachutic—and the springs on which a deck rests are systematized with the bottom's concavity to resist a drop from some particular height. Hence I rose before falling —forgive!—it was done to test the foundations on which you are built. Your sisters knew, the *palmiste* predicted by instructions—to unnerve a king of coolness. Do you forgive?"

I meditated it, and said "All right. Let us go up. I forgive."

I did not tell Linda that, as we had begun to fall, I had understood that our fall was her doing—that I was being tested. Indeed, I inwardly rejoiced to be an inch the deeper, for I considered it a piece of insolence in my Linda, and my Cicely, and my Thea, to be testing me among them like some stud-stallion. So I did not tell that I knew: but I knew.

As a matter of fact, though it was true that I knew little of mechanism, I knew more than my

Linda imagined, for I like, I suppose, to go posing as a good-for-nothing. So I knew very well that boats' bottoms are parachutic ; I had understood that things were about all right with me : for there had flashed upon my understanding the reason why she had not purchased the turkey-eggs at Whiteley's —they'd have been smashed in the shock ; at the same instant I had understood why my Thea had phoned me "*Be brave!*" So I was, ladies; and died smoking.

But Linda has never known that I knew. Never tell, my Clarence. See a phrase in those ancient scriptures : "He that keepeth his mouth (shut) keepeth his life." If I have lived happy, and begotten good sons, it is because in my most fond and doting moments I have "kept my mouth" (shut) ; and been frank in all things, save one.

Yours, AUBREY.

Remark : This Aubrey, writing with no eye to *us*, leaves unexplained the way in which his "vacuum" and "magnet" make those air-boats and towns in the clouds ; but, by reading between the lines, adding two and two together, this may be gleaned. We know that electricity in a wire wound round a rod of iron makes the rod a magnet. Atoms of iron lie higgledy-piggledy, but the electricity drills them, so that we can *hear* the rod *click*, as the trillions of atoms kick and stiffen as to the cry "'tention!" of the current. So, then, the current *lengthens* the rod.

Now, let the current be made and broken, magnetizing and demagnetizing the rod many times a second : then, with every "make," a "back-current" retards the magnetization ; with every "break," a rush of "extra" current prolongs the magnetization. But the "extra" is far more transitory than the "back-current" ; so at "break" the rod contracts far more sharply than it lengthens at "make."

The lengthening, then, *takes longer* than the shortening.

Now, let a box have a lid that can move up and down airtight within the box; let the box be exhausted of air; let the lid be fastened to one end of an iron rod fixed perpendicular over the lid; and let current be made and broken round the rod.

Then, at every "make," rod lengthens, lid sinks; and since it sinks as quickly as air-pressure would make it, there is no air-pressure downward on that much of a boat in which the box is; and as there is air-pressure upward, the boat is rising.

At "break" the rod shortens; there is air-pressure upward and downward, and the boat is falling by her own weight; but as every lengthening *takes far longer* than every shortening, on the whole the boat is rising. The mechanism will be much more elaborate (of course)—multiplying levers, etc.—but this seems to be the principle.

After the end of this story the dumbness of the arbour remained unbroken. . . .

Netta reached aside to switch-off, keeping her eyes averted from Whipsnade Prince, and hers was the only motion, except that every eye but hers turned toward Prince's back where he sat at the cliff-brink on the ground-slabs, legs dangling over, and he was lighting a cigarette, puffing perfunctorily, with a certain skyward gesture of rightfulness, defiance, triumph, as who should say, "God and my right, all's well with the world."

Then Paul Watts called out "Congratulations, Prince!"

And Mr. Killik, the solicitor: "Congratulations!"

And the little Mr. Coward: "Good old Whip! *you* are the boy for raking-in the dibs. Better be born lucky than rich, Sonny."

And the Rev. Mr. Darrel: "But!"—he stopped.

Now Prince sprang upright to drop to lolling in an easy-chair, to say to everybody "Thenks! I do seem to have won the deal, and that is only as Divine Providence should design, since I gave up a cert for an eleventh chance. But, as this poor Greta had the intentions you know of as to the spending of the money, you may depend upon me to respect those intentions, more or less. No one suspects me of being secretly a scientist—philanthropist—don't you know—but I will, I'll meet my cousin's wishes. So now, since it seems that we need not meet here any more on this business——"

"Yes, Sir," Mr. Darrel interrupted—"let's see it through: there is still Monday, Ransom's day, to come—we'll see it through."

"If that pleases you, of course," Prince replied, "though it seems needless: no other tale can so definitely not *have* happened, since this *is to* happen—unless Monday's tale happens in 3073 A.D. instead of 2073; but Monday's tale, named 'Skin-the-Goat,' hardly sounds as if it is going to happen far in the future, when goats will be skinned by magnetism. So what I was going to say is this: that, as we mayn't meet on Monday—I, and Killik, at least won't be here—I'd be glad if you'd keep me posted as to your whereabouts, as I want to lure you to come on a cruise—fact is, I've bought that yacht yonder, or am messing about buying, and when the bereavement that we foresee has dropped upon us, that will be splendid if you help me in snatching Miss Netta Fenton and Lady Dale-Eldon off to fresh interests."

By this time Netta's eyes were dwelling on him with an underlook . . . meditating. . . . Others spoke, she was mum . . . meditating. . . .

He was a Piccadilly-City spark of crack ideas, Whip, Prince of plots, spinner though he toiled not. By the bright-idea of the daily tales he had both stopped her crying, and none the less, hey-presto, had won the lump of money without fail. And before he won it he had spent some, gone yacht-buying, as though sure of winning. . . . Her underlook mused on him ; so did the Rev. Mr. Darrel's, with suspicion. . . .

CHAPTER XI

THE GOAT DAY

AND on the Monday, on the coming together again of nine for the final time—Killik having gone with Prince to meet the yacht-owner at Monte Carlo—Mr. Darrel with a very grave face frankly, through a Beethoven sonata, arraigned Whipsnade Prince of trickery, while every face went as grave as his.

He said "When Prince made it a condition of winning that the tale 'cannot have happened,' he had already conceived the idea of a tale of the future, and foresaw how he could cause a tale of that sort to be the tale of his day: clever, but not straight. Hence his departure ten days ago for London, to see Mr. Keith Richards and somehow win Richards to substitute a tale of the future for Richards' 'Course of True Love,' as foreannounced. All this I scented out, conjectured, but, of course, I am not now conjecturing: last night I 'phoned a man whom I know to be intimate with Richards, to ask if he could throw any light upon Richards' change of tales; he replied that Richards had done it in the interests of some friend; and in reply to my question if Prince is a friend of Richards his answer was, 'Oh yes, Richards has the bad habit of dining with Prince Whip.' So there has been chicane—not fair play."

Now some moments of dumbness, during which Netta's hand slowly rose to cover her eyes.

Then Sir Thomas Ormsby to Mr. Darrel : " And do you say, Sir, that the facts you have given prove your statement of unfair play ? "

" Yes, Sir, I say so "—from Mr. Darrel: " or does it not seem so to you ? "

" No, Sir : your idea and mine of the nature of proof—differ."

" Not proven ! " Paul Watts called out.

And Sir C. Alexander Caxton : " Assurance can be independent of proof. It is a flaw in the English judicature that where formal proof falls short the guilty go scot-free. But where there is assurance, gentlemen need not await ideal proof to refuse to sully their purity by touching a tarnished hand."

And the little Mr. Coward with a certain whoop : " Old Whip ! I had an idea he'd be up to some scheme. And here have I been and dropped a cool seven thousand. . . . What does it matter ? We aren't General Booths, gentlemen."

So everyone in turn had his say, except Harry Ransom, who sat stiff, a little pale, his eyes on that pale face of his love, while Netta's gaze turned, full of earnestness to each, as each gave his verdict ; then turned to stare at Greta's face, at cheek-bones which now seemed more broadened, the chin's pretty point more shortened, the little nose pinched ; and she said in herself " Done with him—done, done " : *she* requiring no strict proof—divined—knew. . . .

But now Beethoven's sonata in C Minor, whose Divine tidings had come unmarked in that arbour, no more sounded, and now someone nowhere announcing " This is the National . . . " " And now for Mr. Lawrence Balcom's tale, 'Skin-the-Goat'" . . . "Mr. Balcom" . . . whose mode and emotion, evoked by magic, like that phantom of Samuel, now arose upon consciousness, and spoke, recounting this story :

Skin-the-Goat had run away from the Hernes clan of gipsies on the Cumberland Moor, to come to the Camomescres (or Lovels), who haunt the neighbourhood of London ; but he knew that the Lovels, too, had a jockey-whip in pickle for his back : so, on reaching a tavern at Finchley which took his fancy, he stopped there to think of it.

He was not really a Rom—though nothing could so deeply wound him as the taunt from a Rom : "You are not of '*the husbands*,' little brother—not really of *the blood*." In reality, he was a child of an English judge—stolen at the age of three.

Now, however, at fifteen, he was as much more a Rom than the Roms as the Roms are more vagabond than a shop-keeper—had seen Cadiz, Naples (by stowing himself away in a brig) ; and his hand was against every man—as much against his friends, the gipsies, as against his enemies, the gorgios (non-gipsies).

He sat on a bench in the bar-parlour—the queerest figure, an albino, his hair white like wool, his eyelashes white, having rather a scorched look, the lids a little inflamed, the eyes pinky, peepy, peering—Chinese—wrinkles at their corners when he laughed with a silly expression of enjoyment.

After half an hour of silence the landlord spoke : "How can I be of service to you, me good feller ?" —a little rat, with one sly and shifty eye, the habit of his cropped head having been contracted in prison : which residence only technically debarred him from holding a licence.

There sat Skin-the-Goat (so-called for his quickness in cutting up animals), on his head a conical hat, such as Irish peasants wear, the rim turned down ; no jacket, no boots, one trouser-leg rolled up to the shin. He made no answer, only screwed up his eyes in a laugh, ran out, cut some semicircles in the air with his feet, and in ten minutes was back to sit in the parlour.

Three times during the afternoon this was repeated : for Skin-the-Goat had determined to rest some weeks from roamings, and to make this inn his resting-place.

Anon he touched in his pocket the bit of loadstone which gave him luck—a bit of the natural rock, rare, hard to get ; anon he tasted a little of the mess of snails which he had in a little bag.

At last, near nightfall, he leant over the bar, to say to the man " Ye told the gentleman a lie! "—referring to a cyclist who had been uncertain whether he had handed over the counter a florin or half-a-crown : the landlord had protested that it was a florin ; and now went pale at this sudden witness.

" Come on, leave the bar, me good feller ! " he said sharply ; and when Skin-the-Goat showed no sign of going, " Ere's a shilling—come on, leave the bar ! "

But still that odd phenomenon was with him for his sins that day; and finally he said " What's it you want, then—a job ? 'Cause, as it happens, I'm on the look-out for a hand."

Whereupon the boy grinned ; and that night slept on some bags in a room behind the bar.

The next day he was induced to wear a jacket which descended to his knees ; but his loathing for boots had to be respected.

Before long he was doing his work with perfect knack and handiness, and stuck to it—the landlord and his wife silently noting him : he was always sober, always hungry ; seldom spoke ; could fall asleep at a minute's notice ; but, whether asleep or awake, by night, by day, hardly a sound, however slight, escaped his ears' awareness ; he had a fondness for frogs and rats ; a habit of rising in the night, and wandering wide ; and a habit of sitting in the kitchen-garden at the back, peering inquisitively at the moon's business, in his narrow-eyed way.

Meantime, he got several blows, and one rather ugly bruise ; but, on the whole, won the confidence of the man and his wife—a tall Cockneyess.

One morning at one o'clock the boy stood outside the landlord's bedroom, listening.

He could hear the wife whisper "This is the night to do it! ", and the husband answer " But the dog, old girl ? "

" Shoot the dog and the man, too, as for that ! " the woman said. " We are ruined in one month more, if you don't put yer hand to this, I tell you ; and to-night's your chance, seeing as his housekeeper is only gone for the two days."

At this point the boy pushed the door open, and stood before them, laughing with his wrinkled eyes and that rictus of his mouth. The man and woman shrank, with sinister looks in their eyes.

" You've heard, you little devil, have you ?" the man asked.

Skin-the-Goat nodded ; adding " I can help you, Sir."

They questioned him with their eyes—how help ? He explained—it was simple : the dog in question was a friend of his, like all dogs ; he would go and knock up " the old man "—a certain Mr. Shepherd, a miser, living alone in an old farmhouse a mile off—and tell him his pony was straying ; he knew Skin-the-Goat well, and would believe ; Skin-the-Goat would then lead him away to seek the pony behind the back meadow ; and, meantime, the robbery of the money from his room, the situation of which they all knew, could be safely effected by the landlord.

There was silence. Then the woman remarked " The boy's no fool."

" 'E ain't," the man echoed, glad of a companion in the venture ; and the compact was made.

Skin-the-Goat then set off, touching his loadstone, for the farmhouse, which stands solitary in that flat country-side of hedges and fields—the night very rough with wind, but dry.

This so-called " farm " was hardly still a farm ; but adjoining the homestead was a loft, from whose doorway still projected a hay-hoist ; and in an apartment of this loft, which was the spot of the farm most shut off from mankind, slept the old Shepherd, who was one intricacy of eccentricities. (Two years after this an account of his death appeared in the London papers, and it was then stated that he had almost starved himself, yet had left thousands behind.)

The landlord, then, waited at a saw-pit some way off the farm, while Skin-the-Goat entered the yard, and began to throw pebbles up at the loft.

Before long a white head, both terrified and angry, appeared—for " the old man " lived in terror of being robbed, for which reason he was said to have left Islington to live outside London.

" It's me ! "—from the boy in a shouted whisper : " Come down and let me in, or ye'll be murdered."

" What ! "

" Yes, I tell you ! "

" Lord in heaven ! "

" Come quick ! "

The old man doddered down the ladder-stair, undid the barn-door ; upon which Skin-the-Goat seized his hand, and in urgent haste hustled him back up to the loft, saying, " It is that dog's-body, the landlord of the Swan ! Don't go out, or he'll have ye : get into that box "—he pointed to the crane-cage—" and when ye see me come and make a sign, like this, then call ' Murder ! ' and he'll be gone like a long-dog."

Meantime, he was turning the crane-handle, and when the cage was up at the level of the doorway, he forced the distracted old man, who was like a lamb in his hands, into it, then swung the arm away, and, with a chattering ratchet-and-pawl, let the chain out a little again.

This done, he ran down and was off for the saw-pit, where the landlord awaited him—and those little legs could flit quick. To the landlord's question : " The old 'un safe ? " he answered: " Aye, I've led his pony astray, and he's away in the orchard, seeking the pony."

At once they were off together toward the farm-house, passed under the crane, up the steps, into the loft ; and the man, having lighted a tallow candle, went prying.

There lay the long, shiny chest which, as was known, contained the spoil, serving also as a step to a pile of feather-beds head-high ; and the landlord, his skeletons and wrenches ready, was immediately rummaging on his knees at the lock.

He was about to finish the job when the boy walked to the crane, put out his head, made the agreed sign : upon which cries of " Murder ! Help ! " from the miser surprised the night.

At this alarum near in his ears the landlord, with a groan of " God's truth ! " forsook all, was down and out, flying for the tavern, at his heels the teeth of the miser's mastiff, quiet till now on account of the presence of its friend, Skin-the-Goat.

The boy was now alone in the room ; and, seating himself in front of the chest, he now proceeded to complete the work of the landlord on the lock, while the miser's cries of " Murder! ", all unheeded by him, continued.

Now the chest lies open : and it was a face of babyish delight that gloated over that sight of silver articles, money in gold, packets of bonds, documents. . . . All his pockets he crammed with gold ; took, too, a parcel of spoons, wrapped in blue tissue-paper ; then shut the chest, descended. . . .

As he passed out into the yard, the old man saw him from over the rim of his cage, which the winds swung, and cried out " Come back and draw me up, you rascal ! Help ! Murder ! "

Skin-the-Goat ran on. . . .

At the inn he ran up to the landlord's chamber, where man and wife were exchanging wild whispers of terror, and, entering the room, held out to them the parcel of spoons. . . .

" I have gotten these."

They started.

" Where from ? "

" Picked them up on the shelf of the loft."

" And that were *all* yer picked up, wasn't it, my beauty ? " the man said.

The boy nodded, laughing in his silly, broad way.

" And yer *didn't* round on me to the old man, and tell him I was coming, and hide him away in case, *did* yer, now ? And yer *did* tell him his horse was strayed, and take him away to the orchard, my fine feller, *didn't* yer ? "

This ferocious species of reproach showed that the beast's blood was up, and boded no good to Skin-the-Goat, for he smelled treachery, and spoke with an eye on fire, bending near the boy, his breath infesting the boy's bent face.

And, as he made a movement to plant a blow, his fingers chanced to touch one of Skin-the-Goat's pockets, bulging with gold : whereupon a chink ; at which the man and woman glanced at each other.

And suddenly the woman : " Let the boy go to bed ; he's done his best."

" Go to bed ! "—from the man.

Skin-the-Goat slid down a banister to his little den, lay on his bed of bags, and in some moments, although he knew that there was but a step between him and death, was asleep. . . .

" His pockets is crammed with gold ! " the woman, meanwhile, had hissed.

"Don't I know?" the man answered: "he's been doing the job on 'is own! I'll tear every penny from 'im——"

"No, don't you! That boy's the devil, I tell you; he'll peach to the police! He'll peach as it is, p'r'aps!" Now she put her lips to his ear: "*Do for 'im!*"

He went white.

"Do for 'im! Self-pertection's no sin. And what are you afraid of? Nobody knows 'im, who or what he is, he's dropped from the clouds. A 'ole in the peas, that's all!"

"Come, then"—suddenly with decision: "you come with me."

"Let 'im get well asleep: we'll get the 'ole ready."

They presently went out, with pick and spade, into the strip of vegetables at the back, a soft rain now falling, wind rough, while only a local luminousness told where the moon flew: in which wild night-weather the two ghouls dug industriously, until a grave gaped there for Skin-the-Goat.

When they re-entered the tavern, the man trembling, the woman pretty self-possessed, she slipped into the kitchen to fetch and hand him a carving-knife; then led him by the arm soft, along the passage, to the boy's door.

There they stood listening some minutes. No sound. And now the woman opened the door as gradually as a glacier drags its mass, and gently pushed the man in.

He drew himself along on hands and knees. . . .

The room was small, his journey short, but to those two hearts the world seemed hushed in a long expectancy : only, there was the man's laboured respiration, pitifully loud. Through that sound, however, he believed that he could hear near beneath him the breathing of sleep, and he put out his hand to touch the sleeper's foot through the covering.

Suddenly, starting upright, he dealt three rapid stabs.

Then the great silence again ; till his wife, close behind him now, asked, in a horrid whisper, " *Done it ?* "

And horridly he whispered " Aye."

On which the woman struck a match to a candle, held the light over the bed, and stood peering, while some grease dropped once, twice, audibly upon the sacking in that silence, her face over the taper looking puffed, demoniac, gloomily illumined by the glare.

But now they started simultaneously in new amazement, new terror : the bed was empty, though the bags had been arranged in the shape of a body. Where the knife had rushed through the bags one could see the ugly gashes.

On his knees, his eye at a knob-hole in the flooring above, Skin-the-Goat was peeping at them.

And, to make their situation worse, as they stood staring at the bed, loud steps were sounding in the passage outside ; the door flew open, and two constables, one of them covered from head to foot in mud, stood before them.

For, at the first click of the pick in the earth among the turnips, remote as it was, Skin-the-Goat had opened his eyes, had divined immediately the meaning of that evil thud, thud, and, before the hole in which he was to sleep was a foot deep, he had stolen through the front, and was well on his way to the Finchley police station, a mile and a half away.

But his appearance was so much against him, that they had been hardly inclined to take very seriously the tale that he told there. Yet he was explicit—explained how the landlord had robbed the loft, had "thrown" the old miser, Mr. Shepherd, into the crane-box, had taken the gold—and the spoons. He could even show them where the spoons now lay, on the chest-of-drawers in the landlord's room; but as to where the gold had been concealed—who could say?

At one instant the officers looked rather suspiciously at him, with the thought that he might be the instrument of some hoax or trick, and at the next moment were ready to laugh at him. They told him to wait on a bench in the outer hall; but the moment he found himself alone, he slipped through the door to be off. Sensitive as a bird, especially in the presence of the dreaded "chokengres" (police), he had taken fright at a look of distrust in the inspector's eye.

Now, not daring to take the gold with him to the station, he had left it at the tavern: it was necessary to go back for it; and he re-entered the tavern at just about the hour when the finishing touches were being given to his grave. He had remained some moments in the darkness of the passage, hearkening to that thud, thud; then had run into his room and again crammed his clothes with the gold. Then, by a ladder-stair that led to a trapdoor, up he had run to the room above, and, after fastening the hook-and-eye of the trapdoor, had put his eye to a hole in the flooring to spy.

Meanwhile, a pair of policemen had been despatched from the station to see the business through ; and first they had hurried to the farm, to discover the old Shepherd half dead in the crane-cage, just in the situation described by Skin-the-Goat, though great was their astonishment to learn that it was Skin-the-Goat himself who was responsible for that situation. They resolved to arrest him, too.

And now they had started for the inn.

It was the darkest hour of a dark morning, and, in passing through the garden, one of the officers had dropped plumb into the grave dug for Skin-the-Goat.

He had picked himself out thick in a complexity of clay, and, intensely exasperated, the pair had then dashed into the tavern, had spied a glimmer shining from Skin-the-Goat's room, and rushed into it just as the two brutes had made the discovery of the empty bed. In an instant " the snips " had been slipped upon the wrists of the miscreants.

" But what've we done ? " demanded the man.

" We arrest you on charges of conspiracy and entering."

" It waren't us ! It was a boy——"

" Yes, the boy : we intend to arrest him, too. Where *is* the boy ? "

" We don't know ! "

" Well, he's here; we'll have him. Come along! "

All moved toward the door. . . .

But the door now refused to open. During their talk—which had contained a threat of the boy's arrest—the door had been soundlessly closed and locked on the outside : for that threat had been heard by Skin-the-Goat, peeping above.

One of the officers rushed up to the trapdoor : but that, too, had been secured ; they put their united force to both the doors, but the woodwork was firm ; then they looked into each other's eyes, and read there that they were prisoners till the morning, at least.

But when the morning dawned, Skin-the-Goat was two good leagues from the Swan Inn—was out in the world, his home and native place . . . a bright day, the storm passed, the country here broken, full of wood and wold, looking more like Bucks than Middlesex.

Near noon Skin-the-Goat was seated high in the leafy thick of a beech in mid-field, seeing where, some miles to his right, some village-roofs rose for a breath out of an ocean of foliage ; to his left four rows of elms led to a country-house.

In his grasp was a frog that looked rather sick, in his other hand a bit of wet bread ; and his being was concentrated on the business of getting the frog to eat the bread.

Just then two country constables, who came trudging along the footpath through the field, passed beneath Skin-the-Goat's beech, where one of them said " By the telegram from town, he's got the gold right enough ; and we're sure to nab him : only a young lout, by accounts."

And the other answered " Oh, ay, we'll have him."

" Eat, thing ! " Skin-the-Goat grumbled above them, rapping the frog's head : " *eat !* "

During the telling of this story, Sir Thomas Ormsby had leant to whisper across the sick to Netta " Not asleep—she's hearing ! ", and Netta had whispered back " Likes boys ! " ; then when at the end tongues were loosed, Lord George Orchardson remarked " Nothing that can't have happened in that : there actually *was* such a miser, I recollect, at Finchley."

And Harry Ransom : " Quite so, Lord George, I am nowhere : certainly, Skin-the-Goat is not a being of the future."

Now Sir Thomas Ormsby began to say " It seems a pity that Mr. Whipsnade Prince was not present when the charge was——" But he stopped.

Someone had uttered " Ha, ha."

Who was it. . . . ?

Everyone glanced toward the *chaise longue*, then darted glances at everyone else, then again gazed at the *chaise longue*.

And now : " Really, I can't help laughing at that boy."

This was merely a whisper, but a whisper in a complete stillness ; and now they were sure : it was the sick who had whispered it.

There leapt from Netta a little scream : " *Sir Thomas !* "

But now Sir Thomas was running.

Running he came back, bringing brandy from the house, the crowd that had now gathered round the sick making room for him ; and though his fingers shook, he chuckled when the lips to which he put the spirit whispered " I am so hungry."

Her recovery, in fact, was as rapid as her collapse had been sudden : the very next afternoon, the Tuesday, she was in the arbour in an ordinary chair, her eyes already bright and laughing, eyes long and narrow, which always had a light of larkiness in their sidling, she seated there interesting like Jairus' daughter, heroine of two worlds, Harry Ransom chronically clasping her hand, and all the rest there to revel in her resurrection, except Killik and Prince. The next (Wednesday) morning she was walking about in ordinary clothes, and soon after noon started running round the garden with Ransom and her shepherd-dog, Rover, they two throwing stones for Rover to fetch, the joy of her new life alight in her eyes ; and, as she arrived breathless, she panted at Netta " Oh ! this isn't bad! Life ! That absurd boy, Netta, with his mess of snails, and his little Chinese eyes—I can't help laughing—he was a match for them all ! "

" Aye," says Netta, " God bless Skin-the-Goat. And did you listen to the tale that came before—about towns in the air ? "

" Oh, yes," Greta answered, " I more or less heard : only, I seemed to be outside, beyond reach, a native in a certain place, without any energy to stir, nor wish to stir, until someone seemed to come a long journey to inform me, 'There is fun on earth, jump up,' and then I made an effort, was up, and away."

And Netta : " Well, that tale of the future about the towns was the tale by which Whipsnade Prince won you. He is coming this afternoon, so do it this afternoon, what we have arranged—keep him to his winning, offer yourself before everybody, put him in a tight corner—let's hear what he says."

" And if he takes her at her word ? " Ransom objected : " isn't the thing too risky, Netta ? "

But Netta : " No, Greta will at once see how the wind blows, and, if necessary, draw back. . . . As to that yacht which he has bought without money, you won't forget to be merciful about that, Greta."

"Right you are," Greta replied, and they went into a luncheon to which came Paul Watts, Gerald Jewson, Lord George Orchardson, these with Sir Thomas Ormsby passing out to the arbour about three o'clock, where Greta was standing at the cliff-brink with Ransom, overlooking the sea, when Prince and Killik came together.

At that sight of her back, Prince, who, just arrived from Monte Carlo, had no knowledge of her recovery, stopped stock-still, peering narrow ; and even as he peered uncertain, she turned, he was aware of that wide architecture of her face, her wicked little eyes with their twinkling. . . .

He had come opulent, a winner; all in the calamity of some moments he saw himself poor, a loser ; but there were not two ticks' interval between his calamity and the insolence of his coolness : immediately he was stepping toward her with his extended hand, with his "I say ! . . . by Jove, I *am* pleased——"

Nor during an hour of ordinary talk was the slightest sign of the cark that must have been at his heart to be divined in him ; nor did he seem to notice, though he must have, a coldness in the men's manner toward him; as to his win in the competition, he uttered not a word : it was Greta who referred to it when they were seated in a semicircle near the cliff's brink, she in the middle divided from Netta by Prince, Ransom at her right hand ; and she said "Well, only friends are present, no reticence is necessary, Mr. Prince. It appears that you have won me. . . . Of course, my sister's undertaking when I was like that, expected to die, is not, strictly speaking, binding on me now ; still, she is my other self : her undertaking engages me to you."

Upright sprang Prince to put his lips on her left hand, which she held sideward toward him, and says he "I am overwhelmed with distinction! Can you by chance mean this?"

Warily she eyed him before replying "Why, yes."

He took a minute to reseat himself, in a seizure of uneasiness, not looking at her, looking at the seat, as if he saw thorns on it ; then : "I am—er—yes—overwhelmed. But, then, how about my friend, Ransom? I thought—doesn't he rather come in somewhere?"

"I am resigned to being a loser, Prince," Ransom remarked : "you may leave me out."

"I see"—from Prince : "I am a winner. But, then——"

"A girl does not like 'buts,' Mr. Prince"—gravely from Greta.

And now Prince's agility failed to hide the shyness of his eyelids. "No—ha, ha—naturally doesn't like 'buts.' Unfortunately there doesn't seem to be any other word which one can say, if one wishes to say 'but.' I never was so awfully honoured, but——"

"Ah! you say it again."

"Ha, ha, that does not mean——"

"Perhaps you don't want me, Mr. Prince. Am I to think that?"

"Want . . . Naturally one wants you—don't you know. You are even more charming than you are rich ; but, then——"

"Ah! you say it again."

" Deah me, I feel a Briton bereft of his rights, if I mayn't say ' but ' ; I wish I could invent—I'll say ' tub.' It is quite true that I won in our kind of a gamble, but——"

" Ah ! you didn't say ' tub '."

" No, ha, ha, I was going to say—You must understand that there was never any question of my marrying, whether I won or not—I have a habit of not marrying, even when frantically looking about for money——"

" You mean, then "—Greta gazed gravely down at her nails—" that you do not wish to claim your win now that I am well ; you win me, then you let me acknowledge that I am won before my friends, then you don't want me. Ah! that is not flattering."

Now Prince, sitting on prickles, threw his eyes to the sky, muttering " Ah, heaven, how excruciating!" and now he whispered at Netta's ear " Oh, Netta—pray—rescue me from this."

But firmly Netta murmured " No ; do as you should."

And though he did not know what she meant—" do as you should "—unconsciously he did it : for his next words were a confession, when, with a sigh of " Heavens ! " and a face bent, pestered with shyness, he said " Not that I really won—in fact, I—so to say—yes, cheated—procured that that tale of the future should be told on my day. Though I was horribly cross with myself, saw the dishonesty——"

" No, no, not dishonesty, Prince," came promptly from Sir Thomas Ormsby : " there was no undertaking among us, man, that that should not be done ; maybe you alone did it because you alone thought of doing it—a bit sharp, eh ? rather smart : but we can't have you saying ' dishonest '."

" And gamely admitted, Prince "—from Lord George Orchardson, springing up to proffer his hand.

" We knew before ! " Paul Watts called out, "and thought it—furtive : not at all ' dishonest '."

" They knew "—this bowed Prince lower, his brow now on his palm—" deah me, even my confession is a fiasco."

But now Netta was saying near his ear " Never mind, cheer up, Whip ; your sins, which are many, are all forgiven you."

On which Prince stared round at her, then suddenly snatched her hand to his lips, breathing " Oh, you, good and beautiful ! "

And Greta : " Oh, very well, I am not wanted, I must only marry a certain broth of a boy who buts me no buts, but butters me with tubs of love ; then, on marrying, I shall have the money, Mr. Whip, to buy the yacht that you have half-bought, if I may."

Whereat a load of care rolled off Whipsnade Prince, and, his face radiant, he threw himself round to look at her, saying, " Now, how thrillingly decent of you ! "

And this was done. Within a fortnight the yacht was bought and ready for sea, Greta was Harry Ransom's, and with the married pair, and Netta, and Prince, and Lady Dale-Eldon, sailed Paul Watts, Gerald Jewson, Mr. Coward and Mons. Pascal, while Lord George Orchardson, that " tough guy " at motor-racing, was gone to the Lombardy Lakes to break some record, Sir Thomas Ormsby was off to Wetterhorn in the Bernese Alps, and Mr. Darrel, Mr. Killik, and Sir C. Alexander Caxton took train in a group for England. It was not till the yacht-party had watched the Acropolis, the pyramid of Cheops, a choppy sea at Joppa, that, on the return voyage, Netta let her lips shiver to murmur "Yes," upon which the English church at Palermo saw her joined with Whipsnade Prince ; then afresh for Villefranche ; and eventually for Prince's native Mayfair.